INSPIRED BY YOU

A SMALL TOWN ROMANCE

VETERANS OF SILVER RIDGE SERIES

CLAIRE CAIN

CONTENT WARNING

Dear reader,

Inspired by You is a closed-door small-town romance about two people falling in love while healing and growing. While it's generally lighthearted, it may contain content not suitable for some readers.

The characters' pasts include divorced parents. The storyline of the book includes stalking and kidnapping of a main character. A secondary character's history of suicidal ideation is also briefly discussed.

I've added this so that readers who might find this content to be particularly sensitive can make the best decision for their health and happiness when choosing to read this book. I want you to walk away with only happy, lovely feelings, and I hope you'll feel safe proceeding with this information in mind. If you have questions or need more information, don't hesitate to contact me at claire@claire-cainwriter.com.

My very best to you,
Claire

*To those who need some Joy. Distraction. Love. Light.
Beauty. Hope. May you find it here for a little while.*

CHAPTER ONE

Jo

Tall, bearded, and beautiful Adam Carter stood in my doorway smiling at me, and he'd just used a name no one else in the world knew was mine.

Josie Wade.

Not a remarkable name by any stretch, but miraculous in that it was my supersecret pen name for a part of my life literally no one but this brain-meltingly handsome man in front of me knew about. I, Josephine "Jo" Malcom, was living a lie.

I mean, not really. I just wasn't telling anyone about this part of my life, and it was my choice. Adam's discovery of the truth had been accidental, and he'd promised to keep it a secret. Six months later, he'd kept his word.

In doing so, he'd tucked himself close to me, even though he didn't mean to. He'd stitched himself a pocket in my life no one else had access to. He couldn't possibly understand what it meant to me that he knew this secret no one else on earth save my accountant did. It was the difference between eating alone at the lunch table and having one friend to talk to—a small change but with infinite impact on the isolation that had been the reality before.

"Come in," I said, smothering the crush of giddiness pinging around inside me like someone had dropped a bowl of bouncy balls on tile. *He's here! He's heeeere!*

The immature interior squeal would've embarrassed me if it had emerged into reality, but fortunately, my excitement and completely manageable no-big-deal crush didn't betray me.

Could anyone blame me? He stepped through the doorway, and I failed to shield my eyes from the perfectly fitted olive green polo shirt clinging just enough to a defined chest and clean, worn-in jeans hinting at long, strong legs and lean hips. He had on gray-and-black sneakers, and his beard was trimmed close and matched his light brown hair he'd styled in a careless and yet somehow orderly look, tidily trimmed on the sides and longer up top.

I swallowed hard and forced my eyes away, refusing to indulge in admiring the fit of that shirt around his muscular arms or the way his jeans did great things for his b—body. *No.* Because one doesn't check one's friend out, does one?

No, one definitively does not. Especially when one had banished the crush on one's friend when said friend very clearly announced he had no interest in relationships or marriage and had done nothing in the almost-year since meeting to indicate a change of heart.

So.

None of this pining after a man who wasn't an option. No Scarlett begging Ashley Wilkes to notice her charms. No Laurie waiting for Jo to settle down for him.

No more admiring. No more bouncy balls. No more nonsense.

Business.

Friendship.

Books!

See, there it was. I could focus on the book, and my frustrating physical response to him could take a flying leap. Grabbing my computer, I let the cool metallic shell of the laptop ground me into this reality—not the shared secrets, fluttery heartbeat one I'd momentarily lapsed into. This man had come to share his insights on life as a military medic and answer questions I could use about my character, and I shouldn't keep him waiting.

"So, I thought we'd sit and I can kind of tell you about the character and you can tell me if it's a bad idea? And then I have a whole list of questions for you if you don't hate the concept."

Now having said it, the thought he may in fact find my character laughable made worry tangle in my chest. I'd written much of the book already but needed to add details that would lend credibility to his medical knowledge and give those specifics romantic suspense readers loved. He didn't need to know the bones of the hero were based on him and I'd pictured *him* as I sketched out scenes. *That* info would stay with me.

"I highly doubt I'll hate the idea," he said, taking a seat at the small two-person table in what I generously referred to as my breakfast nook.

In reality, it was simply a small table set by the lone window in my living room. My one-bedroom rental above the bookstore was rather minuscule, and it'd never struck me as problematic because I lived alone, and I'd never planned to be here this long. But after staying for closing in on a year, I'd settled in, and I couldn't seem to summon the will to leave Silverton.

I plunked down across from him in front of my computer and launched in, stoutly ignoring the thrill of even this simple action—sitting close to Adam in my apartment. As small as it was, it felt smaller... *intimate*, even, with him here. He had broad shoulders and the aforementioned arms and chest and—

Ahhhh!

But also, *Focus, Jo!* With a mental slap to my cheeks, I dove in. "So this guy is on the same team as the other characters in the series. He's their medic." Adam's pleased smile left me no choice but to return it. He had lovely teeth and lips and— "Right, so you know something about that."

"I do indeed," he said with a nod.

Well, crap. Even his most basic speech was attractive to me. He had that touch of a Southern accent, and paired with his rich, low voice, smoke curled in my belly at the simple phrase.

Slap! Another mental reminder to focus.

Adam had been a medic in the Exceptional Mission Unit, where he'd served with most of the people who worked at Saint Security. Wilder Saint had grown up here and his mother and two brothers still lived here, so that's what led him and Bruce Camden, his business partner, to Silverton as their retirement destination. Since then, a whole slew of veterans, retired and otherwise, had made their way over to work for this local security firm or other businesses in the area.

Including Adam.

I rattled off more basic information about the character and the gist of the plot. Adam watched, eyebrows slightly pinched as I explained the bad-guy organization that would infiltrate the small town where my heroes lived, and he blessedly refrained from pointing out the flaws in the general concept. We'd already been through the fact that active duty military wouldn't be living in a small town separate from a base and never deploying. Yes, this concept didn't hold water in the real world, but it's how I'd set up the series before I'd met any of the actual veterans here in Silverton.

Adam had graciously consulted on a few small things in my previous book, and even then, he'd chuckled kindly when I admitted I knew the whole series concept wasn't realistic, but it was too late. He'd been unfazed and still willing to help, bless him.

Ultimately, that's how we'd ended up here—first, he'd discovered my pen name secret, and then he'd been so generous, so helpful. Since meeting him last summer and learning a little bit about him, I'd created a character lightly modeled after him who was, like he'd been, a combat medic.

My hero also had gorgeous blue eyes and brown hair and a jaw begging the heroine to run her fingers over it and lips that practically screamed *kiss me!* But he was completely fictional and any resemblance to real-life people was purely coincidental, obviously.

"He sounds like a compelling guy," Adam said with a half smile. "Let's hear your questions."

Compelling guy. *Sigh.* Little did he know.

Would it be weird if I told him the character wasn't just coincidentally similar to him but actually based on the real-life Adam Carter? *Yeah. Probably.*

Shoving away the thought, I launched in.

It sounds so trite to admit, but the first time I saw him last summer, everything changed.

I'd met his younger brother Ethan and liked him—we'd clicked in a friendly, quick way that made me instantly at ease. We'd even decided to go into business together when I invested in his coffee shop, Joe.

My mind shoved me back into the moment...

"Hey, nice to meet you. I'm Adam."

He had a small dimple and the slightest touch of a Southern accent, so his *I'm* sounded more like *ahm*. His vowels stretched just a bit longer than they would if he were from the western US, and more than Ethan's, for sure.

"I'm Jo," I managed through a flurry of wild heartbeats the likes of which I'd read and written in my own books but had never experienced.

Even with Bruce, whom I'd adored since the day I'd met him, I'd never felt like *this*.

"You're new to Silverton, too, right?" Adam asked, a small smile on his ridiculously handsome face.

And it was. Ridiculously handsome. The stuff of romance novels, and actually, not unlike a character I'd been thinking about writing—

"Jo?"

I startled, realizing I'd just spaced out while cataloguing this man's beautiful features. I knew he'd be handsome, because his brother was certainly good-looking, but *wow*. And now, said brother—adorable, sweet, more and more important to me, Ethan—was looking at me like I was turning green.

"Right! Yes. I'm new. I mean, my dad moved here a few years back and opened All Booked Up. I was in grad school in Salt Lake City until about three months ago, but I've been visiting regularly since my dad moved here." Were those even normal words? Had I lost the power to converse?

I'd never been particularly smooth in the face of someone like him—just ask anyone who'd seen me try to chat with Bruce before my crush had eased off.

Adam nodded, the small smile and dimple trying to murder me. "That's a great shop. Good history section."

"Good romance section, more importantly," I said, because I couldn't not, and because if there was one thing I could talk about without cliff diving into the awkwardness of such immediate interest in a man I'd just met, it was books.

Ethan chuckled. "Jo's a staunch advocate for romance."

He grinned like this fact about me made him proud or charmed or *something*. I'd had more than a few moments of feeling Ethan's *or something* in the last few months since we'd met, but I'd shied away from it and drawn the lines at friendship because I hadn't felt anything more than affection for him.

I'd never felt anything like I did right now, a shimmering sense of possibility paired with actual pulse pounding in my veins, simply standing next to his brother.

My romantic little heart ran away with itself. *What if he's here because of me? What if the reason he's here is for me?* And when normally, I would've curbed those thoughts, would've covered them with logic and reality and all the things that could blow out a spark, I let it glow.

"She's all in for the love, marriage, babies, lifelong soulmates deal, right, Jo?" Ethan said, nudging my arm with his elbow like this was a chummy moment.

I grinned a little too big, probably, and admitted, "Guilty as charged."

But then, it happened.

Adam's brows dipped, and he winced. "Ah."

In that fraction of a second, that little spark didn't ease into something bigger, something with the burn of a flame, but rather, it stuttered, on the brink of blowing out altogether.

Ethan explained then. "Adam's more of a cynic."

Throat narrow, I swallowed against the tightness of disappointment and the odd feeling of a premature ending. "Oh?"

Adam nodded once. "Hard-won lesson, though I'm always happy when others find love and prove me wrong. But for me, I've made a go of it, and once was enough."

And there it'd gone. The spark snuffed right out.

I might've been struck by his features and his voice, how he had that little accent and his brother didn't. I liked his manners and his style and how he knew so many of the people at Saint Security I admired, including my own step-brother, Wilder, but that beat in my chest slowed, and the woman who was ready to fall for someone, to give him all of her heart and make a home with him where we'd love each other endlessly until Heaven took us… that part sobered, stepped back, and offered him a soft smile.

"Good to know. I won't fault you for learning your lesson if you won't fault me for never learning mine."

I meant the romantic in me wouldn't, but the girl who caught crushes and let them billow into something unwieldy like bone-dry brush in the high desert had caught fire? That girl had learned her lesson. I wasn't going to hope for anything with this man beyond cordial acquaintance because no one has time for the exhaustion of burying feelings.

Or so I told myself every day, especially after he found out my biggest secret and then offered to help me with it.

Months ago, when he surprised me while I was writing in what I'd thought was an empty store, I'd nearly had a panic attack. But he'd had no idea I was hiding anything. It wasn't until I'd run into him and splattered the mail from the PO Box where I got my Josie Wade mail forwarded that everything changed.

His soft touch as he'd inspected me, looking for harm. His insistence in making sure I was safe, that he'd do anything to help me.

And then the moment when I'd dragged him to my car, where I knew no one would overhear, and told him the truth in these closed confines that built the bubble between us and stitched the little pocket he'd so easily slid into.

My heart still fluttered in my chest just thinking about it. Every bit of me lit with that same sense of possibility and promise.

So I reminded myself of the little hole I'd dug the first day we met and shoved in all those messy wishes having to do with him, even though it didn't always feel deep enough. Sometimes, things seeped out, especially when he'd snuck his way into a part of my life no one else shared. But then, I'd heap on more turned-over earth and tamp it down, maybe stick a plywood board over top of it and *not* let myself long for things I shouldn't want.

If only my mind and heart could agree about him.

CHAPTER TWO

Adam

How had I ended up in this situation?

How had I become the only person Jo Malcom had shared her secret with?

And then, how had I ended up sitting at her tiny table in her postage stamp of an apartment brainstorming plot points for her upcoming romance novel?

How had I put myself in a situation that made me want to do anything this woman asked of me when I knew what I needed to do was stay far, far away from her?

It started out innocently enough. Really, it had all been innocent and coincidental.

First, I happened upon her typing furiously on her laptop at the store. She'd been wildly flustered and clearly hadn't wanted to talk about what she'd been working on, like she'd been caught doing something bad. I'd even worried she might go into a panic attack in front of me—the way she blanched and her eyes grew wide were a telltale start to the beginning of something bad.

It had struck me as odd. She didn't seem the type to be doing anything actually sketchy. But, fine. I was still getting to know her at that point. We might've loosely been called friends if you were one of those people who claimed anyone you'd known for a while as a friend. Kenny was like this—he knew someone for five minutes and they were friends. But he had an ease with people, much like Bruce, that I didn't.

Granted, I had a little more social fluency than Tristan and certainly more than Beast or Dorian.

Point was, I never would've expected to become her confidante. In fact, from the moment we'd met, I'd hoped *Ethan* would become a lot more of that. They'd be so good together. He was a hard worker and had always dreamed of having a family of his own, just like Jo. Well, in truth, I didn't know her *exact* dreams, but she'd said that first time we met she was a romantic and wanted marriage—perfect for Ethan.

They were both wide-eyed romantics, looking for the shine in life. I'd lost that a long time ago, watching our single mom deal with our deadbeat dad while keeping a roof over our heads. She'd gotten her second chance with our step-dad, but at that point, I'd already graduated and moved out to join the Army. I hadn't seen her blissful domestic life with our stepdad, who'd been a good guy. E had, so for him, the shine was still there, intact.

Anyway, the way I found out what Jo was really up to—her secret—had happened at the post office about six months ago. I'd been sorting through a stack of junk mail that had unfortunately followed me in the move from North Carolina, when I ran into someone.

Directly into her.

She had practically bounced off me, and everything she'd been holding had fluttered to the ground.

"I'm so sorry," I'd said, dropping to a knee to help her gather her things.

But this hadn't been the Jo Malcom I was used to—friendly and wide-eyed and alluring like something cellular in me recognized a reciprocal match in her. This was someone frantic, an echo of the borderline panic I'd seen at the store when she'd been typing, only ramped up way higher. Warning had rung in my head instantly. She'd been grappling for the letters like her life depended on recovering them that instant, like she'd face dire consequences if she didn't collect them and exit the building in a matter of seconds.

"It's fine. I wasn't paying attention," she'd said as she stood, eyeing the two letters I'd held.

And it was likely because she'd been staring a hole through my hand that I had glanced at the envelope and the name there registered. *Josie Wade.* Huh.

Maybe she introduced herself as Jo Malcom but she was, in fact, Wade? That hadn't tracked because I would have remembered that detail. Despite my best efforts, I remembered everything about the woman, from the days she'd worn glasses instead of contacts to the color of her dress six Friday nights ago... all irrelevant pieces of information that meant nothing.

Had to mean nothing.

Her small gasp had drawn my gaze to her, and then she'd snatched the mail from my hand.

My mouth had dropped open because it was so odd and sudden, and my curiosity had instantly piqued.

"Sorry. I just—that's private." Her cheeks had darkened

in the most intense blush I'd ever seen, and she'd shoved the letters into her bag.

If I'd been a smart man, I wouldn't have pried. But some idiot remaining brain cell prompted me to say, "Josie Wade?"

The look she'd given me made my stomach drop—anxiety and maybe even fear. Was she in trouble? Witness protection? What was this?

Instincts alight with the need to protect her from whatever was happening, I had grasped her wrist. "Listen, I'm sorry. I won't put you in danger. Your secret's safe with me," I'd rushed to reassure her.

You're safe with me.

Her lips had parted and her long, dark lashes fluttered, and then she'd grabbed my arm and stomped out of the post office, pulling me behind her.

Not what I'd been expecting, though the urgency had ticked up my heart rate.

"Jo?" I'd asked, because what else could I have done? I'd spent most of my life around men, and I hadn't been particularly fluent with women beyond fellow soldiers and patients. I'd had a few female friends, but they all tended to be on the terse side like Eddie and Jess, and never were they women I'd felt this incessant curiosity about.

Not that it mattered. Curiosity was normal when meeting new people. It meant nothing. *Could* mean nothing.

She had stopped at a small white sedan and released me by the passenger door. "Get in."

I'd followed her orders, more than willing to obey and see how I could help or at least make some sense of... whatever this was. She'd shut the driver's-side door once she'd nestled down into her seat, and I had folded myself up as well as I could considering my large frame hadn't fit all that well in the two-door sedan.

"Listen. I am going to tell you something no one else knows." Her voice had shook, and her hands had, too, until she'd clasped them and shoved them between her legs like she needed to anchor herself.

"I'm listening." *This couldn't be good.*

"No. I need you to promise me you won't tell anyone. *Anyone,* okay?"

Her brown eyes had held starbursts of gold I'd never noticed because I'd never been this close to her. And close we'd been, not more than twelve inches apart in the tiny front of her compact car.

Instead of waxing eloquent about her beautiful eyes or the pleasing laundry and light floral scent of her, I'd admitted, "I'm not sure I can promise that."

Her brows had shot down, so I'd rushed to explain. "If you're in danger, I can help. Saint can help, for sure. And—"

Her hand on my wrist had stopped me, a stream of buzzing attention flowing from her touch.

"I'm not in danger. It's not that kind of secret."

Relief had washed through me, and I'd exhaled. "Okay, then yes. I can promise you I will not tell anyone whatever you need to say."

She'd nodded and swallowed hard.

"Okay. So." She had grabbed a water bottle from the center console and gulped down a drink, then straightened her shoulders. "I'm a writer."

"I figured you might be, based on the writing I've noticed."

She'd dipped her chin. "Yeah. I'm a romance author."

My mouth had kicked up on one side. "Makes sense."

With one last exhale, she'd added, "My pseudonym,

which no one on earth besides you and my accountant knows, is Josie Wade."

And then it had clicked. *Josie Wade.* The name hadn't been familiar because of her mail. It'd been familiar because I'd seen it in All Booked Up. I'd heard Tristan talking about reading her because his friend loved her and... "Wow. That's... she's kind of a big deal, right?"

She had chuckled, seemingly relieved. "No. Not really. I'm small potatoes. But I do have a loyal following. And some of them live here. And, again, no one knows."

Her gaze, so full of trust in me, had sliced me open. It shouldn't have felt like something big, not at all consequential, but I had seen the importance of the moment for her written all over—her wide eyes and the tense set of her shoulders. I had felt the gravity of this moment for her, and because of that, it had weighed heavily on me.

"No one will ever find out because of me. If there's anything I can ever do... just let me know."

And it was probably that moment that had set us on this path. Because not long after, she'd started asking me small questions about work and how we did things in the EMU when we were active duty. We'd gotten more comfortable with each other and had swapped phone numbers, and suddenly, we'd been thrown together even more when Winnie had married and moved in with Tristan. A few more months and we'd been dancing together at their real wedding, and then the very next night, well, here I sat.

Now nestled into one end of the love seat in her apartment above the bookstore, she sank onto the neighboring cushion and set her laptop on her knees. We'd planned this a few weeks ago—our first concentrated private session for her to generate ideas and help her with the details of a main character I had a lot of personal insight into.

"I have so many more questions," she said, biting her lip like she could barely contain herself.

I chuckled to cover the sliver of discomfort—the twinge of unease at being this close to her. Or rather, at how much I enjoyed and wanted to prolong being this close to her. We'd started at her table, and then once she'd ordered lunch—something she'd insisted on—we'd moved here.

I wasn't romance material. Fine, I knew most women could draw the line between real men and fictional ones, and an author especially would be well aware of the differences. I wouldn't call myself an antagonist or even an anti-hero. I was just... a man who'd been burned enough by life and relationships to have lost the shine—the sparkle a woman looking for a hero would look for in a man's eyes.

Jo might be looking for this. Even if she wasn't, she deserved this. Whatever it was that made up the opposite of jaded, burnt, weary...

But I smiled genuinely, because even with all the rest of this mess, Jo was my friend. I wanted to be here. So I spoke honestly. "I hope I have answers."

And my mind added quietly, *I hope you know what you're doing.*

CHAPTER THREE

Jo

Adam smiled gamely at what had to be my hundredth question of the hour.

"I wouldn't use QuickClot in that scenario, no. I'd do a tourniquet and then—"

"Ohhh, and then you'd use the—"

"Exactly." He nodded, an expression I was reading as pride but which had to be relief I was finally understanding. His brow furrowed then. "Are you sure these are romances, though? This is a lot of blood for a romance, no?"

I laughed. "Oh, you sweet summer child. Depending on the subgenre, there's not nearly enough blood." His eyes widened, and I burst out with a cackle. "Not any books *I* write, of course. But there's always a little intensity. And this one features a medic, as you know, so there's a bit more in the medical vein."

His lips twitched.

"It's okay. You can be delighted by my excellent pun." His reluctant smile made my heart flip, which I studiously ignored. "Anyway, thank you for your help."

"You know I'm always happy to help, and I'm glad we found a time to do this."

He stretched out his long legs and ran his hand along the back of my couch. I'd been considering getting a full-sized sofa so I could have get-togethers more often and actually have more than two seats here, but I usually hosted book club in the reading room downstairs at the shop. I was fleetingly both delighted by the lack of space at present and exhausted by his nearness.

Because in truth, the man smelled so good. He had this fresh, clean scent that was a little woodsy, like he'd showered in an icy waterfall with Irish Spring and then hiked through a pine forest. It was on par with a margarita on an empty stomach in terms of the intoxicating effects.

Okay, so that was *not* helpful thinking.

"I really appreciate it. Lunch should be here soon, and then I'll let you be free." We both knew he had better things to do, but he'd set the time, so I had to trust he was okay being here.

And already, I did trust him. He'd given me a gift, even if he hadn't meant to. He'd widened my writing world by one hundred percent, and even though I'd drawn a thick line around what I was allowed to feel for him as a person, the pure relief and pleasure of sharing this part of my world with him had made said line perilously wiggly.

He'd kept my secret, and he'd answered every question I'd peppered him with over the last few months. Small things about what kind of weapon a special ops guy would use in a certain situation to bigger things like help on tactical ideas.

Before Adam's help, I'd gleaned details from the other Saint Security personnel by being a little snoop and listening in on their conversations, sometimes even daring to ask a question if I felt it was general enough it wouldn't seem weird for me to be asking, but having him as a resource had been incredible.

And now, writing this hero who happened to be a medic and happened to have a touch of a Southern accent... well, having the real deal right here with me was nothing short of magic. I could gather more real-life details here in my living room, adjusting them enough so he wouldn't see right through me.

"You really didn't have to buy me lunch, you know that, right?" he said.

I closed my laptop and stood, needing a little space and lapping up the way the words came out, his *buy* a little loose and flat like "bah" and his brows pinching. "You think I'd have you come here and give me an hour of your time for nothing? Not happening."

"It wouldn't be for nothing," he said, standing by one of my bookshelves and perusing the titles.

"Yeah? You charging me the hourly Saint Security consulting fee?" I joked, checking the food-delivery app.

When I looked up, he was frowning at me.

"No, Jo. I wouldn't be charging you, because you're my friend."

I swallowed reflexively and a weird laugh snuck out. "Right. Of course. But it's a lot to ask."

"No, it's not."

With a huff, I moved to the door. "Will you grab silverware and plates from the kitchen? I'll be right back."

I hustled out the door and down the stairs, then around the hallway to the exit of the building, which spit me out between the bookstore and Scoop. Javier's youngest son had just started delivering for Guac and he was adorable, so I always made sure to tip him generously. He deserved a bonus for coming when he did and saving me from any more awkwardness in the wake of Adam's *friend* comment. Why had it thrown me? It shouldn't have. My crush had jumped into a zombie book and had taken on the life of the undead, crawling out of its place in the hole very much without my permission.

"Thanks, Jo."

"Sure thing, Robby. Did you pick up your coding book yet?" He'd ordered some super-advanced book on coding and something else I didn't understand, but when I'd worked yesterday, they'd still been waiting.

"I'll grab it after my shift today. Don't worry, I didn't forget." He winked at me, the little charmer, and took off at a jog. The restaurant was only a street over, so apparently, he hadn't even bothered with his bike today.

"Have a good one!" I said, waving after him, then turning back to my building. Food in hand, I climbed the stairs slowly and couldn't keep my mind from sliding back into the memory of Adam finding me writing at work. Is this what made us friends?

It had been a normal Sunday afternoon at the bookstore, my first fall after graduate school, and I'd been alone with my books and my words for an hour. Sundays could be quiet, and all the more so in the shoulder season between major tourist times, or so my dad had noticed since opening a few years ago.

This provided a perfect stretch to get some words written on my novel, particularly because I only ever wrote when I was alone. Since no one knew my pseudonym, I wanted to keep it this way and took every precaution.

I'd started out writing in grad school as a way to pass the time and to placate myself. I'd set out on a course to become a communications director for a non-profit or do something that would be impactful, but the further into my master's program I got, the less interested I became. And so, after hours of studying and writing for my coursework, I'd turned to romance as an outlet.

Honestly, Bruce Camden had inspired me to write at least two books. I'd met him when my dad had moved here, and he'd been so stunningly beautiful and charismatic and capable, and then I'd learned he'd been a special operations soldier and it just felt a little like that moment when we all discovered Henry Cavill is actually kind and both a dog person *and* a genuine computer nerd. It was patently unfair and yet, the stuff of dreams.

Something about him, and even simply the existence of these burly, gorgeous men retiring and starting a business together to keep other people safe after literally giving their youth to that very end was deeply, grippingly romantic in my mind.

Granted, Wilder Saint, Bruce's partner in the business, was already married, so I hadn't gotten moony-eyed over him, thank goodness. Especially considering he later became my stepbrother after my dad married his mom, but still, he had an air of romance hero about him I knew his wife, Sarah, greatly appreciated.

Since leaving grad school, I'd found solace in my writing even more, and I'd made zero progress on figuring out what great use of my master's degree I was going to pursue. How to handle the wrecking ball realization that I had no interest in finding a job in my field? Write a new chapter! How to face the reality that abandoning the plan I'd made with my sister and the justification for my move I'd given my mother would hurt my family? Another chapter! There were people who needed me—fictional, for sure, but the need was real.

How to face the vast unknown of my own life—professional and personal? Why, ma'am, ye shall write yet another chapter.

The plan to come back to Silverton, help my dad through the summer tourist season and maybe stay on through one winter ski season before starting a full-time job in Salt Lake City, felt less and less appealing.

A job doing what? The answer wouldn't be in another chapter of my current work in progress, but it kept me from spiraling.

Staying snuggled here in this cozy bookstore and surrounding myself with friends and the comforts of this small town while I wrote book heroes and romances into existence... that sounded downright perfect. Especially when paired with the true joy of being partial owner in a local coffee shop and, well, small-town life suited me more than I ever could've imagined.

I'd never figured out how to use the small inheritance I'd gotten when my grandmother had passed away during high school, but investing in Ethan's business in my favorite small town had just made sense. Dad had refused to let me invest in the bookstore when he'd started, so I still had some left.

I'd earmarked it to start my life in Salt Lake—security deposit on a place, savings for rainy days, that sort of thing. As I had initially settled here, it'd given me a safety net if writing dried up or didn't progress the way I'd hoped. It'd also provided the escape hatch from having to get a full-time job, even though I'd been working at All Booked Up regularly enough that I could live frugally on the income and no one would wonder how else I was making money.

My thoughts had veered to the fact I might've subconsciously used most of the money in Ethan's venture to remove this safety net from my life. In a way, if I didn't have the funds to get a place in Salt Lake, well, then I couldn't in good conscience make a go of life there, right? Almost like a reverse self-sabotage. Instead of keeping myself from success, I was metaphorically pulling the rug from beneath myself in order to guarantee I followed my real dreams... or something like that.

"What are you working on?"

I'd nearly jumped out of my skull at the sound of Adam's voice behind me.

"Whoa, sorry. Didn't meant to startle you. I figured you would've heard me come in." He'd nodded toward the door where, yes, hung a cheery little bell to alert me whenever someone entered.

I'd fallen into my thoughts, into the book world and the solace of words, then my own cesspool of internal thoughts about the future, and I hadn't heard him. Hand over my racing heart and panic receding now that my brain had registered it was *him* and not—well, not anyone else, I'd turned to face him fully. "I'm sorry. I think I was in my own world."

His blue eyes had swept around the empty store, though something about the way his brow had dipped made me think he sensed how shaken I was despite my feeble attempt to hide it. He'd watched with a frown for a few seconds, like he was looking and really seeing me, all of what was going on inside, putting it all together... then when he had seemed satisfied with whatever picture he'd come up with, the frown had lifted, and he'd inhaled as if his lungs had needed it.

"I can see how this is a perfect place to world hop," he'd said.

My heart had flipped, and before I'd thought better of it, I'd agreed. "Yeah, it's pretty perfect."

He'd lifted his chin toward my laptop. "So what are you writing?"

I'd slammed the lid shut. "Nothing exciting. Just... work stuff."

I'd refused to cringe or roll my eyes at how poorly evasive that had sounded and staunchly ignored the little flicker in my mind asking, *"What if you just told him?"*

I'd had the thought of telling someone about this on and off since feeling the lack of drive to do much else. My sweet friend Dove would have been the perfect person to share all of this with, and I didn't actually think anyone I knew here would criticize me for writing romance novels. Or, if they did, did I really want them in my life? Likely not.

And yet... the thought of revealing how I spent my time, how I'd shifted my focus from becoming someone impressive and impactful to something so... frivolous, had me frozen. My heart sank even considering it.

My heart absolutely shriveled thinking about Elizabeth, my sister, who was the most formidable person I knew, and how she'd feel about me choosing something small and unnecessary like writing romance instead of changing the world like she did. If anything kept my mouth shut about all of this, it was dreading her finding out and hearing the disappointment in her voice.

"Oh, right," Adam had said, a small smile covering any awkwardness he might've felt. "Well, I just stopped in to get these." He'd handed me a pile of books.

I'd scanned them and admired the titles—two World War II histories, something on a more recent conflict, and a hiking guide for Northern Utah.

"Are you a big hiker?" I'd asked, reminding myself the only person currently obsessing about what was on my computer screen was *me*.

He'd leaned an elbow on the bar-height counter of the check-out desk. "I love it. It's one big reason why I didn't hesitate to come out here with the guys." His gaze had shifted to the windows where we could just see Silver Ridge Peak over the tops of the building across the street. "Hiking in my off-work time is unbeatable here. I ran into Danny Morrison during my first few weeks, and he's kept me in hiking routes ever since."

"Ah, Danny's great. Hiking's pretty amazing around here. I love it, too, though I am definitely a fair-weather hiker. We're entering my no-go zone any day now." The October weather would mean snow and freezing temps making the adventure of hiking less fun.

"Yeah? You don't like the cold?" He'd tapped his card for payment while I bagged his books in a little paper sack with the All Booked Up logo on front.

"I have basically zero survival skills for cold weather. I don't mind being outside and being bundled, but there's nothing like being *inside* and reading a good book while it's snowing." I'd flashed him a wide smile.

He'd chuckled softly. "I shouldn't be surprised the daughter of a bookstore owner would be a bookworm."

Tell him. Tell him how much of a little nerd you are.

The thought had whispered into my mind more clearly than it ever had before. Normally, I felt just fine about keeping Josie Wade to myself. She was my secret, my joy, and yes, sometimes my stress. She was a source of triumph at times, and she was also still, in so many ways, the stuff of dreams.

What was it about this guy that made me want to spill my guts? Probably the last vestiges of the crush I hadn't quite killed based on the way every cell in my body had woken up when I realized it was him standing in front of me.

And so, no. I would not tell this man, however handsome and nice and appealing he may have been, a secret literally no one else in the world knew.

"I am a bookworm indeed, especially if there's romance involved." I'd handed him his bag of books. "And it seems you are, too, since I'm fairly certain I saw you in here last month stocking up."

"Just patronizing my favorite local businesses to stimulate the Silverton economy. Everyone's gotta do their part, right?" He'd held up his bag in a little farewell. "See you soon, Jo."

I'd swallowed hard against too many reactions, one of which was, mortifyingly, *you can stimulate my economy any day.* Thank goodness I did have an internal editor.

"See you, Adam."

I'd convinced myself to return to the fictional hero in my story who did believe in romance and not dwell on this real-life human being who, devastatingly, didn't.

If only Jo then could see me now, turning the knob of my door to find Adam setting my table for two with forks and knives, napkins folded into little triangles, then smiling up at me like he was glad I'd returned.

But not for *me,* or anything romantic. Because I held Guac in my hands.

And also, because we were friends. And as ignorant as I felt asking him a million questions about life as a special operations combat medic, I had a suspicion he actually enjoyed this. He talked a little faster, leaned closer, and his eyes lit up when he recounted details he thought might fit. He'd clearly loved his life as a medic. I wondered how often he got to do medic-related duties at Saint Security.

I set the bag down and let my thoughts loose. "You know, I never would've seen this coming, but I have to say, I'm really glad we're here."

He grinned at me. "You know? Me, too."

I shouldn't have been so pleased by this, but no amount of denying would change how a soul-deep satisfaction wound through me at his words. He liked being with me, too. He was happy he'd come.

And so maybe this was all we'd have—this secret shared between friends—but we could both enjoy it.

I'd made peace with that.

Definitely.

Completely.

Right?

CHAPTER FOUR

Adam

Due to a packed week of work for everyone, we wrapped up an all-staff meeting late in the day on the Friday after Tristan and Winnie's wedding weekend.

Also five days after my small handful of hours spent at Jo's. I wouldn't overtly admit to myself I knew exactly how long I'd been there, because I left her little apartment feeling like something in me had shifted, and I'd checked my watch to make sure I hadn't warped into another time zone or briefly lost consciousness on the stairs before exiting her building.

The time flew and I'd enjoyed every second of it. In truth, I'd been itching to leave because I felt so comfortable in her space with her calming décor and pleasing scents hanging around us—I'd recognized the need to escape.

To survive.

Because being near Jo like this was a bad idea. No need

to explain it out because even completing the thought of why it was would be problematic.

I could simply acknowledge my friend Jo was a wonderful woman who deserved a better man than me. Someone like Ethan, which I'd been working on for months with little success.

Bruce's meeting recap corralled my attention back to the now.

"We've got Jess back full-time next week," he said, eyes slipping toward Beast's hulking form leaning back in his chair. "Cookie's here with us for another few weeks as well, right? And Hijack and Boots will remain out, as will the Washingtons." He ticked down the list of other personnel we had abroad, then brought it to a close. "Anyone who wants to join us at Craic, please do. Anyone who has to run home and enjoy the good life, go ahead and do that, too, and we'll see you Monday."

The room burst to life, the ten of us seated around the large conference table gathering notebooks and other items, chatting about weekend plans.

I nodded at Bruce, feeling the burn of his words. *The good life.* He'd found it with Nikki, his fiancée, and we'd just watched Tristan marry the love of his life. The Washingtons had their own version, always off on an adventure being international badasses for the Saint family. And Eddie and Bri were downright ridiculous.

And of course, our patron Saint, Wilder. We'd joked about *Saint Daddy* more than once, but the man loved his family, and as someone who'd surrendered any plans for his own, watching him jabbed at me sometimes. Holding his baby or catching a moment between him and his wife, Sarah... it made some long-numbed place in my chest awaken.

It'd happened more and more, but at least there were a few of us still single and ready to... grab a beer on a Friday night.

And, to be fair, Bruce, Tristan, and occasionally even Wilder came out with us. It helped that Nikki and Winnie got together with their girls at the same place and time, but I'd take my friends however I could get them. I missed them, even though it made me a little pathetic to admit. I didn't like the idea of being a man who begrudged his friends their happiness, so I fought against the missing. Mostly, I was thrilled they'd found what they wanted, elated they'd found women who loved them. They were excellent men, and I was grateful to Sarah, Nikki, and Winnie for making my friends so deeply happy.

"You checked on Stone lately?" Bruce asked, patting my back as he came alongside me in the hallway.

"I was going to take a jog and swing by tomorrow. I usually check in every week or so."

Bruce nodded, his gaze revealing relief.

"He's not giving me much." He held up his phone, likely indicating Dorian "Stone" Forrester's tendency toward terseness or lack of responses altogether when it came to calls and texts.

"I got him. I'll let you know how it goes."

I slipped into my office after a farewell from Bruce—I'd see him in a few minutes—and set down the folder I'd tucked under my yellow legal pad. This meeting had been a bit less about planning and a bit more of a state of the union now that we'd made it through Tristan's wedding and things were going to be ramping up over the summer and eventually launching into a busy fall.

That was why I hadn't made my proposal. It just hadn't fit in with the content. When Danny Morrison, chief of ski patrol at Silver Ridge Resort and my low-key hiking buddy, had suggested I lead a survival skills course, I'd loved the idea. It felt like the answer to a question I hadn't verbalized. I'd been looking for how to develop my angle on life post-Army. Bruce had his leadership and the business itself, as did Wilder. Tristan had his self-defense classes. The other guys had their interests they'd folded into work or developed outside it, but I hadn't hit mine, save hiking.

Survival classes would let me take my years of practical knowledge and pair it with helping people in my new community. It would let me take *Doc* to the mountains.

I'd never been a coward, but it felt like so much rode on whether everyone liked the idea. They would—it would bring in new clients and business but shouldn't create wear and tear on the already very busy staff save me. Still, I had doubts. So not today—I didn't want to force it. We'd meet again in two weeks, and I could do it then. If my idea got approved, I could get it rolling by mid-July, maybe, and still have quite a while before I'd have to put the program to bed for the winter.

And if they hate the idea, I'll just bury my head in other work and not think about it.

"You coming, Doc?" Kenny asked, sidling his way into my office without so much as a knock.

"Yep. I'm just walking, though. No reason to battle the lots." The main parking lots at the far end of Main Street and the one practically next door to our building would be full by now, plus we were only a few blocks from the bar.

"Same. Beast is waiting on us, too." He flared his eyes. "He's extra sweet, as you can imagine."

I heaved a sigh as I cut off the light in my office. "Of course he is."

One mention of Jess Korbel starting back here, and

inevitably, the storm clouds descended. She'd gone abroad nearly five months ago—she'd done her time away. I sincerely hoped we wouldn't need another meeting reminding him to be civil and professional toward her, but maybe tonight I could slip it in.

Outside, we wandered the bustling streets of our small town together, me and Kenny side by side and Beast like an overgrown linebacker tailing us. June in Utah was nothing short of magnificent, and I couldn't wait to spend some time on the trails tomorrow. Tonight, the evening was cooling off and the sun had started to slip down but hadn't tucked under the horizon just yet.

But first, a drink or two with my friends and coworkers, and maybe a glimpse of other people, too.

No one specific, of course.

Just... people.

As the only Irish pub in town, Craic could get pretty busy on weekends, and evidence the summer season was picking up broadcasted in the buzz tonight. Locals and tourists were cramming around the bar already, and it was only six.

Bruce and Cookie set pitchers of beer in the center of the two high-top tables we kept reserved for our Saint team. It had started as an unspoken understanding, but once the tourist season began last winter, the bar's owner, Kieran, made sure to denote these two tables were taken. It helped that he and Bruce were in book club together and that we always tipped generously.

"When are the lovebirds back from their honeymoon?" Kenny asked as he eyed Bruce and Cookie filling pint glasses from the pitcher.

"Late Sunday," Beast said.

"Is Juniper having withdrawals yet?" I asked, genuinely curious how his week with Tristan's beloved dog had gone.

Beast scowled.

Kenny snickered into his pint glass before asking, "She hasn't ever been away from them this long, has she?"

Bruce and I shared a look as we waited for what would come. Beast was a man of few words to say the least, so he was not likely to detail the ins and outs of keeping Tristan's dog for a week. That said, if there was one thing Beast melted for, it was Juniper Donnelly. Well, and his giant cat.

"No, she hasn't," he grunted out.

Kenny raised his glass. "Well, here's to a great week, to our friend returning, to Beast's excellent dog-sitting skills, and to his cat being willing to share him for a while."

"Hear, hear," Bruce said, raising his drink.

Cookie, Beast, and I followed suit.

"Well hello, gentlemen," Nikki said, sliding an arm around Bruce and pressing a kiss to his cheek.

In seconds, he had her by the waist and captured her mouth in a quiet kiss, then released her.

"Come on, man, that's not fair," Kenny whined.

Cookie and I shared a smile, and Beast maintained his usual affect.

"Sorry," Nikki said, her cheeks blazing.

"I mean, I can't blame him, but it's just mean," Kenny said, still pouting.

"How was your day?" Bruce asked, his voice tender and his focus still fully enveloped in his fiancée.

I looked away, something pinching in my chest I didn't like to think about. Movement caught my attention at the corner of my eye, and I turned to see Jo's long ponytail flick behind her. She stood at the usual high top she and her friends occupied most Friday nights and laughed along with

Catherine Hewitt and Dove Jensen at something Elise Cordero was cheerily gesticulating about.

Maybe it was the single beer on an empty stomach, or maybe it was the fact that this woman tied me in a knot, but I had to crush my hand into a fist to forget said knot existed and banish the bone-deep desire to bury my hands in her hair and guide her mouth to mine.

If she were mine, she would already be over here, wrapping her arms around me. Maybe she'd press her lips to my jaw and I'd tuck her as close as possible before taking my time doing the same to her, breathing in her fresh linen and flower scent. And I wouldn't stop until I'd claimed a kiss, satisfied the need building in me every time I stood in the same vicinity. I'd—

I caught the fantasy running away with itself.

Okay, yeah. Definitely the beer.

Should probably order some food because that's not a thing. Not on the table. Not in the bar. Not in this small town. Not in this lifetime.

Jo was my friend and that was all I could or would ever give her. Add to that the age difference between us—somewhere north of ten years—and the fact that I had nothing to offer her even if I wanted to. I had no idea what a healthy relationship looked like, let alone a marriage. I couldn't give her that, and she'd made it clear that's what she wanted. She didn't even know about my failed track record. Those threads braided into a knot I couldn't untie with attraction and even good intentions, because at the heart of it, I'd shown I didn't know how to love someone and prioritize them the way they needed. I wouldn't ruin someone the way I had before.

So? I shouldn't be thinking like this.

Jo needed someone like the heroes in her books—yes, I'd

read the first two in the series she was working on now. She needed someone emotionally available and ready to shower her with love and affection and attention the way she required it. She needed someone like Ethan, who'd wanted to settle down and love a good woman since I could remember.

All this thinking about her as anything more than a friend had to be due to spending time with her recently and no other reason. I cared about her, wanted her safe, had a little insider knowledge no one else had. That certainly didn't mean she was interested in me, and again, if she were, I couldn't do anything about it. She wanted love, marriage, family.

I'd proven I wasn't made for those things.

Like my mind had warned me—not in this lifetime.

Jo Malcom wasn't for me.

CHAPTER FIVE

Adam

I checked my watch amidst the din of the after-work crowd decompressing, wondering when Ethan would show, and speak of the devil, an arm came around my shoulders.

"Got a head start? I would've thought security guys would be working harder than a coffee-shop guy."

Kenny hollered out an "Ehhh!" and raised his hands in celebration of Ethan's arrival. They'd met before life in Utah, when Ethan had visited me at work in North Carolina, but they'd discovered a real bromance here in Silverton. It helped they were closer in age than any of the rest of us old fogies—most of us who'd come to Saint were retired at twenty years out, which put us squarely in the "late thirties to early forties" category, whereas Kenny had left on a medical discharge at a spry twenty-six, and that was almost a year and a half ago. Ethan was ten full years younger than me, clocking in at twenty-eight.

After a nice little bro-hug, they parted, and Ethan folded into our group. He wasn't a Saint employee, but he knew everyone around the table and they'd accepted him as one of us for all social purposes. Since he'd been focused on opening his business for the first few months he was here and then working nonstop to keep it open as he'd navigated hiring and management and all the things a small business owner had to juggle, he hadn't exactly been a social butterfly.

So seeing him accept a beer from Bruce and watching Beast nudge him with an elbow and give him a rather friendly nod... it filled me up. Yes, that was the older-brother syndrome talking, but it did, and I'd take it.

Ethan had coordinated all of this, ultimately. When I'd told him I was thinking about following Wilder and Bruce out here after retirement, he'd asked how I felt about him coming, too. He'd been in the Army for one stint after college, but we'd never managed to be stationed together. Then, he'd gotten out and considered moving to North Carolina, but I'd been in a nonstop cycle of deployments and he'd had a girlfriend. When that had fizzled, he'd gotten the itch to move, and it had lined up well with my decision to call Silverton home for the foreseeable future.

And here we were.

Nothing gave me more joy than seeing him figure out his life. The Army hadn't been right for him—not like it had been for me. He'd served for three years after getting his degree and that was that. I never would've pegged him for a coffee shop owner, but he had so much pride in his place and he'd worked hard for it, so I couldn't be anything but impressed by him.

"When are you going to ask her out?" Kenny asked in a low tone I only heard because I was standing right next to Ethan.

"Who?" Ethan asked, but his dark eyes went straight over my shoulder to the table of women I'd just been forbidding myself to look back at, then he took a sip of his beer.

Kenny shook his head. "The woman you've been pining for since you moved here."

Ethan choked on his swallow. "I—no. We're friends. It's cool."

I patted his back. "No aspirating your beer."

He coughed out a "Sorry," then took another slug before glaring at Kenny.

Kenny raised his hands in innocence. "Just strikes me as a great time. We've got great weather for a date. Night in Bloom is coming up. Fourth of July makes a great date night... opportunities abound."

Ethan and I both gave Kenny an annoyed look that must've said enough. He begged off, saying he was going to get some waters, so I focused on Ethan.

He'd been cut deep with his last relationship, and I'd tried to respect his space. But Kenny had a point, and maybe Ethan needed a nudge.

"He's right, you know."

Ethan huffed and stared at his beer. "Sure."

"I'm just saying, she's a great girl. You guys are already friends. And you're a good man. You deserve someone..." I searched for the right word. "You deserve someone *good* like her. Sweet and smart and, you know... emotionally available."

He sighed long and slow, then glanced at me from under his thick brown lashes a few shades darker than my own.

"You're forgetting the business partner aspect here. And the fact that I kind of *did* ask her out last summer and she shifted me right into the friendzone. I'm not the kind of guy who's going to try to wear a woman down. She said no? Loud and clear, I heard her. There are a lot of beautiful women here in Silverton, so there's no reason to put pressure on our friendship."

This was the part that never made sense to me—why he'd taken the rejection in the first place when I wasn't certain she'd actually said no. But it did get murky with the business setup—what if she'd felt like she had to create such a boundary if they were going into business together? And sure, it made sense then, but it'd been a year, and it seemed she was mostly hands-off. She attended a meeting with him once a month or so, but beyond patronizing Joe like it was her favorite store aside from All Booked Up, she wasn't in there getting her hands dirty.

"I'm not saying wear her down. I'm just saying—" My fool eyes dragged themselves over to her, where she grinned at her friends, but then her gaze shifted, met mine, and she sobered.

My stomach dropped low and twisted tight, tighter, a rag wrung out in opposing directions. She blinked, then smiled softly and notched her chin up in the way all the Saint guys did.

A rough laugh tripped out, and I returned the gesture, then swallowed hard and wrangled my focus back to the table. My heart clanged around in my chest, and I reached for my beer and guzzled the last few sips in one gulp.

As I set down the glass, Ethan's eyes were boring holes into the side of my head.

"What?" I asked in my best impression of Beast to date.

He didn't speak, so I finally glanced up and met his narrowed eyes.

"What were you saying?" he asked, as though the question made perfect sense.

"What do you mean, what was I saying? I wasn't saying anything."

He chuckled and shook his head.

"What?" I asked again, irritation at the smug look on his face rising.

"You were literally in the middle of a sentence."

I eyed the bar, where Kenny was turning back toward us with a pitcher of water and another round of pint glasses on a tray like he worked here.

"And your point?" I sounded more irritable than I felt, though I had the distinct feeling of being caught doing something wrong and it didn't make sense.

Maybe you shouldn't be mooning over the girl your brother likes—that's pretty wrong. Well, damn. True enough.

"Adam, look at me."

I did as he asked and found him giving me his earnest, serious look, which never failed to get my full attention. This was his *this is important* face.

"Maybe you should think about—"

"No. And that's all there is to say."

He glared. "That's not how life works. There's always more to say."

"Not about this."

His jaw ticked, the telltale sign he was formulating his plan of attack and had every intention of continuing the argument.

I set a hand on his shoulder. "Nothing else to say here, okay?"

He held my gaze, studying me and likely looking for another angle, but thankfully, relented. "Fine."

"We got a Carter-brother standoff?" Kenny asked, sliding pint glasses of ice water toward each of us standing around the two tables.

"Of course not. My big brother is being a stubborn ass, as usual, and I'm choosing to nobly save my next point of argument for a private conversation." He shot me a crusty look, and I could've sworn he was sixteen and not twenty-eight.

I didn't rise to his bait, and thankfully, Kenny ran away with the conversation, which eventually morphed into stories of bodyguarding and the worst people we'd had to professionally babysit.

I didn't turn around again the whole night.

CHAPTER SIX

I'd been at Joe since it'd opened at seven this morning. I loved getting here before anyone else because most early morning customers on a Saturday were stop-ins or a few other dedicated people who hunkered down with their laptops and disappeared into their own worlds.

No one was swinging by to chat and see what I was up to. No one was asking about whether I'd found a job in Salt Lake. No one was interested in me at all here in my little corner, and that suited me just fine. The small thrill that hardly anyone knew Joe was partly *mine* added to the simple pleasure of sitting here.

My close friends knew I had a stake in this adorable shop, and my dad knew, but most everyone else didn't. Ethan had suggested I do whatever I wanted and maybe because I'd already been keeping one secret, adding another came naturally. Granted, Elizabeth would probably love that news since her passion for international relations was just about the only thing burning hotter than her love of coffee.

"You must be in the zone," a warm, deep voice said next to me.

I jolted and looked up to find a very handsome Adam Carter watching me with a soft smile.

"Oh my gosh, I'm sorry. Clearly, I was," I said, laughing lightly at the miraculous focus I'd had. Frankly, *not* noticing Adam the second he'd walked in was absolutely something to be proud of.

"I'm sorry for interrupting. Just wanted to say hi and I hope it's going well."

No mention of what *it* was, bless him.

"Thank you. It is." My cheeks heated at the thought of the first kiss scene I'd just been working on for my heroine and her medic hero. Feeling his eyes still on me, I gestured to his paper bag and the small drink tray. "What are you up to so bright and early?"

"Dropping some breakfast off to a friend, and then I'm heading out for a hike." He glanced out the shop window toward the mountains as though he could hear them calling to him.

"Lucky friend," I said like an idiot. I was not jealous of whoever would receive the Saturday morning breakfast. I wasn't at all.

Why would I be, when Adam was my friend and we weren't... anything but friends? And why was I being so weird about this while he was still standing right here in front of me?

"Yeah, he used to be my trail buddy, but lately he's not up for much other than a stop in." Worry clouded his eyes when he glanced back at me.

"I'm glad you're checking on him, then," I said, wondering who this person was and how Adam had come to care for him so much. Without a doubt he did, though, because this was genuine anxiety I was seeing etched on his face. For a man who didn't broadcast his feelings, this was loud and clear.

"Yeah, me, too. Maybe I can get him back out there this summer."

"I hope so. And, you know, if you can't, I'm happy to be a trail buddy. If you need a substitute for a while."

Why did I say that?

"Yeah? You want to be my hiking buddy?" he asked, the little half smile on his face alluring enough, I could hardly stand the escalation of my heartbeat.

I reached for my drink, only to find I'd finished it and there was nothing left in the large cappuccino mug, so I rerouted to my water and took a sip before answering. "Yeah. I mean... not today. Like you said, I'm in the zone. But... sometime."

Cue mental spiral—I'd just invited him on a hike. Or myself on a hike with him. A thing I knew he valued deeply and provided him sanity and joy and all kinds of things, and I'd just tried to weasel my way into his life by joining him.

Could I be any more desperate? I shuddered at the thought he might realize how much I wanted to be around him—that he could feel the drive to spend time with him wafting off me in freaking needy waves.

"Fair enough. Maybe next weekend?"

His response was casual and friendly and so of course, I agreed. If I backtracked now, it'd be even weirder than inviting myself along in the first place.

"Sounds good. Just let me know how much nature to expect and I'll mentally prepare by then." I fluttered my lashes, hoping he'd know I was joking even though part of me was definitely not joking. I liked to hike, but it took some gearing up.

He chuckled low, the sound rich and something I wanted to hear again in another context. "I'll be sure to let you know. Have a good one, Jo."

"You, too. Hi to your friend, if I know him."

With that, he sent me the Saint guy nod and I gave him a parting grin, then glued my eyes to my laptop until the bell on the door jingled and I knew he'd be out of sight. Without an audience, I sighed and let my head slump to the table.

"Wow, that bad, huh?" Ethan set his messenger bag onto the seat at a two-top to the side and slid into the chair diagonal to me. Close enough to talk but not to invade my space.

"Bad?" I chuckled and clickety-clacked on my keyboard as though I was actually typing something and not still feeling the burn of embarrassment after inviting myself to hike with his brother.

"Talking with my brother was that bad?"

I straightened. "What? No. He's fine."

He chuckled. "I know he's fine. I mean, you clearly like him."

My mouth dropped open. "Um. What? Yeah. He's definitely a nice guy."

That sounded casual, right? *No big deal, nothing to see here, no character-inspiring crushes to report.*

Ethan pulled the brim of his hat lower on his head and leaned over so his elbow rested on the table. He had wavy hair that flipped up just over his ears and at the back of his head, and his face was almost never clean-shaven, though usually, he kept something just north of stubble instead of a true beard. It worked together to give him a boyish quality that was so appealing and nice.

He really was so handsome, and it made no sense that I didn't feel all fluttery and mind-melty around him but I did for his older brother. His darker hair was longer at the sides, but it had the same carefree texture—I'd never wanted to run my hands through it like I did with Adam's lighter locks. Same strong chin and cut jaw, but I felt no impulse to trail kisses along his trimmed beard until I reached his full mouth like I did with his brother.

Shockingly enough, same thicker lower lip, but I didn't have to check the longing to brush my thumb across it, maybe nip it just a little just to see what he'd do, whenever I entered a room with Ethan in it.

When Ethan spoke, his words came out quiet enough no one else busily typing would hear, nor would Jeanine currently pulling espresso for the person at the counter.

"I think maybe you think he's more than nice," he said.

"*You're* more than nice."

He laughed. "Yeah. But that's not what I mean, and you know it."

I could admit it—I pouted back at him, not returning his smile and feeling all kinds of squiggly in my chair. "I don't know anything."

He leaned back and observed me as I hurriedly packed up my things, not interested in staying here under his scrutiny.

"I'll just say that if you did think he was a little more than nice, maybe someone you'd like to spend more time with..."

Slinging my bag's strap over one shoulder, I huffed as I pinned him with my glare. "What, you'll warn me away?

Tell me he's out of my league or too old or isn't interested in dating?"

His smile widened and something in his eyes flashed like I'd just told him a secret. "No, none of those things."

I grabbed my basket and the cappuccino mug, which he took from my hands before pulling my attention back to his face.

"I'd tell you I don't know of a better man, and that he's worth the trouble." Then he winked and turned, hollering a "Have a good one, Jo!" over his shoulder like he hadn't just turned me completely upside-down.

I scuttled out of there and down the street, avoiding eye contact with the small number of wanderers, and slinked into my building without stopping by to see if my dad had come in early for his time at the shop today. I couldn't see anyone else who was going to look me in the eye and read what I apparently broadcasted for all to see.

At least, for Ethan to see.

Yes, I thought Adam was more than nice. I... I liked him a lot. But I'd also been telling myself for coming up on a year now that he wasn't for me and I didn't like the idea of just ignoring my own hard-won wisdom. It was sound logic, and all the reasons I'd expected Ethan to warn me away from his brother were real items on the list of points against Adam, not the least of which I didn't even mention—he's not interested in me like that.

"I don't know of a better man... he's worth the trouble."

I slumped down on my couch and shoved the heels of my hands into my eyes. I didn't want any trouble. I wanted... simple. Straightforward. No obvious disinterest and stated anti-marriage stance. I didn't want a hero I had to reform and shape—these never worked out in real life, anyway—plus that was more a trope for historicals and their roguish men.

But Ethan was telling me something, wasn't he? He was a friend and I doubted many people knew Adam as well as he did. He wasn't warning me away or telling me the feelings I apparently clearly broadcasted for all to see were foolish. He was telling me... well, he was essentially saying go for it, right?

Because Adam was worth fighting for. That was Ethan's point. He wasn't a reformed rake or a guy who'd never committed to anyone before. He was... what? He was a reluctant hero. He didn't see himself as a main character in his own story—it was like he'd taken a supporting role to all his friends, his brother, and even me. He didn't realize he could so easily become the hero in my story and his own just by being himself.

But even as I crushed my eyes closed against the foolishly hopeful thoughts, they emerged clear and bright as a single word on a new page.

I knew Adam was a good man already. He'd helped when Kiley had been taken last fall and again when Winnie had been kidnapped—and yes, technically, that was his job. But he'd also voluntarily helped me with my writing, and he clearly cared about his friends and his brother. He was already wonderful, and there was no need for him to become someone new in order to appeal to me, let alone be someone I wanted beyond the chemistry between us.

Ugh, and this other thought ringing out like truth came in hot, even though everything in me that hated the idea of foisting myself on someone who didn't want me shriveled at the same time.

He'd be worth the trouble.

CHAPTER SEVEN

Adam

Dorian's front door was open when I knocked. A text arrived seconds later directing me to come in.

Not unheard of for Stone to refuse to answer the door but still let me in, and yet worry soured in my gut. He'd been even more reclusive than usual lately, and I didn't know what exactly I'd be finding today.

"Stone?"

A low, clipped *woof* came in response, which explained why Bear hadn't been at the front to greet me. I padded through the entryway and down the short hallway to the kitchen. Lights were all off, no sound coming from anywhere. This, still, wasn't entirely unusual, but the stale scent in here, like the windows and doors hadn't been opened in weeks, set my teeth on edge.

I entered the living room slowly, knowing Bear wouldn't

appreciate me bursting into his space, even if he had sent the response to my call. When I saw him, I swallowed hard.

Bear lay parallel to the couch, giant head tucked into his paws, and inspected me with his forlorn set of amber Alaskan Malamute eyes. On the couch, stretched out under a blanket, was Dorian, who didn't so much as shift to look at me as I slowly approached the chair.

"Hey," I said, speaking as quietly as I could.

"Doc."

No shift of his head to look at me, but at least he'd responded. There had been a time or two when I'd come and thought maybe he was catatonic, but once he'd been asleep with earplugs in, and the other... well, I didn't like to think about that time. It'd been a year since then, though. He was doing great.

Maybe not great, but he was doing okay.

"Brought you breakfast." I set the bag onto the table and Bear perked up enough to sniff around the bag. I pulled the homemade doggy biscuit Ethan stocked from its waxy sleeve and set it on the ground for him.

"Thanks." Voice gruff, Dorian likely hadn't spoken aloud to anyone but Bear in days.

Guilt slashed through me, piercing my chest. *I should get here more often. We all should.*

His gaze set straight ahead, I went about my business removing items from the bakery bag, trying not to let my internal chant willing him to move bleed out into the space between us and spook him.

Bear wandered over and set his chin on my leg, studying me with mournful eyes again. I ran a hand over his head, the black-and-white pattern of his fur making his vivid gaze almost haunting, particularly since I could feel his expression.

"I know, bud. That's a good biscuit, isn't it?" I said as though he was thanking me for the treat and not begging me to help his dad.

"Ethan makes those?" Stone asked, shifting forward and slowly rolling to the side to a seated position. He moved like he had a pounding hangover or like he'd aged a hundred years while lying there and everything in him hurt.

"He gets them from someone local, but he's not the mastermind. Seems to be a pretty good little snack for this fellow." I petted Bear's head again, imbuing as much tenderness into the gesture as I could.

Stone made a sound of acknowledgment as he lifted the cup from the drink tray and brought it to his lips. Just before he took a sip, he pulled it back.

Brows scrunched, he asked, "Is it—"

"Decaf. Of course."

With a nod, he finally took a drink.

We'd need to talk, but I could give him some quiet with his coffee before I dove in, so we sat in silence, only the low hum of his air conditioner out back to accompany us.

After a few minutes, he finally made eye contact and nodded. *Ready*.

"How are you?" No point in pretending this was simply a social call.

He took a moment to breathe through his thoughts, measured and careful, but not avoiding, I didn't think.

"I'm okay."

I chuckled lightly, and one side of his mouth tipped up a fraction. I'd take it.

"You seeing the doc still?" His therapist, but doc felt less invasive.

He nodded but said, "Been a few weeks since I made it in."

His chest rose and fell, and I recalled how he'd describe feeling like words and emotions got tangled up in his chest and couldn't find a way out. How they piled up until it felt like so much pressure in his body, he couldn't stand it.

"Hard to get out right now?" I asked, knowing that leaving his home was often extremely difficult for him.

His jaw flexed under his scraggly beard. "Yeah, worse the last few days, too."

My heart dropped. "I'm going to call Dr. Corrigan. We'll get you set up with a virtual session, and I'm going to get you an appointment to see about your meds, too."

His lips thinned ever so slightly and his nostrils flared. My throat tightened and I moved to sit by him, Bear settling in with his head on Stone's knee.

"I'm tired of this," he said, teeth gritted against the crushing weight of things.

"I'm sorry it's bad right now. Have you had any—"

"Not really."

Pain lanced through me, but I pressed on. "No plans?"

"No. No plans. Just... tired."

Not the reassurance I'd prefer, but he'd answered honestly. There'd been a time when he'd said yes to both. There'd been a time... I shook that off. "Thank you for telling me. I'm sorry it's so hard right now. It will get better."

His chin dropped in acknowledgment, just barely, and he blinked away the tears that'd glossed his eyes. With a gusty swear, he shook his head. "Thanks for coming."

"Should've come sooner. You seemed good at the wedding." He'd been there before the wedding, early enough to give Tristan his support, and then stood in the back until the ceremony had ended. I'd checked in, confirmed he was doing okay...

But you were distracted by Jo and there's no denying

that. We'd been paired up in the wedding party, so I'd escorted her down the aisle. I'd danced with her a few times, too. It was the closest we'd ever been, but in the haze of the celebration and everyone dancing together, it had mostly felt fun and light and beautiful.

I was glad I'd enjoyed the moment, but guilt pressed in on me for how I'd missed the signs that Stone had not been okay.

"I'm glad I went. I'm happy for him." He didn't really know Winnie, but he loved Tristan, and he'd shown up.

If I thought about how difficult it must've been for him to show up to something like that, it made me want to curl up in a corner and weep. It was the curse of empathy and also the challenge of being a person who cared about his family. Stone and I might not share blood like Ethan and I did, but he was my brother.

"Sip your coffee and eat that breakfast sandwich I brought while I start your dishwasher and check out what kind of nonsense you've got in your fridge. Then you can get showered up while I run to the store."

He sniffed again but focused on the bag in front of him. "'Kay."

And so we did. I cleaned up his kitchen and tried not to let the fact that he'd clearly been living off tuna and dry cereal for at least a few days, since Beast or Barbie had checked, decimate me. I texted the guys with an update, set up a meeting between all of us, and then I got some laundry started while he got in the shower. With a quick run to the market and back, I settled everything I could before leaving him.

"Cookie's coming by tomorrow, okay?" I said as I hauled him into a hug. No surprise, but he'd lost some weight. He'd been doing well, had bulked back up a bit and he'd even been coming into the office a few times a month there for a while, but something had shifted for him, and I hated it.

"Yeah. Thanks."

"No thanks needed. And the doc's calling you at three. Answer, okay?"

He nodded rapidly. "I will. I swear."

With a hand on his neck, I looked in his eyes. "You are not alone. I love you, and I am back here to couch surf the second you tell me you need that."

He blinked—all the acknowledgment I'd get for now.

"Let me hear from you later if you can," I said and released him.

"Wilco."

This little twinge of sass made me shoot him a smile. His "Will comply" response was an old joke between us. When he had it in him, he liked to tell me I was a bossy nursemaid. And I could be.

"You better. See you soon, Stone." I patted Bear one last time.

"See ya, Doc."

Out into the small yard and then to the trail of pines that made up a fraction of the sprawling tree farm he'd bought before he ever moved here, I breathed in deep, steadying breaths as I stomped my way to my car. I'd never been more thankful that he'd hired a manager for the farm than I was now because seeing these trees fail would kill him. Outsourcing their survival while he focused on his own was the right call for now.

A hike would do me good. Fresh mountain air, the sun, the trees, the glory of creation... it'd clear my head and maybe, ease my aching heart. I prayed it would, at least, and yet something else was nudging into my peripheral thoughts, which I couldn't allow.

By the time I got to the driver's-side door, it was everything I could do not to head into town. Not to search for Jo and find her and wrap her in my arms and bury my face in her neck and seek solace in her.

She'd hold me until I was ready to talk, and I just knew she'd be patient if I didn't get there—if I couldn't find words to pour out what seeing my friend like this did to me. She wouldn't push or guilt. She'd just let me find peace for a moment.

She knew nothing about this. She hardly knew *me*. But something in my gut told me seeing her would help. *Everything is better with her*.

I couldn't do that, though. It would be completely unfair to both of us to use her this way—and wouldn't that be what it was? Seeking comfort and deep breaths from her when I had no way to give her anything more than I already had?

Good thing I knew how to deny myself—I could be a bossy little nurse to myself just like I could be with my friends. What I needed was fresh air and sunlight and time on the trails. I didn't need a woman who wasn't mine to need—who deserved a future I couldn't give her.

I couldn't.

CHAPTER EIGHT

Jo

It didn't bother me that Adam hadn't been at the Saint Security cocktail hour last night or that I hadn't seen him since last Saturday. It *didn't*. It was just... different.

And as I'd tapped away at my keyboard this morning, it'd taken a great deal of energy to keep myself from glancing up and checking to see whether he'd popped in for a coffee. Of course if he *had,* he would've just come said hi. It wasn't like he was avoiding me. What reason would he have?

As far as I knew, we still had plans to hike tomorrow. I didn't know how well that would go, especially after not seeing him for what felt like way too long, but it was just a friendly activity. Neither of us had any expectations for it except to do something he loved together. And ideally for me to stay alive and intact during it and not betray the full measure of my indoor cat-ness.

An afternoon call with my big sister hadn't helped my sense of anxiety about life.

"How's the job hunt coming? Any good leads in the city?" she'd asked, like she always did. She'd been a staunch encourager of mine during college, and then as I figured out what masters to pursue, so she was eager to see me put all this education to use.

"Uh, not really. No luck yet."

And that was only a partial lie. I hadn't applied or interviewed anywhere, so in this regard, it was true, I'd had no luck. But it was a big fat lie of omission because I hadn't even attempted to obtain any.

"Seems like it's been a while. Is Dad pressuring you to stay there and help with the store?"

She'd had the edge she got whenever she spoke of either of our parents. She didn't dislike them, and as far as I knew, she didn't even have an awful wound in her past that I'd somehow missed. But whenever she sensed someone was holding me back or influencing me in a way she didn't like, she got this tone. The *I'm a badass secret agent and I will destroy anyone messing with my baby sister* ring in her voice.

I loved her for it, but it also made telling her the truth kind of... terrifying.

Yes, I was a grown woman and should be able to say, "Lizzy, I want to write romance novels and sell books at the shop and live in this small town forever." But in reality, what she'd hear is, "Dad is making me stay here, and I'm too scared to say no." Or worse, she'd think I was being selfish. She'd think less of me for choosing to do something so... so *small.*

This woman worked for "The State Department." And yes, that was in quotes. Because she wasn't exactly in the business of diplomacy as we think of it. She'd told me once years ago and sworn me to silence. I didn't even technically know what she did, but I knew she lived internationally, worked with all kinds of different ABC agencies, and she made a difference.

She kept our country safe. Our people safe. And she was amazingly strong and independent. So much so, I often wondered if we came from the same gene pool. None of us had ever been like her—Dad had been an accountant until he'd moved here to open a book store. My mom had been a home-maker until she and my dad had separated, and then she'd gone into real estate. These were fine jobs, fine lives, but none of them were being a spy for our country, or whatever she did.

And certainly, she wasn't out there writing romance novels about hot soldiers and the women they fell first and hard for.

I hated the part of me that felt ashamed to tell her the truth. And so, like I'd done once every other week since last summer when I'd started saying it, I repeated what I always did.

"It's not Dad. I'm just hitting dead ends. I'm sure some-thing will come along soon."

And then, as usual, she'd sighed and evaded any ques-tions I asked about her life and work, telling me she loved me with a kind of stiffness that sometimes made me chuckle and sometimes made me cry.

"Bye, Jojo. Love you."

And I'd returned it, missing her with half of me and relieved she was so far away with the other half. "Love you, too, Lizzy."

Imagining her discovering that every one of my books included a special thank-you to her, to "L" in the acknowl-edgments made my heart race—with dread or a little longing, I couldn't tell. If she knew, though she'd never read the books, she might... I didn't know. She might understand how much her opinion meant to me, how amazing I thought she was—how much *she* meant to me, even though we'd been apart for so long.

It always took a while to recover from the frustration and guilt I felt after calls with her. I loved her and respected her, and I wanted her respect in return. I dreamed of her coming to visit and sharing the truth of my life with her—of showing her those acknowledgments. And every so often, they stayed dreams. More frequently, they turned to nightmares and I'd see her face twist in disappointment, I'd hear her wondering why I'd removed myself from making a difference, and so on.

Those thoughts simply had to be shut down. I couldn't reason my way through them because most likely, she wouldn't say that. If anything, she'd be silently disapproving. But more likely than all of those possibilities was the reality that I hadn't seen my sister in person in years, so worrying about her showing up on my doorstep wasn't a real issue.

I sent a text to Adam asking what time we'd be doing our hike—a nice mental shift before I moved fully away from my messy feelings in the wake of the phone call and into a fun night with my friends.

What I needed more than anything was some solid time with my girls, good books, champagne, and snacks. Fortunately, the time had come.

Adam's reply came through and my heart slipped.

No. Bad heart. No flipping for a simple text about the time for a friend hike.

Silver Ridge Romance Reader Book Club and its

beloved members couldn't show up and distract me soon enough.

"Are we ready to Romance?" Dove asked, skipping down the street as I opened All Booked Up's shop door to let them in. The store had closed a few hours earlier, so I'd had plenty of time to prep things.

"We absolutely are," Elise said, right as Catherine and Nikki pulled up. Winnie had gotten here early and was already inside, and we were only missing...

"Jess! My beloved! You have returned to us!" Dove dropped the little basket she was using as a purse and ran with arms flung wide toward Jess, whose crooked smile grew into something blinding and delighted as she received Dove's bear hug.

"Why are we acting like you didn't see me at the wedding?" Jess asked, ducking her chin and squeezing Dove, who was only an inch shorter than her. "For such a small person, you give a great hug."

Dove pulled back and coughed dramatically. "Well, for someone so small, you are freakishly strong and I think you squeezed out all my stuffing."

Jess chuckled, as did the rest of us.

"And as for you being back, this is the first book club you've been home for."

Jess grinned. "I *am* freakishly strong, but it's part of the gig. And... true. I'm glad to be back." She elbowed Dove lightly in the ribs, and we all chatted loudly as we got settled in the reading room.

"Okay, I know we have a ton to catch up on, and I want to hear everything I missed, but can I just submit one thing for our agenda?" Jess asked as she snuggled into her favorite soft chair in the room.

"Please do," I said, waving her on. We'd missed her so

much these last few months—it felt like half a year since the last time she'd been able to attend a book club.

She bit her lip, excitement outright flaming in her eyes. "I just saw Josie Wade finally posted the release date for her next book. It's next month. Can we *pleeease* have a release party for her?"

My smile stretched thin and my brain scrambled. Release party? What did that mean?

"What would we do? Try to invite her to come? Ohhh!" Dove clapped. "What if she did a signing at the store? You guys have done a few signings, right?" Her big blue eyes swiveled to mine with such hope.

"Uh, a few. Mostly smaller, local authors. I... I don't know if it's enough advanced notice." *Just tell them now. Tell them now! It's no big deal. You can just tell them now.*

I could. I could just sit down and say "Ta-da! No need to invite her because she's already here! Weee!" But then...

Then everyone would know. They would keep the secret if I asked them to, but wouldn't that be virtually the same thing as everyone knowing? Right now, only Adam knew. That was fully contained. My family didn't know.

Elizabeth didn't know. And I didn't want her to know. And until I figured out how to accept whatever fallout happened from that, I wouldn't be telling anyone else.

"Listen, I know you've got a million things to juggle with the store, especially since your dad and Jane are traveling soon. I would be happy to track down her contact info, if any even exists, and reach out. We'll see what she says. Worst case she says no, right?" Jess said with so much hope in her voice, I couldn't ignore it.

The idea that I had more to deal with than any one of these women was laughable, but I acquiesced because what else could I do? If I kept objecting to something that would be both exciting for our group and fun for the store, it wouldn't make any sense. "Works for me."

Jess fist-pumped and everyone else clapped or cheered. Honestly, it was the nerdiest little celebration I'd ever seen.

"But I wouldn't get hopes up. It's short notice and you never know how authors will be," I added, as though I had so much worldly experience hosting authors for signings. *As if I wasn't the very person they wanted to meet.*

The wild mix of total thrill that my closest friends loved my books and piling guilt for not telling them "I *am* Josie Wade" swirled in my gut. I hated the feeling, but it'd become familiar since the last book came out and we'd all started sharing our thoughts on books more purposefully. As long as my own family didn't know, it'd feel like even more betrayal if my friends knew first. And with the way things were going, I didn't want Elizabeth to know, not just yet, so the guilt at not telling my friends? Stuck with it, and I only had myself to blame for it.

I couldn't accept the invitation, but I'd do everything I could as Jo to their faces and Josie behind the scenes to make them feel appreciated.

"I love this. I *love it!* Now Jess, tell us how you are and..." Dove's smile slipped a touch. "How things are going at work."

Jess sighed. "It's fine. Right now, I'm giving him a wide berth and he's basically pretending I don't exist when we're in meetings together. That's fine by me." She swallowed hard. "I was really mad when I left, but I've cooled off, I think."

"You think?" Catherine asked, cupping her wineglass like a mug. Winnie huddled next to her with the same anticipation in her eyes.

A sad smile flitted over Jess's face before she banished it

and gave a shrug. "I've just realized it's one or the other, you know? I stay here at Saint and suck it up but deal with… *him*, or I leave. And I'm not ready to leave for good yet."

Nikki's brow was furrowed, and I would bet a thousand bucks she'd be discussing this with Bruce when she got home. Winnie's face told me she might talk with Tristan, too. *Maybe I should mention it to Adam?* We hadn't really talked about his work and that might be overstepping. I'd have to feel it out next time we talked.

Elise was unusually quiet, though she had been a bit quieter lately in general. But the tenseness in her shoulders and the pained expression on her face spoke to how this news affected her, too.

My heart squeezed at the defeat in Jess's voice. She was a fighter and she was made of steel and fire, so hearing her surrender to being miserable here made me want to scream.

"I wish you didn't have to deal with him at all, or anything that makes you feel bad." Dove reached over and clasped Jess's free hand. She brought it up and kissed the back of it in such an oddly sweet way, it made Jess chuckle, which soon spread to all of us.

"You're an odd duck, Dove Jensen." Jess hauled her into a hug, then released her.

"Well, you are, too. We're all kind of weirdos." Dove beamed around the circle at each of us, and the merciful moment allowed us to ease away from the thought of Jess having to choose between staying here and happiness.

My heart practically overflowed with love for these women who'd become so special to me even as it ached with something like regret that I hadn't shared a moment of closeness like this with my own sister in well over a decade. These friends had become my family, and in some ways, I'd lost what family I had—at least the one I'd been born with.

I'd gotten adopted into an amazing one in the Saints, but that was different.

Shoving the thought away for examination another time, I raised my glass.

"To this beautiful pack of weirdos and to our support of each other through thick and thin. To the books that give us escape, and the joy we have sharing them."

Everyone touched glasses, their faces lit with joy like mine must've been.

"Hear, hear! And now, let's talk about books."

CHAPTER NINE

Adam

Jo answered her door wearing hiking boots, shorts, a lightweight zip-up jacket, and her hair in two long braids snaking over her shoulders. Her expression was serious, but I couldn't read anything particular there, maybe because my head was filled with relief at being near her again.

In fact, just the sight of her had some wayward antsy piece of my mind settling.

I swallowed hard.

I hadn't seen her in so long. I'd specifically stayed away from her, the bookstore, and Craic on Friday, just to remind myself what this was—friendship. That gut-deep longing to see her after I'd left Stone last Saturday, the utter *need* I'd felt to seek comfort in her... that'd required burying.

But not in a hole so deep I couldn't see her today, obviously. I didn't want to be a jerk and break the plans we'd already made.

"Hello, Josie."

Her mouth dropped open, then shut, and her eyes widened and skated around, likely taking in the absolutely empty sidewalk. No one was up this early on a Sunday here, but I'd planned it this way so we'd get ahead of the forecasted heat.

"Hello, Adam."

Despite myself, I stepped a few inches closer. "Should I not call you that?"

Her lashes fluttered and she pressed her lips together before saying, "I guess you can. But only when it's just us."

Oh. *Bad.*

Bad news.

Some visceral part of me reached out and grabbed onto the idea. *When it's just us.*

Like a ravenous little beast, the feeling gripped me—I wanted more time with just us. I wanted all the time with *just us.* At the bar, on the street, at home. Especially at home, and not just a bedroom... though I wouldn't mind some time with *just us* locked away there, too.

I wanted an us with Jo in a way I'd never wanted anything.

Yeah, and that's exactly why you've stayed away.

With a prayer she hadn't seen all of this idiocy written on my face—because I absolutely was not the man for her—I forced a casual smile and stepped back. "Fair enough. You ready?"

She smiled, too, but it slipped for a second and she glanced around behind me. Was she nervous to be out so early with me? Something tapped at my protective side and I took in the street quickly, confirming there were no visible threats. It was likely too much and my gut was reading everything wrong, but better safe.

Before I could give voice to the thought, she stepped out and shut the building's door behind her. "Absolutely."

We loaded into my car, where I'd parked it right in front of the bookstore, then drove in fairly companionable silence to the trailhead.

Fairly because something was bothering her, but she seemed to be fighting it. When I parked a few minutes later, I turned to her before she got out.

"Hold up a sec."

She startled from where she fiddled with her backpack.

"If you don't want to do this, for whatever reason, you don't have to."

Her lips parted and her mouth moved, struggling to find the right word before she could actually speak.

"I'm so sorry. I didn't mean to make you feel like I don't want to be here. I do." She fiddled with one of her long braids. "I've been looking forward to this."

Our gazes held, her beautiful dark eyes pained and so earnest, it killed me.

"Alright. Let's get out there, then."

We made our way to the trailhead, and I forged on, forcing myself to give her space to work through whatever was going on in that beautiful head of hers. But half an hour in, when she hadn't spoken a word, I couldn't take it anymore.

"Let's stop up here for some water." I pulled off into a little wooded alcove with two giant stones perfect for sitting down.

She shucked her pack and let it drop, then sat and fiddled with her water bottle, still unusually quiet.

"Here," I said, handing over a small thermos and a pastry bag.

"What's this?"

Finally, her eyes met mine and confirmed what I'd suspected—something was up. This wasn't the Jo I'd come to know. I might not have had any right to know what was going on, but I'd never been good about seeing someone in pain and walking away.

Need to patch up whatever wound had opened, to calm a racing heart or soothe an ache, yawned wide and unavoidable in me. How could I fix this—whatever *this* was?

"It's some coffee and a croissant from Rise and Shine. Thought you might like a little something, and Joe doesn't open quite as early."

A tiny laugh escaped her. "You don't have to justify going to Rise and Shine. It's amazing."

I nodded, happy to hear her voice. Later, I'd spend some time examining why I'd gotten so wound up about her quiet and that little pinch in the center of her brows this morning. For now, though, I'd just try not to be an overstepping weirdo.

"To a morning spent in the wild with you," I said, holding up my thermos.

Her teeth flashed with a quick smile. "Cheers."

We sipped coffee and ate our croissants in more quiet, but it didn't feel quite so desolate now. The birds chirping and the small stream trickling through the woods with runoff from the snow slipped into my consciousness while the earthy-sweet scent of wild sage and the still-cool air of the morning filled my senses. I used the calm to channel a version of myself who could help without being wild-eyed and needy to right her wrongs. I could simply... help.

"Ready?" I asked, sensing we'd rested long enough and

hoping maybe once we started moving again, she'd talk to me.

"Sure."

Still small. Shrunken, even.

I eyed her as subtly as I could while tucking our trash inside my pack and slipped the coffees in, too. Her lips were pressed together, and she looked so distracted, I wouldn't have been surprised if she'd completely forgotten I was here. It wasn't what I found so troublesome, though. It was that Jo wasn't one to shrink from problems, and I didn't think she usually kept things to herself.

Except her secret identity as an increasingly popular romance author...

Well, right. Except for that.

She took one more long slug from her water bottle before slipping it into the pocket, then hauled her pack over her shoulder and looked up at me, ready to go.

And... nope. I couldn't take it. I literally *could not* take knowing something gnawed at her. I had to do something. Brush a hand down her arm, tuck the wild strand that had escaped her braid behind her ear, or just... hold her. Maybe I didn't have the power to help by contact, but what were hands for if not to heal, to help... to hold? Even a friend.

So instead of turning and trudging on, and long before I could think better of it, I was asking, "Can we actually wait a sec?"

"Sure. What's up?" She looked around like she might spot the issue on the dirt path.

I stepped into her space and set my hands gently on her shoulders, the drive to touch and soothe whatever I could compelling me. "Can I hug you?"

Startled, her head reared back just slightly, but her eyes lit in the same moment. "Of course."

So I slipped my arms around her and pressed her close, hands on her backpack. She gripped the shirt at my sides, not quite touching me but close enough it sent my heart skittering. She exhaled audibly, and my insides wound tight. The edge of my jaw brushed against her ear, and I could instantly imagine this hug in another circumstance—without our backpacks and hats, without whatever was troubling her, without all my baggage piled up between us.

For now, I squeezed her, imbuing the moment with as much care and wishful healing as I could, then released, stepping back to find her eyes glassy. I couldn't take it another second, this twisting in my chest as I witnessed her in pain, so the pushy nurse stepped in as I brushed a thumb over her cheek.

"Jo, honey, you've got to tell me what's going on." My hands ached to haul her back to me, to keep her close and safe, even though I had no idea what was wrong.

"I'm sorry. I didn't sleep much last night and I'm kind of a baby when I'm tired." She blinked the tears away, shaking her head.

Maybe it was that simple. I didn't want to be a man who couldn't take a woman at her word, but I had to ask. "Is that all?"

She nodded. "Yes." Then she exhaled and stretched her neck side to side. "I promise I won't be such a sad sack anymore."

"You can be however you want to be. I just wanted to make sure you're okay." The urge to stroke her cheek was a patently unhelpful one in the moment, so instead, I tugged lightly on the end of one of her braids. "Let's go."

She chuckled. "Did you really just pull my pigtail?"

"That doesn't sound like me."

She laughed in earnest now. "It might not *sound* like you, but it just *was* you."

I glanced over my shoulder and winked at her before saying, "I'm not sure what you're talking about."

She snickered, and I allowed myself a laugh, too. I was being an idiot, but it'd worked—whether it'd been exhaustion or some *thing* troubling her, she was loosening up. And I'd make a fool of myself all day if it meant she could enjoy herself.

She was every good thing. She was a sunrise on a crisp summer morning. She was the rustle of the breeze at high noon, a reprieve from the desert heat. She was the sunset painting the sky with pinks and oranges, light refracting into air and somehow opening my soul to possibility.

So yes. I'd be an idiot for her.

CHAPTER TEN

Jo

The valley overlook at the top of the trail Adam had chosen for us this morning felt like something out of a storybook.

At this elevation, spring came late, and the summer had only just taken hold. Thatches of wildflowers dotted the landscape, not unlike they had at Tristan and Winnie's wedding weeks ago farther down. The trees had thinned out, and the sky was crystal blue with cotton-ball clouds. It warmed up as we went, and two hours after we started, we sat at the scenic spot, just breathing.

Beside me on the ground, Adam's head rested on one of his arms for a pillow, and he looked so relaxed, he might've been asleep except he'd just asked me to join him.

I took another moment to inhale all this wild beauty and exhale the anxieties plaguing me. I pushed away the concerns about how hard it had been to snap out of my fear this morning and how hard Adam had worked to get me to let go of the mood that'd kept me from much more than basic responses to his questions.

And the hug... the hug that tilted my world on its axis. The hug that felt like so much more than a simple embrace. It'd had words in the pressure of his arms around me—*I'm here for you.* It'd spoken clearly with his hand brushing along my back—*I'm sorry you're hurting.* It'd caught me by surprise and spelled a truth I knew in my gut but had *felt* so powerfully, I'd choked up—*I care about you.*

Yes, all that from a hug, his soft caress of my cheek the exclamation. That *"Jo, honey,"* in his low voice, the *honey* reminding me of those Southern roots I too easily forgot about.

Like so many things, the man had understood the assignment and done it well.

With one more giant, cleansing breath, I situated myself a foot or so from him, settling into the space. I wasn't usually the kind of woman who would just lay down in the dirt, but I'd need a thorough shower after this anyway, and it looked so peaceful, any concerns I might've had were nowhere to be found.

"Here, up for just a sec," he said, leaning to ball up his jacket and slide it right where my head would go.

I snuggled into the lumpy material, not caring it wasn't comfortable. I felt relaxed and almost drowsy now that we'd stopped, and the full weight of our exertion and the exhaustion of the night before hit.

"Thanks for coming with me," he said, voice low and close enough I could tell he was facing me.

I rolled toward him, tucking my hands under my cheek on top of his jacket. "Thanks for letting me tag along."

He smiled softly, his face so stupidly handsome I probably shouldn't have let myself keep looking at him from this close range, but I did nonetheless.

"I'm glad you did."

I wouldn't presume to read his thoughts, but the way his expression darkened tipped me off to what I thought he might've had on his mind. He kept his mouth shut, though, studying my face with those heartbreaking blue eyes and not speaking.

So I did. Because I remembered Adam was my friend and I'd felt the truth of it in everything from the moment he'd picked me up this morning to this very second gazing at him next to me. And he was on my side. He wanted me to tell him what was going on, and he was virtually the only person I could talk to about this, anyway.

"So part of the reason I wasn't able to sleep was that the girls want to do a release party for Josie Wade's next book and invite the author."

His eyes widened. "Oh. Tricky."

"Yeah. So I'm just trying to figure out what to do about it."

He squinted, glancing at the trees or whatever he could see past me before asking, "Could you tell them? I mean, I know this is a secret, and I'm honored to keep it for you indefinitely, but I wonder if you might enjoy having people know? At least your closest friends?"

With a sigh, I rolled onto my back and spoke to the sky. "I've been wondering that, too. But there are..." I glanced over to see him still focused fully on me before continuing. "There are real reasons not to. And yes, they absolutely make me a coward, and they have nothing to do with my friends. But it's still just not..."

When I couldn't find the word, he stepped in. "You can do whatever you want, Jo. I don't want to seem critical. I just want to see you happy. If the way things are is doing that, then ride your pen-name pony."

I chuckled at his turn of phrase. "Well, that sounds so simple."

"I'm sure it's not. But you certainly don't need to worry about *my* opinion on the matter, and I suspect that when or if you ever tell your girls, they're going to understand... at least eventually."

With a laugh, I agreed. "Dove, Nikki, Catherine, and Winnie will be fine. It'll be Elise and Jess I have to worry about. And..."

When I didn't finish, he tried, "And?"

My gaze fell to meet his before bouncing away. Whenever our eyes locked, I felt a little lightheaded or dehydrated or *not normal* enough to be reminded I should probably be getting more protein or whatever it was that would help with this feeling.

"And family."

"Your sister?"

I nodded at the sky, wondering if he'd heard about my illustrious sister from anyone, or if she was still an unknown in his circles. Eddie James would likely know her, but did she know Elizabeth was my sister?

"She works for the State Department," I explained into the listening silence he'd offered me.

"Is she at an embassy?" he asked, clearly trying to piece together why my sister would be such a hang-up.

"Uh, she moves around. In fact... you might've worked with her on a mission or two. Maybe." My eyes cut to his and he registered it.

"Not on the diplomacy side, then," he confirmed.

"No. And so far from the frivolity of writing romance novels, I just... I need to know what I'm doing is just for me.

That it's not going to be evaluated for world-shaping mettle and found lacking."

He leaned up on an elbow so his face interrupted my view of the sky. "You know what you do matters, right? I'm sure you get fan mail and you can see what your friends think, of course, but you know it's not a competition?"

I grinned up at his genuine concern and pushed away the little flare of fear at the mention of fan mail. "Thank you for your gentle mansplaining, *Doc*, but yes. I do."

He cut me a nasty look. "I wasn't trying to *mansplain*. I was just trying to... reassure you. To remind you that whatever you choose to do has value, and it doesn't get more or less value imbued upon it in comparison to what someone else does."

His words rang true, and they also cut close to the truth I'd grappled with for many years. Did my work have value in the scheme of things when there were people like Lizzy out there literally changing the world? Or like he'd done for twenty years before retiring, rescuing people and stopping abuses and more?

"I appreciate the reminder. I really do. Thank you," I said, directing my gaze away from his handsome face. We lay there in the summer morning breeze for another ten minutes before he suggested we head back down.

We chatted amiably enough on the way, the two-hour climb halved on the descent because it was a loop trail, not an out and back. As much as I wanted to spend more time with Adam, I felt a little bruised today. Probably due to the lack of sleep, but if I was honest, it also had to do with feeling like he was here, fully engaged with me and yet still so far away. He was inaccessible to me, and all of this over the course of the morning—his hug, his concern, his wisdom

—it was all meant for someone he *could* see a future with. But he didn't want that.

And so, I was caught up in my thoughts as we hit the last quarter mile, and that's when I took a clumsy step and only realized it when my ankle went very, *very* wrong.

I cried out and lost my footing entirely, dropping hard to my knees.

"Jo!" Adam yelled and turned back for me, sprinting to fall at my feet and help me ease back from my knees onto my butt.

Blood ran from both of my knees, but it was the throbbing, almost blindingly bright pain in my ankle that'd made me cry out and now kept me from catching my breath.

"What is it?" he said, shuffling in his bag for a first aid kit even as he asked, squirting hand sanitizer onto his palms on a reflex.

"My ankle. I stepped wrong." My voice came out thin and reedy, gritted between my teeth.

His warm hands slid down my calf and gently pushed at a few places over my sock. My hiking boot hid my ankle, so he couldn't see it.

"Should we take it off?" I asked, worried it might be broken. I couldn't remember twisting an ankle and having it hurt this bad.

"No. Your boots are going to stabilize it and keep the swelling at bay better than if we removed it for now since we still have to get off this trail." He dabbed at my bloody knees with clean gauze until the bleeding stopped. "We'll get you cleaned up and bandaged better back home. Soap and water is best for things like this, so we can skip the stinging antiseptic for now, if that's okay with you."

"Yes, definitely." Though how to get from here to home had become more than a small mystery in my mind.

He gathered the trash into a baggy, sanitized his hands again, tucked the kit away, and zipped his pack before sliding it on his front. Every action was filled with calm, purposeful movement. The hysteria rising in my chest from the pain and the "crap, how am I going to get up and down my stairs to my apartment now?" spiral eased in the face of his confidence.

He stood and pulled me to my uninjured foot, turned, and crouched low in front of me. "Get as close as you can and slide on. If you can get even one knee up by my hip, we'll be able to get you up here just fine."

As close as you can. Knee. Hip. Why did these words sound so profoundly suggestive at a time like this? The man had just cleaned up my bloody knees, and he was offering to piggyback me down the mountain, and all I could think of was body parts sounding sexy?

The pain must've gone to my head. But mounting my gorgeous hiking buddy proved to be equally mind-melting. Hands gripping my hamstrings just above my knees, bodies bouncing in an alarmingly regular rhythm, I begged my mind to think of things other than his hands on my skin and how solid he was and the fact that he somehow barely seemed winded after carrying a full-grown woman down a mountainside.

And then I remembered. I wrote a scene like this in my book, and as he reached down to gently pat my calf, I realized I'd gotten several details all wrong.

"I'm not going to say this is a good thing, but having you giving me a piggyback is going to help me edit a scene I have just like this in my book."

"Oh, yeah?" He glanced back, but since I was literally *on him*, there was no way he could make eye contact.

"Yeah, so really, we can just pretend I meant to do that because I needed help with a scene."

And maybe we needed to run through exactly what he'd do in other scenarios. I'd talked through the more severe things my hero dealt with on missions, but maybe some of the moments between him and the heroine should be things he showed me, not just told me.

We chuckled at my lame joke as the parking lot came into view, and soon enough, he'd gently set me down on the passenger side and helped me ease into the seat before shutting the door. When he loaded in himself, he handed me my water and watched me drink before taking a few sips of his own and backing out.

It wasn't until we were a ways down the canyon that he said, "Next time you need help with your book, just ask."

CHAPTER ELEVEN

Adam

Though the day hadn't turned out anything like I'd anticipated, I wasn't mad about the turn of events.

Well, actually, that was a messed-up thought because for Jo, it'd likely been long and painful. We'd made it to the car, and I'd convinced her to go to an urgent care when I saw how swollen her ankle had gotten in such little time. She'd looked at me with those big eyes and asked, "What good is having a former special operations medic if I still have to go to urgent care?"

She'd gotten a stern look from me, even though internally I was laughing. I explained I didn't have a personal X-ray machine and she'd benefit from knowing her ankle wasn't broken. She'd acquiesced, and happily, there was no break, so I'd brought her home.

And as I waited for her to get out of the shower—*yeah,*

not thinking about that too closely—I distracted myself with the details of her living room.

Of course I'd noticed the floor-to-ceiling bookshelves lining the living room wall, and we'd sat at her tiny table and on her love seat during our meeting. But I hadn't fully appreciated how beautiful and colorful her shelves were or how she had little bookish items that seemed to coordinate with the books they sat by. A small bust of Fitzwilliam Darcy perched by not one or two but *seven* different versions of *Pride and Prejudice*. She had collections of poetry and small prints and verses and quotes sprinkled throughout. It was a peek into her book-loving brain.

But it also reminded me how much she wanted a love story of her own—not just a love story, I'd recently been corrected by Dove, but a *romance*. One with a happily ever after. *One I can't reliably offer her.*

"Enjoying my booknerd-dom?"

Her voice came from the doorway to her bedroom and sent my pulse racing, feeling caught admiring her things like a snoop even though they were here on display.

"I am greatly enjoying it, yes," I answered honestly. "Most of my books are black."

She grinned and started to hobble over to the couch. I bolted to her, slid an arm around her back, and took as much of her weight as I could since she hadn't wrapped her ankle again after her shower yet.

"Thank you," she said as I helped her ease onto the couch.

"Feeling any better?" I asked, taking in the brightness of her scrubbed-clean cheeks and the way her hair looked a few shades darker when wet.

"Yes, thank you. And thank you for staying with me all

day. I really didn't plan for this to be such a process." She gave me a miserable look.

"I didn't mind, and I'm the one who insisted on the urgent care. If anything, blame me and my terrible lack of X-ray equipment." I sat next to her, now painfully aware of the coating of dirt and sweat on me as I perched next to her and basked in her lightly citrus and floral clean scent. "It does make me want to double down on survival training at work, though."

Her head ticked to the side. "What's that?"

Running a hand through my hair, I looked anywhere but at her. "I want to put together some survival and first-aid training, kind of like the self-defense classes we hold. It's this kind of situation today that could get someone really injured if they don't know what to do." I turned to find her watching me intently. "What would you have done if you'd been alone?"

She tsked. "Well, first, I know better than to hike alone. But second, I would've called for help, I guess. I couldn't have gotten down the mountain without you."

The tenderness and gratitude in her voice gnawed at me, begging me to give in and touch her again, hold her, try to rewind time and undo the hurt she'd endured today. "Good. Exactly. The concern comes when, uh-oh, there's no service, there's a storm coming, or whatever. So a class would run through all those scenarios plus do basic first aid, and we could have different levels of training for each. Maybe even culminate in a short trip for graduates."

"That's amazing. You should definitely do it. I feel like people here would love this kind of thing." She seemed genuine about it.

"I think so, too. I talked with Danny Morrison—as you know, he's head of ski patrol up at the resort and also an avid hiker. He cuts trail in summer and such. Anyway, I've been talking with him and he's interested in partnering on it if Saint gets it going."

She beamed. "I know Danny. I *love* his wife, and his kids are the cutest. I love the idea of partnering with Silver Ridge Resort!" She grabbed my wrist and squeezed for emphasis, like her excitement had nowhere else to go.

The touch streaked through me and left a burning heat in its wake.

"Yeah, it'd be great."

"Why do you sound like it's an if?"

I sighed. "I don't know. Maybe it's something Danny and his guys should be doing, you know? I don't know if it's a fit for Saint."

Her gaze hooked into mine and a beat passed. "You won't know until you propose it, right? I challenge you to be brave."

I chuckled, wishing it felt that easy. "Well, you were certainly brave today, so that's a fair request."

She smiled and settled back. "I'm sorry for being so grumpy, and I'm relieved to know it's not broken."

"No need to apologize. I'm glad, too, but remember, you do need to keep off it, ice and elevate it. Can I have a look?"

She lifted the leg closer to me, and I guided it onto my lap. Tugging at her sweats, she revealed a thoroughly swollen and already bruising ankle. Gingerly, I pressed into the skin surrounding and finally, relieved she hadn't reacted to any of it, wrapped it with the ace bandage. I'd told her to remove the one urgent care had put on so she could shower more easily since I could redo it for her before I left.

"This is only going to help stabilize you, and the biggest thing to help with pain is going to be your anti-inflammatory and icing on and off. Did you hear back from your coworker yet? Can you get your shift covered?"

Her gaze was fastened to where my hand now rested on her bare shin and gently cupped her heel. I'd never been uncomfortable touching people, but maybe this seemed proprietary to her? I couldn't tell and I didn't want her to face even more discomfort by having to ask me to stop touching her leg now that I'd wrapped her ankle, so I stood and settled her foot on the cushion next to her, moving to get the ice pack I'd made while she began speaking.

"I've got coverage until noon, but after that, I'll need to be there until four. Monday's our early day, but it's also the day I usually do my errands—post office, grocery, all that." Her brow furrowed as though she was trying to figure out how she'd stay off her foot and still accomplish everything.

"Why don't I grab your groceries and mail? You can put in an order online and authorize me to pick up, and I can definitely handle the mail if you trust me with your PO box key."

Her head fell back to rest on the couch and she eyed me. "You're doing too much. This is..." She shook her head. "It's too much, Adam."

She didn't say my name very often, and hearing it now in the quiet of her space after a day spent so close to her, caring for her, made something inside me hollow out and fill up at the same time. Looking at her with those wide, lovely eyes and concern for me while she was the one laid up with an injured limb... it cut through a layer of the protective shell I'd wrapped myself in.

"It's not, Josephine."

Her lips quirked. "It is."

I slowly shook my head no, back and forth. "It's not. And while I'm sure your friends could help, something tells me you won't bother them since it's Jess's first day back at Saint and Winnie's only just now back from her honeymoon, and I'm sure you'll find excuses for everyone else, too. I can check your ankle again tomorrow afternoon to see how it's doing, and I usually hit up the market and post office on Mondays, too, so really you're just giving the errands I was going to run more value."

"Oh, okay. Makes perfect sense."

Sarcasm dripped from her words, but I wouldn't waver. Instead, I took the small tray I made from the counter and delivered it to her.

She accepted it, blinking down at the plate of crackers, cheese, and the last bunch of grapes she had in the fridge, plus a cup of tea.

"You'll survive me helping you tomorrow, I promise. That's what friends do for each other." I grabbed my keys and looked around, making sure I hadn't left anything undone. "Ice for twenty minutes on and off, keep it elevated. Eat your snack, drink your tea, chill out, and try not to do much other than sit there. Call me if you need anything."

"Yes, sir."

I gave her a half-hearted glare. "Seriously, promise me you'll let me know if I can help you."

Now it was her turn to glare at me. "You're helping me tomorrow. I can handle this tonight. It's not broken, remember?"

This woman was going to hop up and start bustling around the second I left if her tone told me anything. I stalked back to her and braced myself on the couch on either side of her, then leaned down so I was about eight inches from her face.

"Please take care of my friend, Jo."

She bit her lip and the prettiest little smile snuck through. "You are such a bossy nurse."

I scowled in earnest. "That's what Dorian says, too."

She grinned. "Fine. I'll follow your directions and see you tomorrow."

Unblinking, I prompted her to give me the last bit. "And?"

I could've sworn she wanted to smile again, but she kept it hidden and huffed lightly. "And I promise I'll call you if I need anything."

It must've been something about the day or the fact that I hadn't eaten since that pastry hours ago, or maybe it was the mesmerizing proximity and the soft scents of her shampoo and soap. Whatever the case, without thinking and without any regard for my sanity or the reality of my life, I said, "Good girl," then pressed a kiss to her forehead.

And because I'd shocked myself likely more than I had her, I made an exit faster than I probably ever had, launching myself away from her without a glance at her face for fear I'd just done something irrevocably stupid, and fled with only a "See you tomorrow!" as the door shut behind me.

As soon as I made it down her stairs and outside, I slumped against the brick wall of her building and shut my eyes against the train wreck of the last few minutes.

I'd kissed her.

Her forehead, yes, but... *still.*

Friendly gesture, possibly, but also not... just not. Not something I'd done before. Hopefully a move she'd chalk up to my caretaking tendencies and not...

Well, not...

Anything else.

CHAPTER TWELVE

Jo

Time moved as though the second hand ticked through pudding instead of air. And rather than having that time to myself propped behind the desk at All Booked Up this afternoon during my shortened shift, just a little over twenty-four hours after I'd twisted the ever-loving life out of my ankle, I was staring blankly at a computer screen while Adam bustled around the store.

Yes. Adam.

Him of the *good girl* fame.

The one who'd been so problematically sweet to me yesterday, I was left in a hazy trance, the sensation of his lips on my hairline like burning ash sinking into parchment, and his words lingering in the air.

Good girl.

Good girl.

Good girl.

"Jo?"

Speak of the devil, the man in question's voice penetrated my brain so suddenly I jumped, spilling my water in my lap and banging my knee on the desk.

"You okay?" he asked, hustling around the counter to reach me.

"Yes, sorry. I'm just spacey today, I guess. I'm fine—seriously." I waved him away, and after one disbelieving look, he returned to where he stood across from me at a safe distance. "So, what did you need?"

I sounded kind of rude, honestly, but he'd startled me while I was sitting there hearing his voice say those words on repeat. And the context for his being here made it all worse —not only had he been a freaking angel yesterday, but he'd shown up right when I did today and insisted on "hanging out" at the store. He just so happened to hop up and help reach a book that required a ladder for Mrs. McGuinn, and he found himself bored an hour in so asked if he could, for his own entertainment, stock the newest arrivals.

Basically, he was doing everything in his power to conquer my ability to ignore my crush on him, and the worst part? I genuinely believed he didn't realize what he was doing.

He couldn't possibly.

Or he never would've kissed my forehead.

And he *definitely* didn't understand the far-reaching undertones of his innocent little *good girl* comment. He couldn't know the very bedroomy context of the phrase. No, sir. *Unless he's secretly trying to wear down your defenses with covert romance-coded comments...* No.

"I wanted to make sure you have me listed as an alternate pick-up person at the market." He tapped a pen cap-side down and then slotted it into the little jar sitting on the counter.

"Yes, I do." I still sounded grumpy, so I softened my tone. "And thank you. For all your help today, and the upcoming errands."

"It's my pleasure."

And then he was off, tidying and emptying waste baskets and bossing me into telling him what else I needed done before we locked up. Then he wrapped an arm around my waist and escorted me upstairs, but not before I saw the twinkle in his eye that said he was contemplating carrying me, which I flatly did not allow.

A girl could only handle so much.

Plus, he'd carried me down part of the mountain yesterday and that was enough.

"You're stubborn, you know that? I could carry you up in less than a minute," he said, eyeing me with arms crossed, halfway up the staircase as I slowly ascended.

"Yeah, but that can't be good for you," I said, hoping to hide how winded I was. Apparently, the last twenty-four hours had taken it out of me.

"It can't be good for me to carry you up a flight of stairs?" he asked, a little smirk hidden in his expression.

I glanced up at him, then focused back on the next step. "Yeah. I mean... I'm a normal-sized human woman. And you're... you're..." I exhaled, feeling the exhaustion of the day, my injury, and these dang stairs weighing on me.

Then his arms slipped around me and things went side-ways as he lifted me, cradling me to him and taking the stairs in rapid succession so we arrived at my door in seconds.

"Okay, *rude*," I said as his clean, minty scent filled my awareness.

"I'm rude? You were just about to say I couldn't carry you up the stairs because I'm too old, weren't you?"

I gasped as he plucked the keys from my fingers and, one-handed, opened my apartment door. In a few long strides, he'd reached the love seat, then unceremoniously set me down, but he didn't move away.

Instead, he dipped his head to catch my eyes. "I'm doing just fine, by the way."

I rolled my eyes because I was feeling like a petulant child. "I was *not* going to say you're old. Why on earth would I say that?"

He pulled away and set my keys on the counter, then returned and took my purse and set it next to them.

Hands on his hips, he called me out. "Fine. What would you have said?"

"I don't know! I was trying to find an excuse to keep you from carrying me up the stairs, and I figured everyone has a bum knee or a bad back or something, but I don't know what your deal is, so I just... I don't know." He wasn't actually mad, but he gave me a genuinely skeptical look that had me continuing. "Honestly, I don't even know how old you are, but I wouldn't think of Bruce or Tristan or Wilder as old, so why would I think that of you?"

No, in fact, I'd spent an embarrassing amount of time thinking about the age gap between us and confirming for myself that he must fall around Wilder's age and therefore was no more than twelve years older than me.

Twelve was... considerable. But not untenable. Not laughable or ridiculous. And clearly not a barrier to friendship between us.

"I'm just messing with you, Josie." His soft smile waned as he added, "Though I am considerably older than you."

"Fine. How old are you?" I asked, not really interested in having him explain he was too old for me. Clearly, he had no interest in more than friendship, even if he was throwing around forehead kisses and *good girls* and being all kinds of solicitous and helpful.

"Just turned thirty-eight." His gaze didn't waver.

"Good for you," I said, feeling an unreasonable relief that he wasn't already in his forties. It didn't matter anyway.

"And you? How old are you, Jo?"

I didn't like the part of me that resisted telling him. Again, why did it matter? He didn't want a future with anyone, so clarifying that we did have a substantial age gap wasn't going to make him any less of an option.

"Twenty-eight." I resisted the *and a half* figuring it might make me seem a bit juvenile. But I liked the fact that at least part of the year, we'd only be nine years apart.

And that's the kind of cuckoo-bird thinking that's going to have him running for the hills.

He nodded, as though he'd known before I said it, or like it confirmed something he'd suspected. As he moved around the kitchen, my thoughts spiraled. Did I act young? Childish? Maybe so considering how much whining I'd done since I got hurt.

"Better get to the post office." He handed me a bag of ice and tipped his chin toward my ankle, where I'd elevated it on the coffee table. "I'll be back in about an hour, and I'm bringing dinner."

He grabbed my keys off the counter, presumably so he could let himself into the building and the front door without me moving from my love-seat throne.

The door swung shut, and I bit my tongue to keep my flippant response where he could hear me, but eventually, it had to come out, so I whispered it to myself. "If I eat the dinner you bring me, will you kiss me and call me good girl again?"

CHAPTER THIRTEEN

Adam

An hour later, I mounted the stairs with recyclable grocery totes hanging from each shoulder, a paper bag packed with takeout from Guac in one hand, and Josie Wade's mail in the other. I'd stayed in business mode while I scuttled from place to place and refused to interrogate why I was doing this.

When I'd mentioned to Ethan that I couldn't do dinner tonight, he'd been curious. When I slipped and admitted I was taking a half day from work, he was absolutely ready to pop some popcorn and pull up a seat for the show. He had this doofy look he'd always used to get me to talk as a kid, like he hung on every word I said but was also on the verge of a laughing fit.

For a guy who had a crush on the girl I was hanging out with so much, he was remarkably fine with me helping her. But maybe it was due to my very solid reasoning—I felt responsible. I'd taken her on the hike, so it was my job to help her recover.

He gave me a skeptical look—literally, he sent me five GIFs in a row of various versions of the look—but ultimately told me I was being a good friend. I chose not to read it sarcastically.

Helping friends was a normal choice for a grown man to make. I'd learned how to manage relationships in my life—I'd learned how to care about people. I hadn't always understood that, so why would I feel bad for being capable of it now?

When I opened the door, Jo had her hand on her cheek while she stared at her laptop where it balanced on her lap. The ice I'd put on her ankle was still there.

"Did you keep that on the whole time I was gone?" I asked as I set bags down and began putting food away.

"No, sir. I did twenty on, twenty off, and I'm just about to finish my last few minutes of twenty on again." She arched a brow at me.

"Good." I almost said it again, and clearly, it'd been... notable. And now that we'd discussed our age difference, maybe it was just downright wrong. So... just good.

We chatted while I finished putting groceries away and then plated up our food. Her fajitas looked good, but I was all about Javier's barbacoa tacos and would be unlikely to order anything different now that I'd discovered them. After setting the table, I reached out a hand to her.

She startled, then took my hand and eased off the couch.

"Sorry, I was in the zone again."

She'd had her hand on her face once more, and I wondered what that was about.

"Can you tell me what you're working on?" I asked, easing her into her seat.

"Uh, sure. I'm editing their first kiss scene, and I'm just trying to make sure I get the details right."

Heat flashed through me for some unknown reason. "How do you get the details right?"

She loaded grilled chicken into a soft tortilla as she explained. "Well, most of the time I see the scene in my mind, but actually, when you gave me a piggyback yesterday, I realized I hadn't described it very well in a scene I'd written. It made me want to sort of... check my work on the physical stuff I include."

Physical stuff. In a romance.

Check her work.

Check it like try it? Check it like... reenact it? That sounded dangerously appealing and also like something I shouldn't be thinking about, but oh, I already was. Images flashed through my mind at warp speed: laying her down and kissing and touching and—

I cleared my throat.

"How do you—" I cleared my throat again. "How do you check your work?"

Wait, did she do the things that'd just seeped into my head with someone else? Who? How did I not realize she— Who was it? And was jealousy actually problematic, because it squeezed my chest mercilessly at the thought of someone touching her... of someone else *checking her work.*

After swallowing a bite, she fit her hand to her face like I'd seen her doing. "Well, for this, it started with the hero's hand on her face, so I was just trying to mimic that and see if I could describe it more effectively. It's tricky with other things since I can't mirror everything, of course, but in this case, I can just use my right hand on the left side, and it's the same as the hero's hand, if that makes sense."

She lifted her right hand and settled her fingers under her opposite ear, thumb at her cheek.

My hand twitched.

"Good idea."

She shrugged as she chewed another bite. "Maybe. It can be frustrating, but I don't really want to be like, 'Hey, Winnie, can you and Tristan make out in front of me so I can take notes on where you put your hands?'"

I coughed, only managing not to eject the food from my mouth because I'd covered it with a napkin as I blinked against the desire to laugh and breathe until I could swallow first.

"Okay, didn't expect that," I said, voice strained from the coughing.

She tucked a wisp of hair that'd escaped her bun behind an ear. "Well. The glamour of writing romance, right?"

I grinned, enjoying her humor and the bold side of her, then remembered her mail and jumped up to retrieve it. "Speaking of, you have some devoted fans. You've got a whole stack of fan mail."

It wasn't until I returned to the table and sat down that I realized she'd gone completely quiet and her face had paled.

"You don't like fan mail?" I asked, holding it out to her.

"Uh, yeah, of course. I just... I try not to open it unless I'm going to respond so I don't lose track. So, you know... maybe after dinner."

An edge had entered her voice, and she didn't move to take the letters.

More than odd. Concerning. "What's wrong?"

She shoved a bite of food into her mouth and chewed, raising her brows like, "Huh? I can't talk now, gotta eat!"

"Josephine, tell me what's wrong with the fan mail."

She guzzled down her entire glass of water before wiping her mouth and saying, "Nothing. Really. It's fine."

For a woman who seemed to truly love being a writer and marveled at the bourgeoning success she was experiencing, this spotlighted the presence of an issue.

"Listen, you can tell me. Are you being harassed? Did someone send you something inappropriate?" I would find them and give them a little lesson in etiquette. Or at least, I'd help her report it if necessary and help her figure out if she could file a cease and desist.

"Not... harassed. Just... yeah, some inappropriate stuff." She kept her eyes on her food.

"When? How often? What kind of stuff?" I demanded.

She exhaled sharply. "About once a month for the last six months. Mostly it's letters, handwritten, but sometimes there are... weird cobbled together collages of stuff from magazines."

My jaw clenched but I worked to soften my tone. "Have you reported it?"

"I don't think there's anything to report. I mean, he's sending these to the mail service in Arizona and then they forward to me, so it's not like he knows I live here. And... I just throw them away now."

"I can help you with this. Show me the letters and I can use the databases to look this guy up, make sure he doesn't have any history with stalking or—"

"Stalking? No. No, it's not a big deal. Please, Adam, I just... I don't want to think about it." Color had returned to her cheeks and deepened them to a flush.

Everything in me wanted more information so I could help her, fix this, make it go away. But I saw the frantic energy zipping through her, the way her eyes were almost glassy with anxiety, and I accepted that, at least for tonight, we could table this.

"Okay. Okay," I said, trying to calm myself as much as appease her, and then changed the subject.

We talked about some of the books people bought at the store earlier, then after dinner, I took a look at her ankle. It was bruised and still a touch swollen, but not nearly as bad as I would've expected for the end of day two post-injury.

Her energy had fallen since the discussion of mail, and I didn't want to leave her focused on that. I wanted to sit next to her on the couch and turn on a movie, or maybe read while she wrote. Instead, I cleaned up everything I could and grabbed my keys.

"I'll get out of your hair now."

"Thank you so much for everything, seriously. You set me up for the week, and tomorrow's my day off anyway. So thank you."

"My pleasure, truly." Heroically, I didn't cringe at the cliché.

She seemed sad as her dark gaze flicked up to meet mine, then dropped back to her computer, and I spoke before checking the impulse, the need to make things better for her overriding any shred of logic I owned.

"I could help you."

She huffed. "Thank you, but I don't—"

"I mean, with the book. Sort of like I did before, but you can just tell me what you need me to do and I can... do it."

She did the thing where her beautiful lips parted slowly but no words emerged for a few seconds, until finally she said, "Oh. Um... Okay. Yeah. That'd be really helpful, actually."

I nodded, swallowing against a weird tightening in my

throat at the sound of her almost breathless response. "Good. Okay. Well. What can I do?"

She bit her lip, thoughts heavy and unreadable, before finally speaking. "I'm trying to figure out how the hero's hands would be if he was holding the heroine's chin. He's kind of... physical." Her cheeks burned.

Nothing could've stopped me from asking, "How can I help?"

She swallowed hard. "Uh, I guess you could... try it. On me? You know like how you explained things step by step after I hurt my ankle—that was perfect. It kept me calm, yes, but it also helped a lot with knowing what I'd need to write for my character, and why."

Damn, but her eyes were so trusting and sweet. I had to look away as I approached, sucking in a breath and steeling myself against whatever was to come. This was a terrible idea, but if it helped her move away from the upsetting thoughts about the fan mail, I'd do it.

"Whatever you need," I said, as though this was all a normal day and even being this close to her didn't throw me.

She cleared her throat and her eyes flickered around the room before settling on me. "So, um, they've had an argument, and he's trying to get her attention, but he's not.. rough. He's just... tactile, you know?"

You know?

Good grief, did I know.

How many times had I shoved my hands in my pockets instead of sliding my fingers through her ponytail? How many times had I stopped myself from tracing the curve of her shoulder blade or sliding a thumb over the slope of her neck?

Innumerable.

Countless.

Okay, so she was the writer, and it was probably for the best.

None of those things fit the relationship we had, and yet the longing to touch her, to be close her, to *know* her, had been there since day one.

She swiveled on her barstool until she faced me, elbow resting on the countertop behind her.

"So, he just kind of, slides his hand here"—she brushed her fingers along her neck and the curve of her jaw—"and then takes hold of her."

I didn't speak but stepped between her knees and just... did it. If I'd thought about it any longer, I might've heard the objecting, blaring warning signs begging me not to give in to this indulgence, but I didn't.

It wasn't intimate or sensual. It was her work combining with mine. And even *that* thought didn't send a weighty, risky feeling into my gut. It was all just the mechanics of the thing—just like checking her ankle and stabilizing in her boot. Just like that...

My hand brushed past her collarbone and slipped up her neck, grasping firmly but gently with fingers to one side and thumb to the other, and pulled her forward.

Her breath gusted out.

"Like that?" Just epidermis and pulse points and platonic contact. Not skin and nerve endings exploding and racing hearts and *wanting*.

She blinked in rapid succession and nodded. "Yep."

The tension in her voice lit fire under my palm, and I released her, stepping back out of her space and away from the glorious temptation being near her created.

I should've said goodbye, left it there, but my mouth formed words before I checked them. "I'm working the rest of the week, but I can help again sometime—maybe this weekend?"

"Yeah, sure. I just have something Friday, but I'm off otherwise." Her smile was small, but it seemed genuine, even as a fierce blush still painted her face.

"Good. Alright then. I'll see you soon."

And with that, I left, banishing myself from her presence and the chance to do something stupid like kiss her forehead—or her lips—even though I'd just done something far worse.

I needed to get my head on straight before next weekend, or I would have to cancel.

CHAPTER FOURTEEN

Jo

In the end, it was two full weeks before Adam came knocking again. And by *came knocking,* I meant I saw him at Craic for the weekly Saint meeting from my table across the room.

He'd texted last Thursday to say he'd been put on a short-term travel job when Beast had to cancel and was very sweet and apologetic. It wasn't like he was backing out of a date, and I made it very clear I had no hard feelings. But now, seeing him walk in and greet his team after being gone for a full week, I felt practically starved for the sight of him.

I tried not to expect anything. The amount of time we'd spent together lately—barring the last two weeks—wasn't something others knew about. But when all he did was give me a little Saint-Security-dude chin nod in greeting from his table as he slapped Kenny on the back and laughed at something Bruce said, my stomach sank.

The girls had been busy peppering Winnie with questions about her honeymoon since she hadn't felt well enough to come last week, so I focused on that conversation and my beautiful friends. No thoughts veering to the man across the bar, the one who'd cradled my jaw like he wanted to do it and like he was doing me a favor...

Saturday, after a short shift at the store and checking in at Joe, I poured my energy into writing. And *that* was when he actually came knocking.

I answered the door expecting the food delivery I'd decided to treat myself to, but instead, it was him.

Try as I might, I couldn't stop my heart from kicking or my pulse from accelerating, the jerks. I didn't want to have this kind of physical reaction to him or feel a bit giddy that he was here without warning.

He'd been a sweet friend to me a few weeks ago, and I'd let it go to my head more than a little. But he'd clarified things between us effectively when he'd not only not said a word to me last night after weeks away but also sent no communication while he was gone other than the texts to tell me he had to cancel and was leaving town.

"Hey," he said, looking relaxed.

"Hi. Didn't expect to see you," I said, and yeah, that was a *tone* in my words.

His blue gaze studied me, taking in my glasses, the bun crowning my head, and then my schlubby T-shirt and baggy sweats. *Clearly* I wasn't expecting him.

Frustration pricked at me, but another sensation did, too —a keen awareness of his proximity. And then there was the reality of his piercing eyes and slightly longer than usual scruff and the way his button-up stretched across his chest and shoulders.... *ugh.*

"Can I come in?"

Oh. Right. Yes.

"Sure, come on in," I said, walking away from the door and letting him shut it.

I retreated to my current writing spot, which was standing at the bar where my laptop sat on the counter. One of my legs had fallen asleep earlier, and even though my ankle was still tender occasionally, standing and normal walking had been just fine.

"How have you been?" he asked as he slowly entered the kitchen area.

Hands on my keyboard, I gave him my attention. "Uh, good. Yeah. Nothing new."

He nodded. "Good." Then, without a moment of hesitation, he stopped less than a foot from me and set his hand on the counter next to my computer. "Why are you upset?"

I looked up and startled at his nearness, which made no sense since I'd been tracking his movements out of the corner of my eye the whole time.

"I'm not upset," I said, a bit breathless.

His gaze didn't waver. "I know you well enough to know that's a lie."

Why did this do... things to me? The fact he knew me? *What is wrong with you?*

For a second, I thought about pretending and being a little snot, but then I remembered I hated that kind of thing. I hated it in books with heroines who were supposed to be all sassy and fun but really just sounded like whiney little jerks, and I hated it in real life when I encountered someone who refused to just be brave enough to be honest.

So I girded my big-girl loins—*ew*, okay, instant regret for that phraseology, and note to self to never use it again—and turned to fully face him.

"I was surprised you didn't even come say hi to me last

night. Wasn't sure if maybe you were embarrassed to..." I didn't finish the thought because what even was the thought? Be seen with me? It wasn't like that. To acknowledge we had a friendship that would merit an individual greeting? That was essentially what I was saying, but it sounded so stupid to my own brain I hated to let it out in words.

His brow furrowed. "What would I be embarrassed about?"

I huffed. "I don't even know. I'm just an insecure, sad baby, I guess."

He chuckled and shook his head. "No, you're not. But I'd like to point out you didn't come say hi to *me*, either."

A laugh jumped out and my cheeks heated. "I am a terrible person." It hadn't even occurred to me I could go say hi to him.

His half smile made my heart flip. "You and your girls were in the middle of a conversation. I didn't want to barge in and assume you wanted me in your face just because I'd walked in the door. Plus, I'd ditched you last weekend, so I wasn't sure if you would even want to see me in the wake of my bad-friend business."

"You had to work—that hardly qualifies as being a bad friend. I was not upset by that—bummed, yes, but not upset."

He squinted slightly, almost like he wasn't sure I could mean those words and was looking for signs I didn't mean it. His gaze flickered over my face, and after a beat, he nodded. "Well, I'm sorry I didn't come say hi. I would've. And that's why I'm here now."

My smile couldn't be tamed. "Just to say hi?"

He grinned back at me. "Yes. And to do what we planned on last weekend—to help you."

I blinked. "Oh, with the... yeah."

My heart fluttered and I was definitely breathing weird. He was close enough I could smell his clean soapy-mint scent, and I was torn between running away from him to avoid touching him and burying my face into his chest and heaving in that smell.

Okay, freaky, time to calm down.

"So, is now a good time?" he asked, still standing *right there* so, apparently, he didn't get a hint of my weirdo thoughts.

"Uh, sure. Yeah." I cleared my throat. "What do you, uh... what should we do first?" I didn't manage to hide my cringe, which he clearly saw.

His amusement glittered back at me in his smile. "Don't look so horrified. We'll start with the hand on the cheek— that's the last thing I saw. Then you can guide us from there."

Swallowing hard, I nodded, begging my pulse to slow so he wouldn't feel it racing.

He caught my eye for a second, then his focus shifted to the side of my face and his gaze grazed over my cheek as his warm, rough hand rose to touch my skin. His four fingers slid under my ear, sifting into the hair there, and his thumb gently swept over the apple of my cheek and nestled in front of my ear.

The frenetic energy in me stilled as his eyes slowly rose to meet mine, his face only eight or ten inches away. *So close, and yet so far.*

"Good. Great," I whispered, then turned out of his grasp and typed frantically on my computer as he stepped back.

"Cool." He backed up again, giving me far more space than we'd started with, but I needed it.

Miraculously, I focused on the words, jotting notes in a blank document about the brush of his skin and how his elbow had crooked and the sleeve of his shirt had stretched over his rounded bicep and finally, how his gaze felt like fire on my skin. *Whew.*

"Another?" he asked from across the room.

I turned to face him now that I'd run out of words to describe the moment and internally scrambled for what might be a good follow-on. Maybe something without touching or I'd be in danger of spontaneous combustion based on the heat simmering in my belly.

I eyed him as he wandered next to my bookshelves, taking in titles I was sure he'd seen before, but again, not minding how he was giving me some time to recover my wits.

"Sure. So... a big one readers love is when the hero cages the heroine in—against a wall or even a counter."

He stilled at the shelf, pushing in a book with one long finger, and then came toward me. His stride was measured and purposeful, his path as direct as it could be considering an overstuffed chair and a barstool stood in his way. But in seconds, he was in front of me, arms bracketing me with his hands gripping the counter on either side of my body.

He pressed close enough. My back brushed against the countertop, and then our eyes met.

Held...

Locked.

He dipped his head slightly, speaking in a tone that felt like a caress. "Like this?"

"Yes."

"Anything else?" he asked, his voice low and delicious.

Okay, so this man was attractive, but I'd never actually imagined he could be... this way. He was so warm and friendly, but this felt... different. Hotter, yes, but also kind of like he was challenging me. Pushing me almost.

Yes, I wanted to say, *so many other things*. I could picture his face coming closer, his beard rasping against my skin, his lips scant millimeters from my ear, warm breath rushing down my neck. I could imagine—

The doorbell rang at a decibel heretofore unexplored by the human ear, and my nervous system exploded in response. I jolted so severely, he set a hand on my arm and squeezed it, then moved to answer the door while I recovered the ability to breathe.

He set the food—ah, yeah, I'd ordered takeout sometime in my former life—in the kitchen and returned to my side.

"You going to make it?"

Hand on my chest, heart still galloping, I laughed. "Maybe? I think eventually I'll return to a normal BP."

With a half smile on his lips, he grasped my arm and pressed his index and middle fingers to the thin skin over my pulse at the inside of my wrist. He glanced at his watch on the opposite hand for a few seconds, fully unaware his touch was not assisting in my recovery.

"One-fifty. Take a breath for me." He let my wrist slip from his warm hand.

I laughed again and rolled my eyes even as my mind screamed *has taking someone's pulse ever been so lethally and destructively hot?!!* "Apparently, I'm jumpy."

His gaze sobered and I knew, I just knew he was thinking about the letters I'd told him about last time we were together, and I was so far from in the mood to go there, I blustered through. "I only ordered enough food for myself, but we could split it?"

I moved to unpack the food before he could bow out—I

could feel it coming and I didn't want him to go yet. How could I make him stay?

But as I settled the dishes on the counter, he interrupted my thoughts. "I can't stay for dinner, but while I'm here, is there one more quick move I can help you with?"

My stomach flipped and I grinned. "Sure, I can think of something."

CHAPTER FIFTEEN

Adam

That smile could fell a man, and knowing this, I glanced away and ran a hand through my hair. "Great. What can I do?"

How about not voluntarily putting yourself in the position to touch this woman? Yeah, apparently, that was too logical for this brain.

"How about something simple—can you just, uh..."

She bit her lip and sent a bolt of heat through me with the small action.

She didn't finish the thought, and I hung on the pause like the biggest sucker of all time. "What? Just tell me."

I hoped she couldn't hear the pleading in my voice. She couldn't understand the whip of need making me want to practically beg her to release that soft lip and end my torture.

Or you could go taste it for yourself.

With a slow exhale, I banished the thought.

"Sorry, so, can you just slowly roll up your sleeves?"

Her gaze tracked down to my shirt. I often wore them rolled but for some reason hadn't today—likely because I'd only thrown on this shirt in place of a worn-out T-shirt before I came to see her.

"Sure." I unbuttoned one cuff, then the other, and slowly rolled the right side to just below my elbow. As I finished the left, I glanced up at her and found her eyes glued to my forearms. "So... that it?"

She bit her lip again, and I could've sworn she wore a hooded expression.

"Yep. Perfect. And now, can you just... lean in the doorway?"

Her voice had gotten soft and low. Her apartment shrank to the size of a dime, and I saw it all in an instant— me walking over and sliding a hand into her hair, drawing her face close and her lips to meet mine. Had I ever wanted something with such a vivid ache?

For that reason, I took her request on the go and walked to her front door, holding it open for her until, with a wrinkle of her brow, she came and held it for me. Then, facing where she stood inside the apartment, I crossed my arms and leaned in the doorframe.

"Like this?"

She tucked a smile away, eyes skating over me from head to toe, lingering on my arms for a moment before nodding. "Exactly. Thank you, kind sir."

After that, I took my leave for fear I'd act on those baser impulses and throw practice to the wind in favor of experience.

"Great. See you soon, Josie." And I bolted, the excuses of her eating before her food got cold and needing to get something unintelligible done tripping off my tongue as I let myself out.

As the week wore on, the image of Jo's eyes turning liquid as I caged her in against the counter had burrowed in and burned itself into my mind.

I closed my eyes and there she was, her full lips parting and her lashes fluttering, those brown eyes begging me to step into her space, to press her against the counter and maybe bend her, force her back just a little, and take her mouth.

And *that* was why I'd asked Ethan to come by and bring me lunch at work. Or, he'd offered to come to me, and I'd accepted, recognizing my own feeble ability to stay away from Jo if I happened to walk by All Booked Up and she was behind the counter. Instead of risking it, I gratefully accepted E's offer and he arrived right on time.

"Hey. I got you an Italian sub and chips," he said, tossing a paper-wrapped cylinder and bag of chips onto my desk between us as he took a seat.

"Thanks. That's perfect. Sorry I didn't respond sooner —we had a meeting."

We had a lot of people international right now, and even more around the state. Since Tristan didn't want to take travel jobs as often if he could help it, and Beast couldn't leave for a bit, we were retooling more frequently. So far, we'd made it work, but it signaled a need for more staff with the desire to travel, and I'd said as much to Bruce and Wilder. They'd both agreed, so we'd see what came up in the next few weeks.

"So is there a purpose for this meeting, or are you just embracing the convenience of both of us living in the same town?" Ethan asked, already taking a huge bite of his sandwich.

"Can't it be both? I do enjoy that we both live here, especially when we take a minute to actually see each other."

In truth, we did a terrible job of it. We should have a standing lunch or dinner, but so far, we'd just worked each other in when we could. Sometimes, it meant going weeks without in-person contact. Other times, we hung out every other day.

Either way, I'd take it over living states apart without question.

"I suppose so. I know a lot of that is on me... the shop's doing well, but it's just... it's a lot." He scrubbed a hand through his hair.

"You don't owe me an apology. You're juggling a new business—you're the boss and the idea man and everything. From what I can tell, you're doing a great job." He really did amaze me. I couldn't imagine doing it all on my own—it sounded awful.

I was used to being given a task or mission and executing it with my team. I didn't want to be the person who figured out which mission to choose, too. I liked leading, but not being the ultimate, buck-stops-here man in charge. I'd leave that to Wilder and Bruce, especially since I knew I could trust them.

We ate in silence for a few minutes, each wolfing down our sandwiches in short order. You could take the Carter brothers out of the Army, but you'd be hard-pressed to take the Army out of the Carter brothers when it came to eating.

Ethan finished first and leaned back in his chair, draped in it like he owned the place. "So tell me... been on any dates lately?"

I shook my head as I finished my last bite. "No, and you know that for a fact."

"Do I?"

His dark blue eyes locked with mine and I studied him, my heart rate kicking up. Did he... did he somehow know how I felt about Jo?

"I'm not seeing anyone, E. You know I'm a mess with nothing to offer."

His head dropped all the way back and he sighed dramatically. "Well, that's exactly why I don't know for sure you're not dating—because that line is just a pile of junk. You're not *a mess* and you have plenty to offer."

I wiped my fingers with a napkin, then tossed it into the trash. "I'm a thirty-eight-year-old divorced ex-soldier with a decent job and a small house and... what? Five hundred pounds of baggage dragging behind me? I don't mean to sound like I pity myself. I just mean practically, for a woman who wants marriage and a future with someone, that's not me, so I don't have that available."

He sobered and stared at me with no trace of humor, so I busied myself with packing up the paper from my sandwich and then studiously drinking water from my bottle.

"I get that you've got a past, but who doesn't? I know you bought the line that it was all your fault you and Marlee didn't work out, but that's just not true."

Teeth on edge, I took a slow breath, held it, then released it. "I'm not going to act like I didn't ruin my marriage. I did. And it wasn't one thing, it was years of not prioritizing it or her. So I can't sit here and act like I know what to offer someone else when I failed the woman I promised to love and cherish."

"You drained the life out of me, Adam. You killed anything good between us, and I don't know if I'll ever be able to trust someone like I did you. But you'll never change

—you'll always want what you want, and God help the woman who thinks she can change you."

I heard Marlee's voice echoing in my mind. My ex-wife hadn't meant to be cruel when we finally divorced, but she'd been so raw. She'd made clear that I'd left scars—my choices had hurt her.

Ethan's hand smacked the desk in a rare show of impatience. "I'm done with this. You got married when you were twenty. *Twenty*, Adam. You're on the dark side of your midthirties, and you are *not the same man you were*. Literally no one is. You were an idiot back then and you didn't do right by Marlee, but she didn't do right by you either. You guys never should've gotten married, and there's no way around that. But just because you had a marriage blow up when you were practically a child groom doesn't mean you can't have a successful relationship now."

The compassion and frustration in his eyes prodded me, but he couldn't understand. He had no idea what it was like to be married to someone I thought I'd love forever and then watch it all crumble. And not in a day or a month, but after five years, to see how we'd both made so many small choices that led us away from each other and so few that turned us back toward each other. By the end, we were resentful and angry and hurt and it was a mess.

And while she did play a role, looking back I could see my determination to work and progress in the Army had been like a mistress to me. I may not have cheated on Marlee with another person, but I'd let her be a distant second to the love of my life at that time—the Army. Damn, but it made me cringe to think of the arrogance and misguided mindset I'd had then.

How could I act like the intervening years had given me some great insight into myself and what I could bring to a relationship? I'd dated two other women for a few months each in the time since then, and in each case, I'd felt the same pull to do whatever I wanted to do and not prioritize them. With Marlee's words always ringing in my ears and the utter brokenness between us as we parted leaving a long shadow, how was I supposed to trust that what she said—what my own choices have proved—had changed?

When I didn't respond, Ethan swore, his frustration doubling. "I just wish you'd give yourself a chance to find someone—the *right* person. At a time when you're not trying to climb the ranks, you're not deploying all the time, and you're not a total idiot anymore."

I chuckled at the insult because it was so accurate. "The 'right' person is a myth. There's not just one person for each of us. If so, you'd never see people who lose their partner find someone else."

Waving a hand, he acquiesced to the point. "Fine, sure. But I do think there are some people we're more compatible with. And maybe there is something to the idea of a soul mate—someone we'll fit together with well enough that when it gets hard, we're willing to try. We're ready to fight."

A cocktail of shame and regret and frustration sloshed in my gut. "Let's worry less about me."

He shook his head. "Haven't you ever learned that all I do is worry about you?"

I could say the same to him. Instead, I attempted logic.

"I wish you wouldn't. I'm happy here. I've got friends and a life and I'm settling in well. It's been a year since I moved." What more did he expect?

What more was there?

Love. Sharing your life with someone. Committing to a person and partnering with them to build a life with them.

But who would be "right" for me?

Josephine Malcom comes to mind...

I didn't appreciate the intrusive thought or the suggestion that my own brain dared to lob at me indicating that maybe I wasn't as happy as I liked to believe. I wouldn't buy it.

Nor could I now entertain a thought like that about Jo. It was too...

Too tempting. Too alluring and something I wanted far too much.

Ethan sighed again. "Listen, I'm not the arbiter of what makes you happy, but you've got a lot of love to give. You love your friends and me so damn well, I hate the idea that you won't ever be a husband or father. It's just wrong, A, and I want you to stop outright refusing yourself the possibility."

He stared at me with this face he'd always had—the one that wouldn't let this go until I gave. At least a little. So I nodded. "Fine. I won't refuse the possibility."

"Good."

"Yeah, good. And now, tell me when you're going to ask Jo out."

His eyes widened and then ping-ponged around my office like I'd genuinely surprised him. "Me? You want *me* to ask Jo out?"

There it was again, this hint he knew something about my feelings for her—or, our chemistry.

Not feelings. Chemistry and friendship.

But he'd had a crush on her since he'd moved here, so why would he think I'd do anything, never mind the age difference and all my aforementioned issues.

"Yes. Don't you want to?"

He laughed, but it came out thin and a little odd. "Uh, I

mean she's great. Obviously. But I don't think she feels that way about me. I've told you this."

"Right, but will you know if you don't ask? I'm not pressuring you, I'm just trying to... encourage you. To be bold."

He huffed. "Be bold."

"Yeah. Go after what you want."

He gave me the most intense, critical glare I'd ever received from him. "Yeah? I should go after what I want? That's your advice for me?"

I swallowed, wondering if somehow I would regret this, but forging on, fully in big-brother mode.

"Yes. Absolutely. Go after what you want—"

A knock came on the door, and then my stomach flipped and dropped.

Because there was Jo.

CHAPTER SIXTEEN

Jo

I made what I considered a valiant attempt to disguise the hurt coursing through me but didn't even attempt to mask my frustration with these two doofuses.

Hadn't we connected these last few weeks? Hadn't Adam felt what I did when we touched? I exhaled out the befuddlement and shoved it down into the same hole my feelings had managed to crawl out of lately. *Curse you, zombie crush!*

"Hey, guys. Just thought I'd say hi."

Jess was finishing up a quick meeting, and I'd thought it'd be fun to see Adam. Stop in to say hi and maybe check out his office, get a feel for his professional life.

Little did I expect to hear my name as I wandered up. *"You want me to ask Jo out?"* This from Ethan, and then all the brotherly nudging I could take until I made myself known.

Served me right for eavesdropping, though I hadn't exactly planned on it. But honestly, why was Adam trying to force Ethan on me? Ethan and I were friends, and he knew that. I'd have to make it abundantly clear to Adam that I didn't want Ethan like that, and I didn't think I ever would. I'd *wished* I felt something more for him more than once, and I simply didn't.

And Ethan appeared to have accepted it. He certainly didn't seem to be taking his brother's suggestion with much enthusiasm, so hopefully what he'd portrayed to me—accepting our friendship for what it was—wasn't untrue.

"Jo! Hi!" Ethan stood and wrapped me in a hug that was a little much, but okay. *Fine.*

Adam also stood, an expression I couldn't read on his stupid, handsome face.

"Hey, Jo. What brings you in?"

His voice was smooth, and if it weren't for the total absence of a smile, I might've thought everything was normal.

I might've believed he didn't suspect I'd overheard his conversation.

"I'm catching up with Jess over lunch. Just thought I'd swing by and say hi while I wait for her to wrap up a meeting."

"Nice," Ethan said, smiling in the adorable way he had that would've put me at ease if it weren't for his brother.

My heart squeezed in awkwardness and hurt, but I shoved the thought away.

"It's not going to be easy, but I know you two can do this," Bruce Camden's voice said as footsteps drew closer down the hallway.

A low grunting sound rumbled, and then Jess arrived in the doorway, her face a mask of boredom.

"Ready?" Her eyes shifted to Ethan, then Adam, and she gave them chin-lift nods. In the hallway, Beast ambled by with a scowl the size of Antarctica, and Bruce gave me a cheery wave as he passed.

"Yes. Let's head out." To the annoying brothers I didn't know what to do with, I said, "Have a good day," and that was that.

Jess was several inches shorter than me, but her stride might as well have been that of Adam or Tristan, or dare I say it, Beast, because she walked with the purpose and rage of a man twice her size who'd been wronged. We didn't speak, and I clutched my purse and lightly jogged to keep up with her as we made our way to the restaurant.

Within ten minutes, Jess and I were nestled into a corner booth at Guac. I'd enjoyed several chips dripping with salsa, but she just sat there, stewing at her water as though she could bring it to a boil given enough time.

The waiter brought a large serving of guacamole and set it down between us, and that seemed to unlock her. After she shoveled more than a few chips and guac and sat back enough to take a big breath, I took my shot.

"So. Fun first few days back?" I dared ask, willing her to open up a bit.

Generally, she kept things close to the vest. Of the women I considered my closest friends and saw regularly, I knew the least about her. Part of it was due to her being gone the last few months, but part of it was because she didn't let anyone get all that close.

Humor flickered across her face, and the anxious energy filling up my chest eased a little.

"So fun."

I chuckled. "Any chance you can elaborate on that, or is it all supersecret?"

She blew out a breath, evidently still working to calm herself. "You know Beast and I don't get along, right?"

I nodded because everyone knew this. If one of them showed up at Craic on a Friday night, the other left. They gave each other wide berths at events where the Saint staff all gathered, and then there was the infamous trip Jess had just gone on because she'd told the Saint leadership something had to give, and apparently Beast had refused to budge, so she left.

"Well, I left and had some time to think. I also did some virtual sessions with a therapist. I was feeling really good… and then I got back here and—" She sighed and rubbed her eyes. "He just infuriates me so quickly. I feel like I'm another person around him."

Treading carefully, I asked, "Can you tell me why? I mean, I don't want to pry, but I've always wondered. You seem pretty chill, so it's a surprise to me you'd hate someone so vehemently."

A hollow chuckle slipped out as she dipped a chip in guacamole. "It's a long story. But I promise it's not for nothing. And I do think I should be honest and admit I'm not actually all that chill."

Her *sorry not sorry* face had me laughing. "I guess I can see that. I mean, you had to be one of very few women in your field, right?"

She widened her eyes. "You can look at Saint's staff and see the mix there—me and Eddie are here, we've got Amani and Sariah overseas. So, four. And that's to the twelve or fourteen men?"

I hadn't realized there were even that many women working for Saint, but it was still a slim percentage. In truth, I hadn't realized there were that many *men* either. They had so many people who didn't work from here in Utah that it didn't shock me, but still. The company had grown so much in such a short time.

"Well, that's a bigger ratio than any team or squadron I served on. A few had more, but in most of them, I was one of two or the one and only woman." She shrugged. "You get used to it. But yeah. Meekness, not speaking up, none of that is an option, and I'm not about to start now."

"Fair enough. I wouldn't want you to." I sipped my water as I wondered how best to ask my next question. "Hear me when I say I selfishly want you to stay here, but would it be better if you kept to an overseas assignment? Is that something you'd want if it was even an option?"

"I could go out and stay out because they don't have enough bodies for overseas jobs right now, but frankly, no. I've lived the life where I'm always on alert, always ready to go, always living out of a bag. I'm not interested in that being my next phase. I want—" She cleared her throat. "I want more for myself." Her cheeks brightened with a blush.

I raised my glass. "I absolutely love that, and I'm right there with you. Here's to asking for more."

She touched her glass to mine and grinned. "Amen, sister."

We both drank deeply, then our food arrived. After a few minutes of blissful chowing down, Jess leaned on an elbow and said, "So, tell me about you and Doc."

I took my time chewing, wondering just how ignorant to play this. But I knew Doc was Adam, and she knew I knew it. I also knew she was a world-class professional operator and had likely read some level of weirdness in the room when she'd walked into his office.

There wasn't much point in pretending she meant Ethan or that I didn't know what she meant in the first place, so I landed on "I'm not sure."

"Okay. But you guys are friends, right? You're hanging out fairly often, from what I've heard."

I straightened. "You've *heard*?"

"Honey, you live in a small town, and your *friend* Adam works with a bunch of ex-soldiers who, I'm sorry to tell you, are the biggest pack of gossips you'll ever meet."

Realizing my mouth had opened and nothing had emerged, I snapped my jaw shut.

"So disappointing to realize, right? All these big, strapping men, literal American heroes, and they might as well be sitting around the poker tables at Silverton Springs for the amount of gossiping they do. Well, except Bruce *does* play penny poker over there with Rosie and Amir, so he's like *double* the gossip."

The image of Bruce sitting at a table with Nikki's grandma gabbing about me and Adam was so ridiculous, I cackled. "Are they really? Why can't I picture it?"

She shook her head but smiled so brightly, she clearly loved this. "Honestly, no idea. If these men are professional soldiers and badasses first, they are gossipy old biddies second."

We laughed for a while, longer than really necessary but enough to shake me out of the weird funk I'd been in.

"Me and Adam... great question. He's been awesome. Helped me with some personal stuff going on. And we've had a few moments where I've thought maybe..." I sighed. "I don't know. And what I *do* know is he's not interested in dating or marriage, and he doesn't believe in romance."

The horrified look that crossed her face made me giggle. "How horrible."

"Right? And I know he's got a past. I know that. I don't know exactly what, but I just... there's this stupid part of me that feels like maybe something could happen between us, but I also know that wishing someone would change who they are and what they want for you is just foolish. It's like I'm begging for heartbreak over here."

Her eyes held so much compassion. I knew for a fact whatever came next would be something important.

"I can tell you that love is often worth the risk." She smiled down at her hands, brushing her thumb over the knuckles of her left hand. "But I can also tell you getting stuck hoping someone will change, or that they'll want you enough to change, is a formula for heartbreak."

I wondered how she'd gained such knowledge but didn't want to push her. Instead, I thanked her. "I'll take that wisdom. And I think from now on, I'm just going to try to give him space. I can't separate out the feelings I have for him and those hopes, so I think I need to let those fade a bit before I can be around him one on one again."

"That sounds smart. And you can always change your mind, you know? You get to choose whether you see him as a friend or whether you make him wish he didn't suck so bad and could man up and be good to you the way you want."

We chuckled and I grinned.

"Okay, now enough about real-life disappointments. Let's talk books."

CHAPTER SEVENTEEN

Adam

After a good check-in with Dorian after work, I rolled into a parking spot in the lot near Main Street. I hadn't heard from Jo since I'd seen her a few days ago at the office, despite my efforts.

Two texts and no dice—absolutely no response. We didn't text all that much, but she usually responded within a few hours. The ice I'd felt coming from her expression before she and Jess left for lunch came through the silence loud and clear.

I should've let it be. If she didn't want to be near me anymore, then fine. I should've taken this and run, victorious over the temptation to compromise my plans and possibly let her down.

But I couldn't. And this had to be the reason I acknowledged my coworkers settled in at our usual table at Craic, but went right to her, sliding a hand to her lower back and hearing her gasp as I dipped my face to say in her ear, "Do you have a minute?"

Her lips closed, but she seemed to say yes, then told her friends she'd be right back. Dove smiled at me, Elise squinted as though she were taking my measure, Catherine gave me a slight nod, and Nikki and Winnie seemed... intrigued. Curious. Like maybe they'd take up a bucket of popcorn if offered. I left them with a "Ladies," and followed Jo outside.

The summer air ruffled her long chestnut hair, which she'd worn in waves down her back, and her white-and-blue floral dress fluttered around her knees.

My mouth dried out.

She moved a few meters from the entrance to Craic, and my pulse hammered in my neck like I'd just lifted a car.

"Did you need something?" She crossed her arms over her chest, hiding the scintillating dip of her dress and—

I swallowed hard. "I wanted to talk. I feel like you're mad at me and I'm not—"

She shook her head. "I'm not mad at you, Adam. I am frustrated and I needed some space, yes, but I'm also a busy woman with a whole life outside of responding to your texts, shockingly enough."

Whoa. Definitely *frustrated* and it was clearly my fault, though I wasn't certain why. Maybe because of how I'd nearly kissed her, then run away? Maybe for how awkward I'd been when she'd come to my office?

"Since you obviously aren't sure what happened, I'm going to make this very clear." She marched closer, her strappy sandals pat-pat-patting against the sidewalk until she stopped inches from my face. "Your brother is my friend. I care about him. I also have no desire to date him and would appreciate it if you would stop telling him he needs to go for the gold or whatever nonsense you've dreamed up that'll force us together."

I reared back a little, but not so much it moved me away. Her eyes were fiery, and the fed-up ring to her words were a slap to my face.

"I'm sorry. I thought I was doing the right thing." It sounded like such a weak excuse, but it was true. Ethan was the best and free of so many things I wasn't.

But if she doesn't want him, maybe…

"Please don't play matchmaker on my behalf, okay, *Doc?*"

I flinched, the nickname sounding awful coming from her. I liked my name on her lips, not the oddly formal sound of my work persona.

"Jo, please. I—I want you to be happy," I said, chest hollowing out and hands aching to touch her, to hold her this close and convince her to believe me.

She exhaled sharply. "Kind of you. Thank you. Please hear me when I say I am very happy with your brother as my friend."

I nodded instantly. "Of course. Yes. And… us? Can we be friends?"

Our eyes locked and everything in me froze. Waiting. *Begging.*

As foolish as I'd been to resist spending time with her, I would no longer pretend I didn't want her friendship, at the very least. *And if you're honest, that* is *the very least.*

It took more than a beat, but soon, her gaze dropped away and she stepped back. "Sure. Yeah. We can be friends."

"Good." *Thank God.*

"I'm going to head back in." She gave me a thin, oblig-atory type of look, and walked past me toward the entrance.

I stayed put, exhaling and shutting my eyes against the mess I'd made and the mess I felt.

"Looks like that went well," Ethan said, shooting me an amused smile as he wandered up to lean against the wall next to me.

"You can shut it."

He chuckled. "I tried to tell you, man."

My head was shaking before I spoke. "I guess you did, but I'm..."

"Stubborn. And pretty oblivious to the fact that the woman you're trying to shove at me is far more interested in *you* than your brother."

I shifted, uncomfortable with the statement, and yet the tightening low in my stomach, the little flip in my chest, suggested I might have other feelings about it, too.

"I still don't know that I have anything to—"

An arm came around my shoulders, and Bruce squeezed me in a side-hug.

"Is this guy trying to convince himself he's got nothing to offer again?" He directed this question to Ethan.

"Yes. He's working overtime at it," Ethan said, settling in with a widened stance as though he had nowhere else to be.

Bruce turned to me. "We've talked about this, my friend."

We had. He'd been so happy with Nikki, and now they were engaged and he was over the moon and he wanted all of us to have that same happiness. I loved him for it, but I'd struggled to embrace his suggestion that my past didn't define my future.

"Your past doesn't—"

"Define my future," I finished along with him because this wasn't the first time he'd made this argument.

He grinned. "Exactly."

"I disagree, though. Isn't that the very thing that defines it? I trained as a medic for years and therefore, I was a great one. I did turns in trauma ERs and handled all kinds of problems on missions, and each of those things in my past built the skills I have now. That's my past defining my future."

Bruce leaned against the wall of the building and crossed his arms, getting comfortable. "No. It *informs* it, yes. But take me. Deadbeat criminal dad. A mom who loved me but ultimately didn't know how to love herself very well and ended up hurting not only herself but my sister. Are you going to tell me that because of that, I'm destined to be a deadbeat criminal father?"

I scowled. "No. Of course not. You had no choice in those things, and that's totally different. That was years ago. I ruined my own marriage. I made the choice to make vows, and then I ultimately broke them by not caring for the relationship like I should've."

Ethan and Bruce shared a look.

"Did you cheat?" Bruce asked, stone-faced.

"What? No. I didn't cheat," I spat, offended at the question.

"Well, you keep saying you ruined it as though it was one moment, and I don't buy it. It also wasn't just you, from what I understand," Bruce countered.

I scrubbed a hand over my face. "It was a hundred—maybe a thousand choices over the five years we were married, okay? It was the choice to work late, the choice to take the TDY or extra training or extra hour at the gym. It was the choice to sit next to her and play video games like a little idiot instead of turning to my wife and talking to her."

"Yes. Absolutely yes. Those were bad calls, especially

repeatedly over time. But what was she doing? Was she asking you to stay? To come home earlier? Was she waiting there next to you to talk?"

In truth, she'd been just as disconnected as I had—out with her girlfriends, working Saturdays at the salon and sometimes offering cuts on Sundays, doing whatever she wanted whenever. And I liked how we had that freedom. At one point, I'd taken pride in how separately we operated, as though it was a sign of maturity rather than a pretty clear red flag we weren't interested in each other enough to prioritize the other.

But she'd wanted to change things, and I didn't realize it until it was too late. She'd asked about a marriage retreat the unit was doing, but I decided to take a training trip instead. She'd suggested I look at other possible jobs instead of wanting to be an operator medic. I'd been so angry with her then, hating how she didn't seem to see me and my goals. But with time and distance, I'd felt the truth needling in my gut. She'd wanted me around, eventually. She'd wanted me to try with her, not just for my career goals.

Yes, she'd played a part in the failure, but I was accountable for *my* actions, and I couldn't forget that. Ever.

Bruce gripped my shoulder and shook me a little. "I know it was complex. But it doesn't define you. It has informed you. My guess is that if you're with someone you really love and not someone you're infatuated with and marry too young, you're going to work harder than ever to pour into that relationship because you know what can happen when you become complacent."

Ethan snapped and pointed. "What he said, A. For real."

I sent him a glare.

"You may not know that person yet. But you're a natural

caretaker, Doc, and you're a good man. You would make a great husband to someone, if you decide to. But that's the thing—you have to decide. And I get that me lecturing you isn't going to do the job. But from one man who thought he had to wait for what was right in front of him to another, I'm saying consider letting yourself change your own mind."

Bruce's words couldn't be ignored, but I could change the subject. "Sure. Yeah. So, uh, can I get a meeting with you and Wilder Monday? I have something I wanted to propose."

Bruce raised a single brow that practically shouted "Really?" but he nodded.

"Consider it scheduled." He patted my back and hollered over his shoulder, "Now come get a beer with your friends!"

Ethan raised a brow and gave me a knowing smile. "He said everything I wanted to say, and yeah, let's go get a beer."

I grumbled but followed. Swirling thoughts jammed my mind so full I wanted to go home and sit on the deck and watch the stars wink into existence as the sun set, but instead, I sucked it up and went with my brother and promised myself I wouldn't instantly reject everything he and Bruce had said. I'd let it sit until I could pull it out and inspect it more carefully.

And then maybe I'd be able to decide if the ways my past had *informed* my future meant I could share a life with someone else.

CHAPTER EIGHTEEN

Jo

I didn't read the three letters. I sent them right into the trash. I didn't need to see this person's thoughts about me to know I didn't want them in my life or mind or anywhere near me.

They'd been coming more frequently. One or two a week instead of each month. Was he threatening me now? Or was it still the awkwardly personal fan mail like it had been the first few times?

Josie, I love your words and the way you write your heroes. Are your hands soft like Shailey's in book two? Is your hair blond like Iris's in book three? I'd like to touch you, to see you, and know how much of yourself I'm seeing in these beautiful stories.

The trickle of unease that usually accompanied seeing the standard envelopes clearly holding a substantial stack of papers inside with the familiar Valentine's Day stamp in the right corner doubled, then tripled, despite having tossed them as quickly as I could.

I rushed out the post office door and fiddled with my phone, pulling up the group thread with the girls in search of distraction.

A body stopped a foot from me, and I only registered it when a hand reached out to grip my arm.

I startled and yelped, dropping my phone in the bushes next to me.

"Hey, whoa. You okay?" Adam's intense blue eyes gazed at me with equal parts alarm and concern.

"Yeah. Of course. I'm just in a rush to get back to writing. Big scenes today." My heart thundered in my chest, the fear from running into someone after thinking about the letters still grabbing at me. *It's just Adam. Everything's fine.* I exhaled slowly, willing my pulse to slow.

"Need any help? I'm free today."

I should've said no, but standing next to him took the edge off my fear, and before I could stop myself, I accepted. "Sure. Come over whenever. I'll be home."

And then, I nearly jogged to my car and narrowly escaped speeding home. In ten minutes, I was parked, up to my apartment, and snuggled on my couch under a soft throw, wishing I hadn't checked my PO box, wishing I didn't care so much, wishing I'd told Adam no.

He'd been so apologetic when we'd talked last night, and I couldn't lie and pretend I'd kept my eyes off him when he'd come back inside Craic a few minutes after I had. He was just so handsome and kind, and I didn't like how hurt I'd been feeling. I hated how I'd been so frustrated with him, I'd almost yelled and I'd definitely lost my patience.

And yet, he hadn't seemed altogether surprised. He

hadn't tried to defend himself either. He'd explained his thinking, but it hadn't made sense. Maybe at some point, I'd need to dig into his statement that he thought he was doing the right thing.

Could he mean he believed Ethan liked me, and therefore it made his encouragement right? Ethan had liked me initially—I knew that. And though sometimes he seemed to look at me a little longer than a friend would, I didn't get the feeling, especially lately, that he still held a candle for me.

But what else could it mean? And why was I still thinking about it?

"Jo, Please. I—I want you to be happy."

I sank into the couch, melting into the cushion at the memory of the pleading in his voice.

He'd said it from his gut. I'd felt it, the way he'd meant it so completely. And it'd stuck with me as I'd agreed to friendship, something that felt like an imitation of what I really wanted and yet couldn't have. It'd floated around in my mind as I watched him at his table, smiling and even laughing with his friends, then later wandering out into the summer night with Beast and Kenny long after Tristan had come to take Winnie's hand and Bruce had pressed a kiss to Nikki's head and led her away.

I was a mess of emotions, and after a poor night of sleep last night and restlessness this morning, I forced myself to focus on work for a while until finally, the words started coming more easily. At some point, the bell rang and I didn't startle quite as dramatically as I had when Adam touched me earlier, so I gave myself kudos for that.

And speaking of, Adam stood at the door with a takeout bag in one hand. "I'm hoping you haven't eaten."

"I just had—" The oven clock caught my attention.

"Wow, I thought it was at most three, but I guess I've been in the zone again."

His smile quirked up. "That's a good thing, right?"

Stepping back so he could come in, I agreed. "Yes. Definitely. I've been kind of stumped for a few days, and it's been like pulling teeth to get words in, so I'm relieved. I should be done and the deadline approaching amps up my anxiety when the writing is slow." It never failed that when he helped me, I wrote up a storm, but this strain between us had made it all feel like typing through mud.

I needed my muse here... my very hands-on muse, *please and thank you.*

"If it's better I go, just say the word. I don't want to keep you from doing what you need to do."

Well, there it was. My out. I could accept what he was offering and tell him it was important I keep writing without him. Logically, with how raw I still felt, I should do that.

But having him here felt so good. I'd missed him these last few weeks between his being gone and then our time together feeling so fraught, then absent. I just wanted to talk with him and hear his stories about crazy ways he'd saved people's lives or which operators had been big babies when they'd gotten small injuries. I wanted to know him and for him to know me, and all of that was... it was probably a little more than friendship territory, but tonight, I couldn't bring myself to tell him to go.

And yes. I wanted more of that muse-level inspiration he brought with him.

"If you went to the trouble of bringing me dinner, you should probably stay." I moved past him to get plates.

"Good. Thanks." He fumbled with the bag and began

removing takeout containers. "I got what I remember you getting last time—hope it's right."

Not that I doubted, but he'd remembered. Even down to no green peppers, he'd gotten the order exactly right. We sat at my tiny table, chatting about superficial things, and I tried not to feel a small thrill whenever our knees brushed.

Once we'd finished, we moved to the kitchen. He rinsed dishes and put them away while I wiped down the table, then packaged the containers up and tucked them in the trash. We worked together so seamlessly I would've thought we'd done this a hundred times, not just twice.

"We make a good team," he said, an oddly pleased smile on his face.

"We do," I said, blushing for no good reason.

Okay, well, maybe the reason was I liked the idea of being on a team with Adam Carter. Maybe I'd dreamed about it a little, even when I'd promised myself I wouldn't. Maybe I'd wondered what it would be like.

"Anything I can help with?" he asked, taking a seat in the chair and notably *not* next to where my computer rested on the love seat.

"Actually, yes. I'm writing a scene where my hero is checking the heroine for a head injury. Can you walk me through that?" I sat down and slid the keyboard in front of me.

"Want me to show you?" His voice had dropped a touch, seemed quieter, and his blue eyes were darker somehow.

"Sure. Yeah. That'd be great," I said, attempting to maintain a purely casual tone and not one that said, *"You can show me anything you want."*

After asking a few more questions about the scene, we determined I should lay flat on the ground, since the heroine's neck and spine were also sort of in question. It made no sense that sliding the coffee table out of the way and lying on my fluffy living room carpet should send my heart rate into a tizzy, but it sure did.

Or maybe it wasn't so much the lying down but the doing it in front of Adam, who was now kneeling next to me and asking me to squeeze two of his fingers to confirm I could use my hands as he checked my pupils and then whispered a little "Perfect" with a wink before he moved on to his next task.

He explained each step. "You'd stabilize the neck, making sure it's in line with the spine. Obviously stop any bleeding, and remember a head wound is going to bleed like crazy, but that can be the case for superficial injuries."

Why did this make my stomach tighten and my breath grow light? Probably the way his hands rested at the sides of my head and the way his eyes were running over me, simulating just what he'd do.

"After basic stabilization, then he'll check pupils, looking for uneven dilation, usually. Then ask questions to get a feel for their coherence—name, what day is it, that kind of thing." He wrapped up his explanation, all that training and excellence waving right in my face.

And all the while, I just kept thinking about how much I wanted something with him, and how he'd begged me for friendship. I kept feeling this pull between us, this attraction sparking in my chest, and I knew it wasn't just me. Despite his early protests about what he wanted and his attempts to shove me off on Ethan, he kept coming back.

Maybe he really did only want friendship, but maybe... maybe he needed a little push.

Maybe he needed me to help him see what could be between us.

CHAPTER NINETEEN

Adam

Her gorgeous eyes had watched as I went through the motions, explaining each step, and then something almost imperceptible shifted.

A sharpening in her gaze, maybe, or a thickening of the air between us. Whatever it was, it felt like a hand on my chest, and my throat grew dry from longing to know what it was and what it meant.

"So that's it," I said, leaning back and rising to my feet, then holding out a hand to her.

She rose to standing and stumbled into me, steadying herself against me with a hand on my shoulder. The press of her body against mine sent a crush of heat through me, and I released her and stepped back.

"Thank you. Are you up for something else?" She knit her fingers together, drawing my gaze to her hands.

"Of course. Whatever you need," I said, my voice

sounding amazingly normal considering the utter thirst pawing at me.

She sat and pulled up a document on her computer. "Okay. Doorframe hang. Jump and kiss. Neck grab—"

My eyes had to be bulging out of my head. "Neck grab?"

She glanced up and gave me a saucy grin. "Adam, honey, you know I write romance, right?"

Sensation cascaded like a refracted rainbow through me, her expression and the word *honey* coating my mind so all I could manage in response was "I do."

She chuckled. "Well, these are things I haven't actually experienced, so it would be helpful if we could do them."

Jump and kiss. Let's do that one.

I silenced the thought, but another one arrived unbidden. *Has she really not done these things? Hasn't she dated? Had boyfriends?* She must've, and yet the thought only made the snap of longing for *me* to be that person even starker.

Also not helpful thoughts.

"Well, we already did the neck grab." She coughed and cleared her throat. "Let's start small for now. So, the doorway hang."

"Wait, didn't we do that already?"

She smirked. "No, that was a doorway *lean*. This is literally just you stopping in a doorway and holding on to the frame on your side of the door but kind of leaning down into the space. Can you try that? Here—" she hopped up and flipped on the light in her bedroom. "Just come in here and then lean this way."

She waved me forward, evidently not thinking twice about having me enter her bedroom, then stepped back. I walked through and took in the view—white bookshelves lining one wall and a cozy little reading nook with a large wicker papasan chair in one corner. A bed with coral-and-white sheets and a pristine white comforter with a bright coral throw splashed across one corner.

It was cheery and lovely and comfortable like its owner. A chest of drawers littered with small items and a perfume bottle sat next to a small closet. And the scent... it was her scent, but amplified in the small space. Citrus and sweetness and clean—I didn't know the right names for the notes she hit, but they were all exactly right.

"Adam?"

I spun, grabbing the doorframe and praying I hadn't looked like a total creep standing there staring at her bed. I leaned against the frame a little and raised a brow. "Like this?"

Her gaze slipped down one of my arms, then bounced to the other, and her lips parted.

She cannot know what that does to me.

"Yes, all good. Thanks," she said, voice a little thin.

I dropped my hands. "Good."

She bent over the back of the couch and typed furiously on her computer. I followed the movement until I realized the peril of doing so, how her skirt slipped up the back of her thighs and—nope, not a good idea.

"Okay, so next... this is kind of like what we did last time, but more intense. It's an argument between the main characters, and she's backed up against a wall and he cages her in but sort of pins her hands above her head." She scuttled over to a section of wall without a bookshelf and put her back against it.

"Uh—" I cleared my throat. "Right."

I approached right as she raised her hands above her head, and a disbelieving laugh tripped out. Was I really going to do this? To punish myself by touching this woman, literally pinning her to the wall?

She gave me a soft smile quivering with nerves, just once. And that was it.

Yes.

Yes, I was going to do this because she'd asked me to. And very quickly, I was realizing I'd do just about anything for Josephine Malcom, even if it cost me.

With one hand, I pinned her wrists to the wall as gently as I could while still making it feel secure. "What's my other hand doing here?"

She bit her full bottom lip, eyes slipping over my shoulder like she might find the answer there. "Hmm. What would seem natural?"

I'd touch your waist, your back. I'd slide a hand from your neck to your shoulder and slip the strap of your tank down so I could trace the line of your collarbone with my tongue.

Okay. Focus.

"Probably here," I said, resting my hand at her waist, the warmth of her setting my fingers on fire. Naturally, I was leaning close, and I couldn't stand to be this close to her lips, so I moved my head to the side of hers.

"Good," she said, a little breathless. "And then..."

A huff left her when I spoke low and soft into her ear. "What does he do next, Josie?"

"He—" It was all air, so she tried again after a little cough. "I mean, what should happen next, do you think?"

I was this far into the exercise and at this point refused to stop. She wanted me to tell her what *he* would do next, so I would.

"Maybe he'd lace his fingers with one of her hands and let the other one down." I released her wrists and caught her right hand with my left, knitting us together and gently pressing her back against the wall. "And maybe he'd beg her to use the other one to touch him anywhere she wanted."

She understood the assignment, her arm floating down and her hand taking up residence at my lower back.

"Good. Then he'd probably want to taste her. Soft..." I pressed a featherlight kiss behind her ear and she sucked in a breath. "Slow..." Another kiss, this one another inch down the smooth skin of her neck. "Savoring every second he got to be this close to her."

She made a sound, something almost like a whimper, but then her free hand moved, fingers sifting into my hair and holding me close.

She smelled so good, and her skin was so soft and she was breathing as hard as I was, as into this as I was. This wasn't the hero and heroine—this was us. But I didn't want to think about anything but Jo. Just Jo and doing whatever she wanted me to do.

"Would he eventually kiss her, do you think?" she asked, eyes closed when I glanced up to see her face.

Good grief, she was beautiful. Lashes fanning out against her cheeks and mouth parted, just waiting.

What kind of help would I be if I didn't answer that questions with a yes?

"He would. But only..." I brushed my thumb over her lips, and her eyes opened to pin me.

"Only?"

"Only when she was aching for it." I dipped my head and kissed the corner of her mouth, then her cheek, then her jaw on the opposite side.

"She—she would be. By now. I'm pretty sure," she said, chest and cheeks flushed and words full of the same need I felt in every inch of me.

I pulled back, meeting her gaze again. The desire there made me go molten with wanting, and I told her the truth.

"Then he'd be sure to give her what she wanted."

Eyes on her lush lips, I finally released her pinned hand and used both of mine to hold her head and lower my mouth to hers.

In some part of my brain, I'd imagined stopping just before our lips met. Maybe I would pull away entirely, as though the playacting and study time were over, but in this universe, where I'd kissed her neck and heard her breathless with need for me, there was no chance of holding back.

Because I didn't stop. Our lips connected, a sure press and release, then another, deeper kiss until she gripped my head with both her hands and I tilted hers to the perfect angle, until I'd pressed as close as I could get and felt myself being consumed by the fire between us.

This wasn't a first kiss. This was... this was illogical. More than nerve endings and chemistry and endorphins, this was a bonfire in my chest, something unfurling into an unwieldy type of wanting that transcended the moment of these touches.

Mine. I captured her lips again. *She's meant to be mine.*

I pulled back as the thought finally penetrated the haze of desire and took her in, this woman who'd kissed me back and stolen something from me in the process.

We stared at each other, breathing heavily and slowly, slowly coming back to ourselves.

"Well. I think... yeah. That's what he'd do," I said dumbly, needing something to fill the space between us so I didn't instantly start kissing her again.

She blinked, then smiled. "Yeah. I think you're right."

CHAPTER TWENTY

Adam Carter had kissed me four days ago.

And when I said kissed, I meant *kiiiiiiiiiissed.*

I sighed and my eyes shut, mind filling with flashes of memory from the minutes we'd stood there, kissing like it was the end of the world.

I did not particularly want to remember the way he'd stepped away and slowly came back to himself, then apologized.

He'd apologized for kissing me like our lives depended on the pleasure generated between us and he'd done the valiant work to save the whole city, and then *apologized.*

I'd stared at him, too dazed to fully comprehend his words.

"I'm sorry, Jo. I shouldn't have done that."

I'd laughed because it'd seemed so wildly wrong. "I'm glad you did."

He was shaking his head before I'd finished. "I'm—I really shouldn't have done that."

"Explain why."

He'd run a hand through the hair I'd just had my fingers in, holding him close to me, pulling him closer.

"I can't give you what you deserve. And I..." He'd reached out and stroked my cheek. "I'm so damn sorry."

And then he'd left—no running out, just quietly going while thoughts swirled and nearly drowned in my head, nothing coming out of my mouth. I'd thought he'd just disappeared again, and anger started at a low simmer as I ping-ponged around my house and tried to figure out how he knew what I deserved.

What did I deserve? I couldn't say what he *thought* I did, but it must've been something truly fictional if he thought he wasn't it. He was kind and thoughtful and generous and a bossy nurse who cared about everyone in his life so much. He was gorgeous and engaging and willing to help me even though it did nothing for him.

All of that was wonderful, but if he didn't *want* me, or want to want me, then it didn't matter what else he had in mind, because for that reason alone, he was right. And that was crushing.

But then, he'd texted me.

"Can we hang out Wednesday?"

And since then, I'd been waiting for today. Tonight. To have time with him and finally pin this man down and make him tell me what he meant with all of that. If he really didn't want to start anything then... then I'd figure out how to move on.

But you don't kiss a woman like that if you don't want something with her. It's just not possible. And until he told me straight out with full sentences and fewer apologies, I wasn't going to assume anything.

The bell on the door rang, and I snapped out of my reverie slash machinations and waved at the customer entering All Booked Up.

"Welcome in," I said cheerily.

When my eyes focused back on my computer, I saw the top email in my Josie Wade inbox waiting there.

From Jessica Korbel. Subject: Invitation to Small Town Release Party

I shut my laptop to avoid any of the now three patrons from catching a glimpse. Not that anyone was looking over my shoulder, but Adam had found me out easily enough.

I hadn't written Jess back. She'd invited Josie Wade on behalf of the Silver Ridge Romance Readers Club and All Booked Up, an "adorable indie bookstore serving the small but avid mountain town reading community" to a book release party on the release day of my next book.

I needed to respond. I always responded to reader e-mails, and I hated the thought of letting that one be neglected. But what could I say? If I agreed, then that was it. The anonymity I'd had, the freedom I'd had, and the lack of judgment from Elizabeth when my dad inevitably crowed about it to her, would evaporate like so much water on a desert afternoon.

Of course, they didn't expect Josie Wade to show. I could easily say I was already committed to another event. It wouldn't be hard to do. So why did I hate this idea, too?

The door jingled again and, speak of the woman herself, Jess wandered inside, along with Elise and Sarah Saint. Sarah came straight to me and gave me a hug.

"Hey, you. Are you coming to family dinner this week?

It's been way too long," she said, her sweet voice and lovely smile always so warm and welcoming.

"I'm planning on it! I can't wait for some baby snuggles." Her son was a little over a year now and the cutest thing on the planet.

"If you can catch him," she said, beaming at the thought of her little wild man who was so much like his dad, it was ridiculous.

"We have a nice new collection of rom-coms that just came in yesterday for release day if you're looking," I said, winking at her. She was an honorary member of the Silver Ridge Romance Readers, as were several other locals, like Dahlia Wallace, who couldn't usually make our Saturday night book club meets for one reason or another but still read along with us.

Jess and Elise approached as Sarah slipped away to browse.

"You three out for lunch?" I asked, delighted to see their faces.

"We all need new books," Elise said, then winked and disappeared into the romance section. Normally, she'd stay and chat a while but again, lately, she'd been quieter. At some point, I'd need to ask her what was going on. Maybe she and her on-and-off boyfriend were off again? Or, on? I couldn't keep track.

Jess leaned on the counter. "And I'm here to check on you."

"Me? Do I need checking on?"

She gave me a kind smile which just made her prettier. She was so entirely gorgeous, I didn't really understand how she didn't date more, although I knew it was a matter of choice.

"Well, we saw you talk with Adam on Friday. Then I've noticed this week he's…"

My heart sank. "Is he okay?"

Her smile deepened. "He honestly seems great. Happier and lighter. And I know part of that is because one of his friends is doing better, but I'm also suspecting it miiiight have something to do with you."

Tiny wings fluttered in my belly. "Happier?"

She nodded, studying me. Good grief, the woman had an intense gaze. "Yes. And I want to know how you are, if you want to tell me. If not, I'm just… checking in. Making sure you're good."

I glanced around, confirming everyone was happily browsing and didn't need help. Once I saw they were, I lowered my voice and spilled my guts. "Um, so, we kissed—like *really* kissed—and then he apologized and told me he shouldn't have done it and then he left."

Her expression hardened, and if I had to guess, this was a sliver of what one would see if faced with Jess in a professional setting where you were on the wrong side of the scenario. The woman was fearsome when she needed to be.

"Please tell me Doc isn't out here acting like a manchild and can't handle his feelings." The level of unimpressed on her face was practically nuclear.

"I don't think so, no. It's honestly why I'm not more upset. I'm not exactly thrilled by what he said, but he initiated hanging out tonight, and I'm hoping there'll be some explanation."

"Good. If not, let me know and we'll find some truth serum and get it out of him the old-fashioned way." She winked and I cackled, enjoying her reference to a scene in one of the earlier Josie Wade books.

"I do love that scene," I said, grinning with her.

She sighed. "If only such a thing would work in real life. I have a few people I could use it on."

Interest spiked. "Yeah? And who would make that list?"

Her eyes cut to me. "No love interests. Mostly just a brutish, idiot man who makes my life miserable."

"Beast?" I mouthed this for some reason, like anyone in the store would overhear and understand what I was talking about.

"Tell you later," she whispered, then patted the desk. "Keep me posted on how things go. Oh, and I haven't heard back from Josie Wade, but we'll still throw a party here, right? Can you get the all clear from Mr. Darcy?"

I snickered at her calling my dad, Darcy Malcom, Mr. Darcy. "I'm positive we can. And I hope you hear back soon, but if not, hopefully it just means she's busy writing the next book."

Hopefully, she'll figure out how to stop being such a coward and tell you all the truth.

Each of them checked out with a few books in tow and left me feeling warm and fuzzy about life here in Silverton. I really did love it here, and the idea that I ever wanted to move back to the city was just ludicrous.

The afternoon wound down, and I found a few moments to work on brainstorming my next book. My current project was with the editor as of yesterday, and in another week or two, I'd be sending off advanced copies. I was sad to see the book Adam had helped me with come to an end, but the possibilities of what could go right—or wrong—between us tonight and in the future made the book seem less essential. We were friends now, independent of the Josie persona knowledge and the help with my work. We had a relationship rooted in friendship.

Maybe tonight, he'd finally explain why he refused to let it change into something more even though he clearly wanted it as much as I did.

My phone buzzed in my hand—Elizabeth. Ah, nothing like another evasive conversation with Lizzie to keep me distracted until I saw Adam again.

CHAPTER TWENTY-ONE

Adam

I waved to Kenny and Cookie, who were waiting on a late meeting with one of our overseas team members to start and shouldered my bag.

Anticipation and a twinge of nerves kicked at me, but I buried all of it. I'd pep talked myself into this evening for the last few days, basically since the minute I'd left Jo's apartment on Saturday, and I wasn't about to let my default settings take over.

I didn't need to fall into the trap of thinking about touching Jo, or kissing her, or being close to her and how much I wanted to do that again. I certainly shouldn't be allowing snapshots of those fleeting moments together pepper my mind at odd intervals throughout the day. I definitely wasn't in a position to be wanting more of that.

No. Because I'd resolved to return to the friendzone

with lovely, intelligent, creative, friendly, kind, beautiful Jo. *Friendzone.*

And while it might've seemed naïve that after sharing a mind-bending kiss like we had, we could return to friendship without anything else in the way, but I had a plan. I'd simply tell her the truth.

First, I'd tell her I was divorced. She might've known this already, but the more we interacted, the more I suspected Ethan hadn't mentioned it. If he hadn't, no one else had. Second, I'd make clear it was my fault.

I could just hear Ethan and Bruce and any number of my friends suggesting that no, it wasn't my fault. Or at least, it wasn't *only* my fault. To be fair, they were right, and so maybe I'd make sure she knew it was a two-way street and it still dead-ended in both directions.

She would likely be disinterested enough by then that it'd be no issue, but if she somehow got past those issues, I'd... think of something else.

Beast waved from his truck, where he piled in but left the door open. I jogged down the front steps of the Saint building and waited until I got close enough we wouldn't be overheard, knowing he was intensely private.

"How's your grandma?"

"She's okay. Thanks."

A thousand realities could be loaded behind those words, and he wasn't likely to tell me. If Dorian couldn't bring himself to find words at times, Jude simply *wouldn't*, although sometimes, I suspected his brutish persona was more a result of a shield he relied on than his genuine personality. Maybe that was the Pollyanna in me, and I could just hear Jess's eyes rolling from wherever she was in town.

"See you tomorrow," I said, and he gave me a signature nonverbal response back.

I didn't worry about him like I did Dorian. Beast showed up, he worked, he communicated when the mission or meeting called for it. He became a lesser version of himself around Jess, true, and we'd need to figure out a way forward now that she was back, and he was still off the travel list. But I hoped I wasn't giving him too much credit—that I wasn't assuming he was okay when he wasn't. He had a lot on his shoulders.

I could've gone home and changed, but we wore utility pants and plaid shirts to work most days, so unless I was going for jeans, I wasn't going to get more comfortable. Sure, shorts and a T-shirt would feel nice on a hot late-June evening, but I didn't feel like waiting. I'd psyched myself up to feel friendliness and affection for Jo, not... other things.

Passion.

Desire.

Hope.

Nope! Not those things.

After dropping my bag in my car, I locked it and walked to Jo's since it was only a few minutes away on foot. I'd never imagined living in such a small town, but now that I'd settled in and felt like it was *my* town, I loved it.

I took the stairs to her floor two at a time, and by the time I reached her door, my heart was racing. From the stairs, obviously.

"Hey. You got here fast," she said, a wide smile on her lovely face.

Okay, let's stop thinking about how pretty she is, because that's not going to help things.

"I came straight here."

Her smile grew impossibly larger. "I'm glad you did."

Something in my chest squeezed mercilessly, the beauty of her absolutely wrecking my composure and the feeble attempts to mind control myself into believing I didn't have any feelings for her beyond friendly ones.

"Me, too." My words were soft, and my eyes fell to her lips and *then* my brain kicked in.

"Come in," she said, fortunately right as I remembered the whole goal of tonight.

Clear the air, then draw the lines. *Clear the air, then draw the lines.*

But then, I registered the silky-looking dress in a navy color swishing against her legs, and I was tracing the line of the zipper up her back to where it ended a hands width from her neck, revealing the delicate ridges of her spine.

Nope. Lines. Drawing lines. Clearing air.

"I was glad you wanted to get together after the other night," she said as she turned, fingers laced together in front of her in the first show of genuine uncertainty I'd ever seen from her.

Okay, we'll dive right in.

"Yeah, I'm sorry about that. And I want to be clear, I'm not sorry because you don't deserve to be kissed and kissed well. I'm sorry because I shouldn't have done it in the first place, and I don't want things between us to be confusing."

She blinked, her brow furrowed. "Can you explain that to me? I'm not sure what you mean when you say you *shouldn't* have done it in the first place. It feels like I'm missing something, especially when you say it like that—with all the 'you deserved to be kissed and kissed well' business."

I pushed out an exhale, willing myself to find the right words and not sound like a total jerk here. When I didn't respond right away, she continued.

"In my head, we're both consenting, single adults who like each other and have a nice friendship and a solid helping of physical chemistry, so this makes a lot of sense. But clearly, I'm not seeing the whole picture."

I nodded to the couch and she sat, then I took the spot in the chair perpendicular to it. "Did you know I was married before? That I'm divorced?"

Her brows popped up. "I didn't."

I nodded. "Yeah. And the marriage failed because of both me and my ex."

"That makes sense. Seems like it's rarely just one person, right?" She tucked her hands between her knees and waited patiently.

"It was a gradual slide into being barely roommates. And in retrospect, we never should've gotten married. But I was young, and going into the military gives you this feeling that you're grown—you've got a salary and benefits and a housing allowance if you move out of the barracks. It feels normal to get married at twenty." I shook my head, remembering the way I felt like I had everything together. I'd been on my own for more than two years by then, so I thought I knew everything.

"That is really young. How long were you guys married?" she asked, the disinterest or shutdown I'd anticipated not hitting yet.

"Almost five years. I deployed a couple times, so that probably allowed us to delay the reality that we didn't know each other. Some of it's a normal part of leaving for a year and coming back—you have to reintegrate. I remember thinking it was normal when I didn't feel close to her, or even like I wanted to be..." I ran a hand through my hair. "Do you see what I'm saying?"

The compassion on her face was almost unbearable.

She scooted to the edge of the couch and reached for my hand. I didn't want to touch her, to be comforted by her, and yet nothing in my arsenal of personal willpower could make me turn her away.

"I see that you were young and tried to do one of the hardest things two people can do, and it didn't work out. I see you accepting responsibility for your part in it, and maybe a little more than your part. And I see you punishing yourself even now, more than a decade later, for something you did in another phase of your life."

Her big brown eyes glittered with so much care and concern for me and not an ounce of the disinterest or worry for herself I needed to see.

"You're missing my point, and that's no surprise because you're so intent on seeing the good in people and being kind, I should've guessed you'd see this as a mistake in my past. But Josie, I've had other relationships, and they failed, too."

Didn't she get it? I didn't know how to do this. I didn't know how to be with someone and give them everything.

"I appreciate the backhanded compliment, I think, but I'd like to point out that I, too, have failed at relationships. Hence the reason I'm single."

I let my face speak for me in response because it wasn't at all the same.

Her lips twitched and a streak of longing shot through me like a shooting star, wishing to see the smile she hid away.

"My question for you is this—are you the same person you were when you married her?"

I laughed. "No."

"Of course not. Because it's been almost twenty years

since then. You're not a spring chicken anymore, Adam, honey," she said, shaking her head and tsking.

It was so ridiculous, I laughed again but grasped onto the thread. "Well, that's another reason. I'm a decade older than you. At twenty-eight, I was fumbling around like an idiot, still obsessed with work and unable to prioritize whomever I was dating enough to make it last."

She shrugged a shoulder. "Well, the good news here is, I'm not an idiot. I've always been an old soul. I'm mildly obsessed with my work, but I admire yours. And handy enough, we work five minutes from each other."

For some reason, this response, of all of them, cut through my determination to shut things down. She had her own life, her own goals, and she wasn't going to begrudge me mine. She was also absolutely one of the smartest people I knew and her point landed—I might've been an idiot at her age, but that didn't mean she didn't know her own mind now.

"You've really thought about this. Us." The thud of my heart nearly shook me as I sat there on the edge of my seat, my hand still cradled in hers.

She smiled softly. "I have. And I think that while all your excuses are understandably concerns, they are just that —excuses. I think we should give this a shot."

My throat tightened and I cleared it. "You deserve so much—"

Her hands squeezed mine and she shook her head slowly, eyes locked on mine. "Let's let me decide what I deserve, okay? I deserve an honorable man who is good and thoughtful and kind of cute."

My brows dropped, and she grinned before admitting, "Okay, maybe more than kind of."

My stomach clenched, the sensation I was standing on

the edge of something huge and deadly and life-giving bursting in my head.

Marlee's words snuck back in. *"You'll never change..."*

Had I given them too much power? For so long, I'd accepted them as fact, and yet I'd just admitted I wasn't the same person. Who was the same at twenty and nearly forty?

Still, the thought of hurting this woman who was so loving and full of life and joy made my heart shrivel up.

"Jo, I don't want to hurt you. I *can't* hurt you," I said, my last-ditch effort here.

Her eyes welled with tears in an instant, the emotion so quick to rise to the surface, I didn't know what to do. But she brought my hand to her chest and flattened it against her sternum. The smooth, thin skin there was warm against my fingers, the silk of her dress at my palm an unfortunate impediment, and the contact drop-kicked my breath.

"You'll hurt me more if you refuse to take a chance on yourself. I know I'm not the only one who feels this..."

Her chest rose and fell under my hand, and whatever part of me that had resisted this, resisted *her*, crumbled.

"I'm going to mess up. I don't know how to do this," I said, my words ragged.

"Me, too. But I'd also like to suggest that the way you've been a friend to me has been wonderful. The way you're a friend to so many people. And I think, if we just do that but enjoy the other aspects of being together, too, it'll work out."

She bit her lip, and a flood of images detailing the *other aspects* crashed through my brain.

There was no way this would work in the long run—was there? She was completely wonderful, and I would never forgive myself if I hurt her. But what if we dated for a while and we got to connect and I could experience what it was like to be with someone as full of joy and beauty as Jo, and then when she was ready, we'd move on. Inevitably and rightly so, *she'd* move on. When she figured out I couldn't put her first in the long term...

I'd let her go.

I could accept that. It would be better for her, too. She could have this, whatever it was between us, like she wanted, and then when it stopped being best for her, she could be free.

It could work.

Or maybe, it could be more than that. More than just for now. Maybe this sense of inevitability with her means more than just attraction. What happened at twenty didn't need to repeat itself at nearly forty... Another shot of hope weaved through me.

So I agreed. "Okay. Okay. Let's... try."

She'd want marriage and babies, and I hadn't planned on that. I'd planned the opposite. And living with a certain plan in mind for over thirteen years couldn't simply shift in a matter of minutes in a conversation.

It wasn't fair to let her think I'd miraculously shed all my doubts and hang-ups born out of very real failure and lessons learned, and I had to make sure she got that. "Jo, you understand what you're getting into here? I'm not—"

"I do. I know. And I'm not scared."

She smiled, and we both moved. I slipped the hand already on her up and around her neck to the back of her head, drawing her closer even as she climbed onto my lap and took my face in her hands. We were kissing before my brain could fully register the choice, like the gravity in the room drew us to each other instead of back to earth.

After far too few intoxicating seconds of kissing, she pulled back, my head still in her hands.

"I think, as much as it pains me to say it, we should move slowly."

I nodded, knowing this was the wise course even though a small insurrection occurred in half my brain and planned to stage a coup on the matter. But realistically, this was absolutely how we should proceed.

I wouldn't focus on that *now*, but moving slow was prudent. Maybe it would last, but if it didn't, this was safer—better for us both.

The look she gave me was so sincere and sweet as she said, "You talked about rushing, and while I think comparing what you did as a twenty-year-old to anything going on here isn't necessarily helpful, I'm guessing you'll trust yourself more if we're more purposeful."

"I want you to trust me, too," I said, realizing the truth of that ran deep.

She pressed another kiss to my lips. "I already do. You just need to catch up."

CHAPTER TWENTY-TWO

Adam

After the conversation that went so far off the rails I couldn't have made it up, we ordered takeout. It was like discovering a new element and then sitting down for a microwave dinner or something—total novelty and excitement and unanticipated joy, and then a banal finish. Though sitting next to Jo, being near her and feeling this peace about the decision we'd made—and the one I'd accepted—would never feel routine.

It was only after we'd eaten and snuggled up on the couch to watch a movie that I realized how tired she seemed.

"Hey, are you okay?"

She paused the movie and angled herself to be able to see me better. "I'm great. Thank you for talking through everything and seeing it my way."

I chuckled, loving this little hint of sass. "It works out

for me, too. But I mean... I don't know how to say this without sounding like a total jerk, but you seem tired. Like there's something on your mind."

Her smile fell and she took a long breath. "I talked to Elizabeth, my sister, today. I love her so much, but it always kind of messes me up for a few days."

"I'd like to understand that, if you're willing to share." I didn't want to press her, but since she'd mentioned it, I could see the weight of it dragging at her shoulders and wrinkling her brow.

"It's probably going to make me sound like a whiney little kid, so brace yourself."

She raised a brow, and I shook my head to show I wasn't going to think that.

"You know Elizabeth works for the government, mostly overseas doing fancy, important stuff."

I hadn't asked around amongst the folks at work, but I should've. Maybe someone had worked with her sister while on active duty since the EMU did occasionally partner with other government assets.

"I got my master's because she has one. And honestly, I thought I wanted it. It gave me purpose at a time when my dad moved out here and I needed an excuse to leave Washington. My mom's great but she and I have never been super close, and I couldn't just follow my dad without creating major drama. But with the purpose of grad school, it worked for everyone—Dad was happy I was closer, Mom was appeased I wasn't just abandoning her for 'no reason,' and Elizabeth..." She sighed. "Elizabeth thought what I was doing could make a difference."

"How much older than you is she?" I asked, sensing there was a sizable gap. It wasn't unlike me and Ethan—I'd always had to be careful about how I talked to him because he took everything I said to heart so intensely.

"Six years. She was out of the house by the time my parents got divorced. She was… she was always so far ahead, and I looked up to her so much. I knew I didn't want to work for the government or live overseas, but I thought I'd found my own path, and she seemed excited for me whenever I talked about it. But the reality was, I didn't love my program, and I didn't love the job prospects—climbing the rungs at a non-profit to eventually aim at director of communications or something like that. I never imagined being in the corporate world, but even that, she suggested, could be a force for good depending on the company. It just… none of it clicked for me. Every time I talk to her since I graduated over a year ago, there's this pause after I tell her I haven't found a job using my degree, and I can just hear her disappointment. I can hear her thinking I'm wasting my life."

The urge to defend her rose hot in my chest, but I could see coming at her sister wouldn't be right. "Is it possible you're filling in those silences with your own thoughts, and not actually what Elizabeth feels?"

She dropped her head and let it hang as though in defeat before she raised it to give me her eyes again. "Yes. It is entirely possible. But it's also absolutely the main reason I haven't gone public with Josie Wade. I can just imagine her laughing, thinking I'm joking or writing on the side rather than making this a business, a life. And I hate the idea of disappointing her or embarrassing her, even though logically I know none of those things should factor into the choices I make for my own life and happiness."

I brushed a strand of hair back behind her ear. "That sounds really hard and frustrating. How can I help?"

She tilted her head. "Help?"

"Yeah. I can give you an inspirational speech about how much what you do *does* matter. I can give you a hug. I can—"

"Hug, please. And maybe table the inspirational speech for another time?"

I took her in my arms, wrapping her up and relishing the way she melted into me. I inhaled her soft scent, and she buried her face in my neck.

Then I felt it. That little bursting burn in my chest I'd shoved away countless times since I'd met her, and here on her too-small couch in the quiet of the evening and the peace of the embrace, I heard it, too.

This is it.

She is it.

I pulled in a breath, pushing away the panic I expected to come, but none came. As we parted and I kissed her forehead and she settled in next to me and started the movie, none came.

As she fell asleep with her head on my shoulder, our fingers entwined, my mind had run out of excuses.

I'd never felt anything like this before, though now that I'd let it in, I could admit I'd been choosing not to. I'd been avoiding it as it barreled closer and begged me to notice that this woman was so much more than beautiful and kind. She was *everything*.

I only hoped her faith in me wasn't misplaced.

And I hoped I could give her everything she needed—everything she wanted, too—and if not, that she could walk away happy and whole. And me?

Well. I hoped I'd survive it if it ever came to that.

CHAPTER TWENTY-THREE

Jo

My dad squeezed me tight and released me. "Thanks for holding things together while I was gone."

"Happy to do it whenever you need. You shouldn't retire from one job and get stressed out doing your next one."

We'd talked about this, and he'd eased up a bit after the first year went well enough that he didn't need to worry about the store going under. He'd worked hard to set up partnerships with the school district and the homeschool community, as well as a bunch of other businesses that supported each other.

"The joy far outweighs the stress here, but I love you for worrying about me. I hope you'll find what you love far sooner than I did."

He gave me one of his signature dad smiles, and I

hugged him again. I'd missed him while he and Jane were gone.

And I ached to tell him I *had* found what I loved. Working here at the store, writing my own books, and living this quiet but lovely life felt like a miracle to me.

If that's true, then why won't you let yourself fully embrace it? Tell him. Tell Elizabeth.

I wasn't quite there yet. Not just yet.

"I'm looking forward to family dinner. Why don't you bring Adam with you?" Jane asked, looping her arm through my dad's.

My eyes must've been huge, because she grinned Cheshire-cat big.

"You thought I hadn't heard? Oh, sweet Jo. Just because I was out of town doesn't mean I didn't keep up with the latest. Anything involving my sweet stepdaughter is absolutely front-page news for me."

I chuckled, marveling at her. Adam and I had been dating for about five seconds—okay, technically three days—but we hadn't even been out on a date. Those three days had started the night he'd come over and I'd ended up falling asleep during the movie. Then we'd only managed to text since then, so I was very eager for the day to wrap up and finally set eyes on him at Craic tonight.

The bell jingled as my dad and Jane left, but they stopped just outside to talk with someone. They were essentially Silverton royalty, since Jane always had been and as the beloved bookstore owner, my dad fit right in. The solitary life he'd imagined for himself when he'd moved here had been stripped away, and now he had more joy and beauty than he'd ever imagined. I knew this because he told me often, and it was a relief to see him embrace it after so many years of living in a grayscale version of life.

In some ways, Adam reminded me of my dad. Maybe I was the Jane Saint in the situation, a woman who had to show the man she wanted that it was okay to want her.

Chuckling to myself as I clicked through screens on the computer, I acknowledged I'd certainly done that. First with the kissing last weekend and then with challenging him to think beyond his past.

I wasn't sure how far he'd let that go—was he sold on the idea of trying but would eventually throw on the brakes when we got closer? Or would he let things ride and see where this chance we'd agreed to take took us?

I hated the idea that we'd date towards a dead end, but the worry lingered in the back of my mind. I wouldn't dwell on it, though, because I wanted to move forward in good faith. Maybe we weren't chugging along toward marriage and babies, but not every relationship had these as end goals. Even though I could see the doubt and concern on his face when we talked, I could also sense the hope—and it matched my own.

While it would be great if we were both certain, how often did anything start out that way? I'd very rarely felt sure of anything until after I got my feet wet. Why would this be any different?

Plus, we didn't need certainty yet. We only needed a willingness to try, and we had that in spades. *I'd like to try everything with him...*

Someone entered and I finishing entering the information as I hollered, "Welcome in! Be right with you."

No response came, which was fine. They were probably browsing, until a shadow loomed in front of me and I looked up to see Adam.

"Hello, Josephine."

Goodness, the smile on his face was stunning. "Hi there, Adam."

He glanced back at the door. "Your dad and stepmom just invited me to family dinner on Sunday."

I cringed and laughed. "Wow. Okay. They were not going to let me get away with not mentioning it."

He grinned, apparently not fazed by this turn of events. "Guess my timing was just right. Would you really not've invited me?"

"I mean, we just—I don't know. We're going slow, but you're going to come meet my entire insane family for Sunday dinner before we've ever been out on a date?"

He leaned on the counter and dipped his head. "You getting cold feet?"

With a roll of my eyes, I said, "No. That does not apply here. I didn't want to overwhelm you. They are a lot, and I don't—" I chuckled at myself. "I don't want to scare you away. I know the too-much-too-soon thing is a concern."

I was trying to be respectful of his desires, but I certainly didn't want him to feel like I didn't want him there. I also didn't want to spook him. That he'd agreed to give us a go already felt momentous. I wanted more of him however I could get him. Having him at family dinner would be amazing. Plus, he already knew pretty much everyone. That wouldn't be a problem.

He lowered a hand and waited for me to take it. I set mine in his and he held my gaze. "Will you go to dinner with me tomorrow?"

"Yes."

He winked. "There. We'll sneak in our first official date before our first official family dinner."

There was no point trying to hide my pleased smile. "Sounds good."

He raised my hand and pressed his lips into the back of it. My brain flatlined for a moment, temporarily paused by the sweet and surprisingly sexy gesture.

"Why are, um, why are you here?" I asked with complete composure and elegance.

His half smile made him look so ridiculously appealing, I stole back my hand.

"Oh, I came to ask you out."

"Really? You came all the way over here just for that?" I asked, again failing to hide how much pleasure this brought me.

"Well, I'm not sure *all the way over here* is accurate, but yes. If we're doing this, we're not just going to get takeout and hang out in your apartment, as much as I enjoy it. If we're really giving this a shot, then we're going out. And we'll see how it goes."

His hand caught mine again and laced our fingers, effectively sending butterflies winging around my belly.

Maybe it was too much, but I didn't want to hide from him. He knew all my secrets, and I didn't want that to stop. "I think it's going to go well."

He turned my hand and dropped his head to kiss the inside of my wrist, then caught my gaze again as he slowly removed his lips from my skin. The look in his eyes—the hope and heat mingled together—made my breath catch in my throat.

"Me, too, honey. Me, too."

It'd been a skeleton crew last night at the pub, so I'd had quality time with Catherine and Dove. I'd also enjoyed glancing over and seeing Adam, Cookie, and Wilder, who'd sent me a knowing look as if to say, "You really dating this guy?"

Sunday dinner would be *fun*.

But this afternoon, after the minutes ticked by like hours during my short shift at the bookstore, I was finally ready for my first official date with Adam.

Excitement buzzed in me, and I'd done my level best not to get my hopes up about anything. In truth, I didn't care what he had planned. I just wanted to spend more time with him, especially now that we were on the same page.

A firm knock came and I skittered into the bathroom on my toes to check my hair, makeup, and dress. *Yes.* I felt good in the white dress I'd chosen, something summery and light that felt a little sexy without being flashy.

In seconds, I was at the door and steadied myself with a deep breath before answering as though I hadn't been pacing my apartment, anxious for him to arrive.

"Well, hi there, Adam."

His low chuckle sent shivers up my arms, and my belly swooped as I took in his trimmed beard and perfectly styled hair. He wore dark jeans and a navy, green, and white plaid button-up that made his eyes look wildly blue. Of course he'd rolled the sleeves to just below the elbow, so he looked effortlessly casual and also showed off grade-A forearms.

"Hello there, Josephine."

"Hi," I said, because I'd forgotten what came after a basic greeting. His hotness had fried my conversational skills.

His smile flashed. "Ready for dinner?"

"Yes."

He leaned against the doorframe and crossed his arms. *Those forearms.* His gaze slipped from my face to my hair falling over my shoulder, taking in my dress and then my bare legs stretching to the floor and feet topped by sandals and toes with bright blue polish.

His eyes slowly returned to meet mine as his head shook back and forth slowly, and the appreciation there nearly lit me on fire. But then, he leaned closer and said, "My goodness, you are unbelievably gorgeous."

I flushed warm and bright red from my forehead right down to my toes. "You're not so bad yourself."

"Thank you. Do you want to head out, then?" he asked, apparently in no hurry.

"We probably better." Because if he kept looking at me like that and flashing those forearms and smelling like fresh soap and something woodsy and delicious, the whole plan to move slowly would be out the door.

"Probably so." He extended an elbow.

I looped my arm through his and out we went, excitement filling every inch of me. We were finally doing this, a year after I'd first met him and wished things were different.

Now they were, and all the other stuff that wasn't going quite right could take a seat while I enjoyed this night.

CHAPTER TWENTY-FOUR

Adam

Silverton's small-town reality came into full effect the moment we stepped into the Silver Ridge Brew Pub. I saw no fewer than four people I recognized within ten seconds of entering, and Jo likely knew far more than me. The place had opened last summer, and the food was fantastic, so it came as no surprise it was packed.

"Guess there was no chance this wasn't getting out," I said, laughing at the fact I'd ever considered we'd slowly let people know.

She squeezed my hand and searched my face. "Is this a problem? We can leave if you're uncomfortable."

I raised her hand and kissed the back of it, holding her gaze to make sure she understood. "I'm good if you are. Just didn't think this through, but I'm happy to be seen with you."

Yes, it'd be painful when all of this was over—*if it has to end,* that tiny voice reminded me—but I'd promised myself I wasn't going to dwell on that aspect while I was here with her.

Her smile came slow and pleased. "I'm happy to be seen with you, too."

Thankfully, she confirmed it just in time. The host gestured for us to follow him, and once we were seated at a booth in a far corner, we had about ten seconds to settle in before the first visitor arrived.

"Well, look what we have here," Kenny said, all delighted swagger. He leaned in and shoved my shoulder. "You look lovely this evening, Jo."

"Thanks, Kenny. Who are you here with—oh." She raised a hand toward Beast, who'd posted up a few steps behind Kenny and gave me a look that said everything from "I tried to stop him" to "Sorry about this idiot" to "Hey, man, good for you." His scowl was infinitely expressive.

"Yeah, had to get this guy out of the house, and now we're heading to check on Stone." He held up a bag, presumably with takeout inside.

"That's great. Tell him hi for me."

Kenny gave us an exaggerated wink. "Oh, I'll tell him more than hi. Have fun, you two." He turned and left, passing Beast as he gave me the chin nod and tipped his head further down to acknowledge Jo.

"That man…" Jo said, chuckling to herself as she settled her napkin in her lap.

"Which one?" I asked, glancing back at them, Beast's hulking mass drawing eyes from at least half of the restaurant.

"Well, good question. I mostly meant Kenny because he's just out there, but he's sweet at his heart, I think." She looked toward the hostess desk, where they'd undoubtedly already passed before exiting the place.

"He is definitely that. But also young." My gaze shifted to hers as soon as I said it. "Not that that's a bad thing."

She tsked and shook her head, though her lips only barely held off a true smile. "Oh, very bad attempt at a save, Doc. The words are already out there."

"It's not that youth is a problem necessarily, and of course that's relative. But your being twenty-eight and his being the same, or actually he might be twenty-nine, it's different. You have maturity and some life experience, and a lot of times it feels like he doesn't."

The waiter arrived and we placed our orders, miraculously fast but likely because we'd both been here before, and then she circled us back to Kenny.

"It's odd to me that you're talking about him as though he *doesn't* have life experience. Didn't he deploy when he was in the Army? And live away from family and... I mean, he had injuries, right?"

"He did. It's part of what makes it feel like he needs to grow up a little, but it's more complex than that. Kenny lost a lot—yes, he lost two fingers on a mission a few years ago, but before that, he lost"—I shook my head, knowing it wasn't my place to divulge everything but also wanting her to understand my friend at least a little—"a lot. I think he's almost forced himself into this super-positive version of himself as though that's his way of coping. Or rather, it *is* his way, but I worry about him."

Her gaze softened and she extended her hand across the table, which I gladly took, a thrill following the contact.

"He and Beast seem to be good friends."

My thumb swept over the heel of her hand. "Funny

enough, they are. The grumpy-sunshine pairing we never knew we needed."

She gasped and then beamed at me. "Adam Carter, are you talking romance tropes to me?"

I chuckled, more than a little pleased to see her response. "Well, not *actual* romance between those two, more like *bromance*, but I know a little about tropes. I can't hang around the Saint Security building and escape it, let alone walk by the All Booked Up romance section and not learn a thing or two."

She grinned. "Very true. We love a good trope tag."

I dipped my head and spoke as quietly as I could. "Plus, I'm dating a romance author."

She covered her mouth, eyes wide, then let her hand drop and gave me the kind of smile that would cue the sunrise.

"So true. You need to be well-versed in things like tropes."

"Guess I do," I said, all nonchalant.

"And probably should have a list of at least a few favorite romance authors," she suggested.

"Sure. Give me a list and I'll read whomever you recommend."

Her eyes lit with a fire only kindled by a man asking a reading woman for book recommendations.

"Oh, I certainly will," she said in a voice so smooth and low, I made a mental note to return to book recommendations and romance tropes if I ever tried to seduce her.

Okay, odd thought, but point was, all of this felt like an oddly sensual form of flirting based on her responses, and I was not mad about it.

"Why is Beast so grumpy? And why can't you guys have him leave town so Jess doesn't have to keep going?"

I squeezed her hand and leaned back as the waiter set our drinks in front of us, then a bread basket full of soft, warm rolls. We each dove in to slather them with butter, and Jo took a giant bite of hers as I responded.

"Beast has been a man of few words as long as I've known him. It's not all that uncommon in our field. Operators are, as a demographic, largely introverted. Some of us are more half-extroverted, like me, and then there are the Bruces and Kennys of the world."

She laughed and dabbed her lips with her napkin. It was such a dainty, delicate move and made me realize how long it'd been since I'd been on a date—even longer since I'd been out with someone I cared about.

After a bite of my own roll, I continued. "He and Jess have history that's more complex than any of us truly know, but from what we do, we get that they do best with space between them. For his part, Beast technically signed on with Saint first, and Jess agreed to work there after the fact, even knowing he was already on staff. But I'm not sure she knew that a, his contract includes a no-travel clause, and b, that she wouldn't want to travel because she actually likes Silverton and its inhabitants quite a bit. I think you're partly to blame there."

She pressed a hand to her heart. "I love Jess. At least, I love what I know of her. She's amazing, and I hate that she's unhappy at work."

I could practically see her mind racing through whether to ask me more about the situation. Jo wasn't a particularly nosy person from what I'd observed, but when she cared about someone, she really cared. She wasn't a halfway kind of person. It reflected in most of what she did, just like her books. She'd started out casual, but now Josie Wade had become a huge aspect of her life.

"I'm sorry she is, too. And I probably shouldn't talk about it much more, but I can promise you that Bruce and Wilder are not unaware of the issue, and they care about Jess and don't want to lose her or Jude."

"Oh my gosh, I always forget he has an actual human name," she said, an embarrassed laugh rushing out.

"Honestly, I think we all do sometimes. But he's a good man, even if he's taken the grumpy nonverbal thing to its limit. I worry about him, but... I'm doing what I can."

Her dark gaze flickered back and forth between mine for a moment. "And Stone? That's Dorian, right?" Her voice was soft, as though she knew this was a particularly tender subject.

I nodded, taking a small gulp of my water.

"Yeah, Dorian." I shifted, wanting to explain my friend to her, and yet knowing how private he was, I couldn't say much without violating what he valued. "We all come with baggage, of course. And it's sort of like, if you serve for a handful of years, you might get out unscathed. Same if you serve twenty—miraculously, there are people who serve twenty and never see anything traumatic. It's unlikely to go without changing you in some way, to grow a person and present challenges and whatever else, but some might sneak out without real damage."

She swallowed, waiting patiently for me to finish. The waiter brought our appetizers, and we ate for a minute before I finished my thought.

"Many of us served, and aside from the big things like how to transition into a civilian life after twenty years in a military one, or how to go from being a soldier in a unit that executed missions that mattered on a national and some-times international scale to something small and sometimes seemingly insignificant, we don't have a whole lot to work through. Others of us... our bodies and minds carry the load differently."

"That makes sense. I'm sorry that, either way, the load you all carry is so heavy."

The compassion in her expression and the care in her voice made me want to jump out of my chair and kiss her until we both forgot we were standing in a room full of people who knew exactly who we were and would report to everyone else in town who knew us.

"Thank you. So, yeah. Dorian's got a heavy load he's carrying right now, and we're all trying to help with that burden in whatever way we can. Still, I worry about him."

But tonight, he'd have friends. They'd make sure he ate. He had Bear, and I think his neighbor checked on him once in a while. Plus, I knew Aidan Wallace went over there about once a month to check in on the tree farm itself. Dorian had been doing better overall, but I wanted him healed completely. Maybe that was my curse as someone in the medical realm—I wanted to be able to patch up everything like I'd dress a wound and then watch the body slowly work its magic. It didn't always go that way.

But Stone would be okay... he would. He had to be. He was one of the strongest and best men I knew, and that didn't mean he didn't struggle, but it meant we wouldn't give up on him. We wouldn't be scared away. We hadn't yet, and we wouldn't ever.

Jo's hand covering mine pulled my attention back to the here and now.

"You have such a big heart. It's amazing," she said, nothing short of awe in her voice.

I huffed. "It's a pretty normal heart, actually." And one that ultimately wouldn't manage to hold on to hers. But that was a thought for another time.

"You just told me how you worry over all your friends, and you have this love and concern for them that I can feel from across the table. You check on Stone and you fret over Kenny—"

"I don't *fret*—"

"But Adam, who worries over you? Who takes care of you?"

I shook my head, ready to tell her I didn't need any care-taking. I'd been fine for years and I wasn't about to stop now. But the warmth of her hand on mine and her beautiful face searching mine for a real answer, not a blow off or something flippant about being the old man in our relationship, made me answer truthfully.

"I don't know, Josie. Are you applying for the job?"

CHAPTER TWENTY-FIVE

Jo

Y*es. Yes, I am.*
I grinned at him in order to hide the "Pick me! Pick meeeee!" internal response. "Maybe I will. And in the meantime, I want you to consider that you're doing so much for these friends and they all love you deeply."

He raised his brows like, "Really?" but nodded. "Fine. I will. But it's probably not going to change much."

I shrugged right back, but more dramatically, prompting a little tug at one corner of his mouth. "Maybe not. But maybe you'll find ways to channel all this worry—more hikes and such."

"I like that idea. I'm actually working on some ways to incorporate more of my own interests into Saint. The transition from active duty to private security has been good... but hard."

He launched into a more detailed explanation of his survival courses.

From there, we were interrupted by two people—Jane Saint out with her friends, and then Wilder and Sarah Saint. My cheeks had to be almost as red as my wine when Sarah hugged me and Wilder shook Adam's hand, then turned and kissed me on my burning cheek.

"This guy treating you well?"

I nodded.

"You treating my baby sister well?" He glared at Adam.

My mouth dropped open before I sputtered. "Baby sister? I'm barely your adult stepsister."

He cut me a dark look. "Doesn't matter how you become a Saint. Once you do, you're in, and that's that. So?" He turned to Adam.

"I believe so and plan to continue," Adam said, not appearing nearly as alarmed by Wilder's big brother posturing as I was.

Honestly, what?

Satisfied, Sarah gave me a look, and we shared a "That was wild, right?" look, and then they left with a "See you tomorrow."

"Is he serious? *Baby sister* like our parents haven't been married for a whopping eighteen months at the ripe age of sixty-something." I was honestly a little shocked.

Adam just smiled at me while he finished chewing a bite of his dinner. "He can be a protective big brother as long as it doesn't interfere in your life or look like he's trying to control you. If it bothers you, though, I'll tell him to lay off."

I blinked once. Verrrry slowly.

"Or, right. *You* could tell him to lay off."

I pointed to him with my fork. "Exactly. I will. But

also... point taken. It's maybe a little misguided, but I get that he's the kind of person—and in fact, the whole Saint family is this way—who once you're their people, that's it. You have them."

Adam was already nodding in agreement. "Yes. That's how he is about work, too. You join the 'Saint family' at Saint Security and you're in. Granted, we haven't had anyone leave, but they mean it when they say they're going to take care of their people. They want to make our lives good, which means we'll do great work for them, and that benefits all of us. I'm seeing it play out with Dorian and—and other people, and it makes me really proud to be a part of it."

I loved that. Loved how he was happy there and loved knowing this growing business in my town was full of such good people trying to make their employees' lives better. Even if it meant my new stepbrother was a little bit of an overstepper.

After recovering from Wilder's big brotherness and chatting a while longer, dessert arrived—a molten chocolate cake with vanilla bean ice cream. The center oozed out lava-like chocolate, and the combination of the creamy vanilla and sharp, deep chocolate flavor had me shutting my eyes in a moment of ecstasy.

When I swallowed and opened them, Adam was staring, rapt.

"Sorry. It's just so good." I scooped up another bite.

"Never apologize for enjoying yourself." His voice was a low rasp, and he definitely hadn't even tried the dessert.

"Are you going to have any dessert?" I hoped he hadn't gotten it just because I wanted it. Maybe he wasn't a chocolate guy?

His gaze zeroed in on my lips as I closed my mouth

around the spoon. "I think I might enjoy watching you eat it more than having any myself."

I swallowed the cake before I choked on it. "Um, wow. *Wow*."

He chuckled as I laughed, but his hooded expression hadn't disappeared. "I admit that might've sounded creepy. I'm just... thinking..."

Would I be able to handle whatever was coming? TBD. But I wasn't about to *not* ask. "What are you thinking?"

He leaned his forearms on the table and let his eyes sweep over me, lingering on my mouth again before finally rising to meet my eyes. "I'm just thinking about other ways to put that look on your face."

My stomach swooped low and my cheeks instantly burned. "Oh. Well..." What does one say to a man this attractive and kind and intelligent and capable when he says something like that?

He grinned, stabbing me in the chest with his ridiculously gorgeous smile. "Sorry. Too much."

"N-no. Not too much. Just... I mean, yes, a lot. But not in a bad way." I laughed at myself. "You kind of scrambled my brain."

With a shake of his head, he said, "I know the feeling."

From the corner of my eye, I saw someone wave and then returned the gesture when I realized it was Winnie and Tristan. They didn't come over—she only gave me two thumbs-up and wiggled her brows, then shuffled Tristan out the door. He wasn't the kind of man who'd insist on interrupting a dinner, and they'd likely seen Wilder and Sarah stop by if they'd been sitting nearby. I hadn't noticed them when we'd first come in, so maybe they'd just gotten take-out. Whatever the case, I knew I owed my friends a full report, and honestly, I couldn't wait to tell them. It'd already been a great night.

"They're good together," Adam said, following my line of sight.

"They are. He loves her so well, and I think she's good for him, too."

Adam seemed pensive for a moment, nudging the chocolate cake without taking a bite. "He does. And she definitely is. They're well matched."

Something about his expression had darkened, and I tensed, wondering if he was thinking about his past, about the woman he hadn't been well matched with. Or maybe, if he was wondering if *we* were as well matched.

Where is this going?

The thought streaked through my mind despite my very much not wanting to face the question. Could we have a future if he was still hung up on the things he'd done wrong in his past? If he was measuring every step of our time together against things that'd gone wrong before?

I didn't know if he was doing that, but an ember of worry smoked in my belly.

"How are you feeling about the book?" he asked, his voice low enough no one would overhear, not that anyone close by was a Josie Wade reader. Well, that I knew of, anyway.

My thoughts veered away from the concern over what his previous comment might've meant, and I mentally caught up to his topic change. "Um, good. I'm ready for it to be out there. Thank you for all the help."

A smile verging on a smirk pulled at his lips. "It's safe to say I'll help you any time. You just let me know."

"I'll start the next book in a month or so."

Would we still be dating? Would we be more than that?

"Sign me up," he said, eyes smoldering. "Who's the main character in this one?"

I launched into my plan for the next book, and he asked really good questions, even acting impressed when I mentioned a plot twist I'd thought up. He paid the check, and though I offered to pay my half, he gave me a look enough to clarify we were not about to go Dutch.

"It's funny, but I don't think I've ever gotten to brainstorm with someone or even talk to them about my writing with the exception of you."

He grabbed my hand and laced our fingers together as we left the restaurant. "Then I'd like to apologize for my shortcomings, but I hope that, with your expert guidance, I'll have more to offer as I broaden my romance knowledge."

I laughed, a lightness in my chest so ebullient I almost felt my feet leave the ground. Not only did he not mind me chattering away about my books, but he wanted to learn more so he could contribute more. *Who is this man?*

"It will be my honor to sponsor your romance education," I joked, grinning over at him as he opened the door to my building for me.

We were quiet ascending the stairs, and my heart began to beat harder with each step we took toward my door. Would he come in? I didn't want our night to end, but it was such a loaded thing to go inside at this point.

Wasn't it?

Or was it?

And did I have to overthink every second of what might be our last few minutes together tonight?

On the landing in front of my door, we stopped. When our eyes met, my body lit up with more anticipation than I'd ever felt, a wave of longing and expectation so overwhelming, I swayed toward him.

Without a word, he moved, too. Taking me by the chin with gentle fingers and guiding my mouth right to his.

It was a relief when our lips met, and it was the reminder that despite eating a full meal and dessert, there existed a ravenous hunger in me *for him*. His soft exploration of my mouth deepened into something searching and demanding, giving and taking, and so completely consuming, I wouldn't have managed to stay standing without his strong arms holding me to him.

He pulled back—too soon, though I suspected it would always be too soon for me—and brushed some hair out of my eyes.

"I think you're sponsoring my romance education in more than one way, Josie."

His blue eyes flickered back and forth between mine, almost like he was piecing something together, or hoping to, and if he just found the right thing there, he'd know an answer to a question he'd asked.

I hoped he'd find his answer.

"My absolute pleasure, Adam," I said, keeping the formality of saying names just like he did.

A hazy smile crept into his eyes, and he shook his head. "Thank you for going out with me tonight."

"Thank you for dinner." *Would you like to come in? Would you like to stay over? Would you like to be mine forever and we'll start that right now?*

With a pause, then a slow inhale, he nodded once. "My absolute pleasure." With a quick peck, he released me. "See you tomorrow."

So that's it. This was right, of course. We shouldn't go inside. I knew we shouldn't, and he did, too, and so here we were, saying goodnight. I fumbled with my keys and unlocked my door.

"Night."

And with that, I slipped inside, biting my tongue to keep from asking him to stay for a movie or just to talk. Commanding myself to go inside and let the night end, knowing I'd see him again tomorrow.

Knowing this was just the beginning.

CHAPTER TWENTY-SIX

Adam

I'd known Wilder Saint for over a decade. I'd known his brothers since I'd moved here a little over a year ago. They were good men.

Seeing them fawn over their wives and kids and nieces and nephews and mother and stepfather and stepsister only drilled that home.

But seeing Jo amidst this madness made my heart squeeze mercilessly in my chest. She was adored in this place, and it made me wish she would tell her family about her writing. No part of me doubted they'd be thrilled for her, and Sarah was a true romance lover and would probably be absolutely elated to learn it, not to mention her book-loving father and stepmom.

I'd arrived late due to a time warp while hanging out with Stone, and since Jo had gone early to help with dinner, she'd made me promise not to worry or cut my time short with him. She knew I worried about him—actually now, she knew I worried about everyone.

"Who worries over you? Who takes care of you?"

I could hear her voice and see the concern on her lovely face. Then later, after I'd diffused the yearning in my chest by asking her if she was applying for the job, she'd said she was considering it.

I'd instantly refuted the idea, mentally screaming at myself for ever putting us in the situation where she'd invest so much of her heart into... me. But there was an undeniable echo in my mind saying, *Yes, please. Please take the job.* And that couldn't continue.

I'd never stop wanting more of Jo. Every second I spent with her drilled the truth home. But I could not let myself dwell there. And for now, surrounded by her family, I was reminded what real love and partnership looked like.

It looked like Wyatt doting on his pregnant wife. It looked like Warrick gazing at Sadie with so much adoration it was clear he'd forgotten the rest of us were in the room. It looked like Wilder tucking a lock of Sarah's hair behind her ear, then suddenly snatching their toddling son from the floor and pretending to gobble her up as their baby giggled so brightly everyone laughed along with them.

It looked like Darcy hugging Jo to his side and dropping a kiss to her head, a fatherly expression of what I knew had to be love and pride and admiration, because who could ever spend time around Jo and not feel those things, much less have a hand in who she'd grown to be?

"It's a lovely scene, isn't it?"

Jane Saint's voice startled me from where I stood just inside the front door of her house.

"It is. You have a beautiful family." As matriarch of the Saint family, she got a lot of credit for raising her sons to be good men and being the kind of people good women would want to tether themselves to.

Her smile was soft as she gazed at the scene. She didn't pull her eyes from her family as she spoke. "Why do I get the feeling there's a little wistfulness in there?"

"Ah. Ethan and I didn't have anything like this. We just... it wasn't warm. And my parents divorced and my dad kind of disappeared on us, and after that my mom was working hard until she remarried. That was right about when I joined the Army. Ethan had a different experience..."

She hummed. "Wyatt and Wilder remember their dad, but Warrick doesn't at all. It's different for each sibling, and there's a genuine burden on the oldest sometimes."

I'd never seen any part of my past or my family's dynamic as a burden. More simply a reality.

"Seems like Darcy fits right in," I said, watching as baby James collapsed on the floor near Darcy's feet, and the man picked him up and nuzzled his nose.

"He does. And I'm delighted Jo's willing to wade into the madness with us, too. I know their house was never like this." Her blue eyes caught mine and held. "But growing up without it doesn't keep you from having it."

I nodded, throat tight. I didn't often feel all that tender regarding what I did or didn't have as a kid. I'd had a good life, and I had a good brother, and my mom was happy and safe, even if she wasn't all that interested in us anymore. We'd built our own family over the years, and it was enough.

But this woman had an uncanny ability to zero in on a forgotten tender place in me. Wilder must've taught her some of his observational skills, or maybe he'd learned his notoriously keen ones from her.

She gently but firmly gripped my wrist where my arms folded across my chest. "And if you don't mind a bit of motherly wisdom, I'd like to suggest that neither does failing at love once or twice. That doesn't keep you from being capable of great love with the right person and a solid helping of determination."

I huffed out a breath, glancing at my shoes to give myself a reprieve from her all-seeing Saint blue eyes as she released my arm, but when I glanced up to explain the reasons I couldn't—the ways I wasn't capable—she'd already walked into the fray.

"Jo! Your man's here!" Jane tipped her head my way, and Jo's gaze snapped to find me.

And then she jumped up, midsentence with Wyatt and Calla, and jogged to me before launching into my arms and hugging me.

"Thank you for coming," she said, her lips brushing my ear.

"Thank you for letting your dad and stepmom invite me," I whispered back, to which she nudged me away and smiled.

"So you're not freaked out?" she asked, happiness etched in every line of her face.

Freaked out wasn't the phrase I'd use. I couldn't quite place what I was feeling except... longing. Grateful. Restless. Wishful. Regretful—not about Jo, but that my reality was so far removed from this—from what she deserved.

"No, honey. I'm not freaked out."

Her gaze went soft and she bit her lip. The air shifted between us, all sound evaporating into the ether beyond us in light of her nearness and her focus on me.

"Hey now, you two. Come join the fun!" Warrick's

voice cut through the moment, slicing like a hot knife through butter.

She blushed prettily and shook her head. "I went from one grumpy, hands-off sister to three ridiculous brothers..."

"Has she ever visited? Met these guys?"

Sadness crept into her expression. "No. Not yet, anyway. She keeps saying she'd like to, but then something happens and she's called back into whatever crazy international situation she's managing and I don't hear from her for a while." She frowned outright. "I honestly think I'm the person she's closest to in the world and that makes me so sad for her."

I kissed the back of her hand, and we walked slowly toward the living room. "Why? You're a great sister."

I hadn't seen them together, but I'd seen her with her stepbrothers, and I'd heard her speak with love and concern about Elizabeth more than once. Honestly, maybe too much concern about what she'd think of her writing, but still.

"I mean, maybe, but I hardly know her. We haven't seen each other in years. I haven't lived with her since I was twelve. I hate the idea of her hiding so much of herself—" She swallowed.

I waited, the sounds of her family teasing at the edges of our conversation. She sighed, her shoulders dropping.

"I heard it. I did."

I dropped a kiss to her cheek. "Good. But no guilt. Let's go hang out with your people."

She pulled me into a hug, steering us behind a wall in the kitchen for a few seconds of privacy. My heart beat steadily in my chest as I breathed in her scent and savored her nearness. I wouldn't ever take it for granted.

She gasped and cupped my cheeks. "Oh my gosh, I can't believe I haven't said thank you already!"

I tilted my head. "Thank you?"

Her smile was wide and genuine. "For the flowers."

My mind blanked and I had a moment of panic. Flowers? Was I supposed to send her flowers? Wait, no. She was saying I *had*.

"I'm sorry, but I didn't send you flowers."

"No, you did. They were outside my building's door addressed to me."

I was shaking my head before she'd finished. "No, honey, I didn't."

Her face fell and she went pale as though a switch had flipped. "He—he did it. He figured out my address."

A chill swept through me, snuffing out all confusion. "Was there a card? When did it arrive? I—"

"Shhh. We can't talk about this here. They can't know. We'll stay for dinner, act normal, and then we'll go back and —" She tucked her hair behind her ears and her hands were shaking. "And then we'll deal with it."

Everything in me warred with her on this. Someone had given her flowers and that might not be a problem except everyone in town had seen us out together, for one, but for two… she seemed to know who it was. Not an admirer, but from the pallid look to her usually pink cheeks, the person who'd been sending her letters she didn't like opening.

"Please. Please let's just be here and then we'll handle it. Okay?"

Her gaze searched mine, urgent for reassurance, so I nodded. "Okay. But then, you're going to tell me everything. No more secrets or downplaying. Not anymore."

She swallowed hard and nodded.

We took a moment—I breathed deep and she followed my lead, then smiled at me like everything was normal. If anyone was truly watching, they'd see the way her eyes didn't light up the way they normally would, but in the chaos of the house, it wasn't hard to believe we'd get away with the ruse.

And then, I spent a lovely evening with Jo's family while mentally counting down the minutes until I could go figure out if her stalker had found her address.

CHAPTER TWENTY-SEVEN

Jo

The closer we got to my apartment, the more my anxiety ticked up like the second hand at the fifty with ten, nine, eight.... Only seconds until reality rammed back into me.

There had been a sense that things between me and Adam had been going so well, maybe too well. Maybe it'd all been too good to be true.

But here came the other shoe dropping. The reality I'd worked quite hard to shove away from my mind and out of my life had arrived whether I liked it or not, and now, it was clear all my hard work to ignore this person had been for nothing.

Or worse, had been the wrong choice. Had possibly put me in danger.

I'd held it together at dinner. Adam had managed to be charming with the family and comforting with me, holding my hand or placing his palm reassuringly on my knee. A touch that would've felt thrilling at another time had served to keep me from screaming.

It sounded so stupid to say the bubble of safety I'd assumed was around me had popped, but the realization this person who'd invaded my life, who I'd worked so hard to forget about and not let affect me, had my personal information made me feel absolutely ill.

Jane had hugged me long and tight, as had my dad, before we left. My dad had subtly asked if I was okay, and I'd said I was just stressed about the job hunt, which was another lie to someone I loved, another part of my life I'd not been honest with myself about.

I hated lying. Hated it. And yet, here I was doing it and everything would still fall apart.

Adam parked in front of the shop, and since I'd gotten stuck in slow motion, he made it around to my door and opened it. My dad had picked me up before dinner, so at least my car wasn't still at their house. *But maybe it would be safer there.* Maybe none of this was anything. Maybe these flowers were from someone else...

Adam stepped into my space, between my legs before I could exit the vehicle, and he cupped my cheeks, his warm hands on my skin instantly steadying me.

"We'll figure this out. You're not alone."

Tears pricked my eyes, but I nodded and forced them down. "Thank you. I'm sorry."

He shook his head. "No. No apologies. Let's just go deal with what we know, and we'll go from there."

We. We'll go from there.

So much of writing and publishing was a solitary job, and that was even more true since I used a secret pen name. I hadn't fully recognized how alone I'd been, even with something I loved, until Adam discovered my secret. The relief and, honestly, joy at being able to share that part of me had shocked me. I hadn't been all that tempted to tell anyone until Adam held my secret and made clear just how much sharing my passion and accomplishments and frustrations about my work could enhance my life.

Knowing he was here with me, ready to help with whatever was going on, reinforced this. I needed to figure out a different way to move forward. Maybe all of this was a sign I should tell everyone.

Fear clawed at my insides at the thought of everyone finding out. What if more weird things like this happened?

What if Elizabeth laughs in my face? What if she's embarrassed of me? What if I let her down? What if the exhaustion I can hear in her voice but she won't admit to gets worse from worrying about me?

I hated how these were the loudest thoughts in a moment like this.

"Hey, you're okay. Walk me through the flowers and we'll gather whatever other information we need."

Adam had led me inside my apartment—he must've unlocked my door, because we were standing in the kitchen, the flowers on the counter behind me.

"I opened my door this afternoon to meet my dad and they were sitting there right outside the building. Sometimes, flower deliveries will ring up, but this one didn't."

"Mind if I have a look?"

He approached the arrangement—a little basket with an explosion of blossoms and clearly Dahlia Wallace's handiwork. There was a bright green ribbon wrapped around one side of the basket's handle, and it had a Bloom pin at the center. Otherwise, no card, no anything.

"We'll talk to Dahlia tomorrow. Maybe she or whoever

was working when he called can tell us his name and credit card information. That will let us go dig a little deeper. I'm assuming he didn't sign his letters?"

My stomach curdled as I moved to the coat closet and pulled out a manila envelope I'd stuffed some of his letters into. "Not usually. I kept these at first because they were so heartfelt, and then when they started turning more... personal, I thought maybe I should keep a record. But a few months ago, they got really weird and I just started tossing them because they freaked me out." I felt ill and so foolish. "I shouldn't have done that, but I didn't know what else to do. You can't just go to the police with unsigned letters, can you?"

He took the envelope and set it onto the counter, then wrapped me in his arms. I breathed in his comforting scent, begging my heart to slow and my mind to clear so I could tell him what I knew and not *feel* so much while I did it.

"Probably not, especially if it's just letters, although it's certainly worth pursuing. This collection is helpful. Do you know if he's contacted you any other way? E-mail or anything?"

I stared at my feet. "I—I filtered out his messages about a year ago. So, I don't know if he still is, but he used to."

He nodded, steady and unaffected. "Okay. I'm going to look at these now."

"I haven't checked my mail in a while. There's probably something new there by now."

I'd been avoiding my box thanks to the uptick in letters from this person. I'd gotten to where just walking into the post office made me feel lightheaded with dread, so I'd told myself I only had to go once a month. I wasn't a fool who thought they didn't matter, but I had nowhere to go with it.

No one knew I was Josie Wade, so how could I tell anyone what was happening?

I'd fallen into the trap of ignoring them being a solution when, apparently, that had only been delaying facing reality.

"Go change into something comfortable while I read these." He kissed my temple and nudged me toward my bedroom door.

I splashed water on my face in the bathroom and took off my mascara. I hoped I wouldn't cry tonight, but I might as well prepare. After slipping out of my dress and into sweats and a T-shirt, I padded back into the living room to find Adam's jaw clenched, face hard as rock and every muscle in his body tense.

He turned toward me slowly. "I need to call Bruce and Wilder. We have some resources at Saint that can help with this."

He'd mentioned this before, weeks or had it been months ago, but I wasn't ready then. I hadn't allowed myself to accept how this was a problem that wasn't going to stay at a distance—it wasn't something I could simply ignore. That pipe dream was no longer viable—I couldn't ignore it. If this guy had ordered flowers to my doorstep, he knew my address. And if he knew my address, there wasn't much stopping him from coming to see me in person.

"Just them, please. I know it'd be easier if everyone knew but—"

"No, I agree. At this point, the fewer people who know you're Josie Wade, the better. It helps contain this and may help us track this pervert down."

I snapped my eyes shut at the word, not wanting to let my mind stray to the kinds of things his letters contained. The ones Adam had read weren't even the worst.

"Yeah, that makes sense."

He shoved the letters into the large envelope, then moved to the sink and washed his hands. After tapping out a message on his phone, he came to me on the couch and wrapped me up in his arms again. The way he rested his chin on my head and held me tight made it feel like he needed this as much as I did.

"I'm not leaving you tonight," he said in my ear, low and gruff.

"Okay. Good."

I felt his nod, and that was that.

Our first full night together, and I couldn't even feel excited.

CHAPTER TWENTY-EIGHT

Adam

The sun warmed the summer morning, and everything was alive—birds, pedestrians, and apparently every one of my coworkers, who'd all arrived early.

"So, you and Jo Malcom make an adorable pair..." Kenny batted his stupid Ken-doll lashes at me from where he sat, chin in his hands, on the stairs.

"Are you really sitting there so you could be here when I walked in?" My voice had an unnecessary edge to it thanks to the larger situation, and unfortunately, Kenny was getting the first hint of it.

His hands shot up in innocence. "Actually, no. Your beloved brother is dropping me off coffee because I won a bet."

I didn't have time to delve into whatever that was, but I made a mental note to follow up later. "Tell him hi," I said and kept moving up the stairs and inside, where I found a visibly fuming Jess and a brooding Beast with Wilder and Bruce deliberating something.

Their attention shifted to me.

"My office," Wilder said, and I followed him and Bruce down the hall.

"You guys need me?" Jess asked, clearly alert to an immediate situation looming.

I was shaking my head, but Bruce answered for me. "No, Jess. Not this time." Then he shut the door and leaned against it while I took a seat and Wilder sat behind his desk.

I'd made clear this was confidential, so I didn't need to preface the conversation with any warnings. "Jo is an author —pen name Josie Wade."

That settled in, both of them recognizing the name since the women in their world loved her books.

"She has someone who's been rather persistent at sending her fan mail, and we're pretty sure it just escalated." I quickly briefed them on the situation as far as I knew it and my current plans—first, a visit to Bloom. Second, a trip to the post office to collect anything new, and third, a visit to the police with Jo.

"Good plan. If we get a name, we can make sure to have more information. I'm not sure if they can do much since he technically hasn't threatened her and there's no name yet," Bruce said, mind clearly running through the details, combing for anything useful.

"He hasn't threatened to hurt her, but he's... indicated other interests." My jaw flexed and I laid out a few of the things I'd seen in the letters she'd kept. If those were the ones she could stomach, I worried what we'd find in anything he'd sent recently.

Wilder swore. "Get to Bloom. Dahlia will do whatever she can to help, and maybe John can write up a cease and desist to send out. If this guy already knows she lives here, there's no harm in it coming from someone local. That gives us more clarity for the cops to show she's asked him to stop and he's not doing it, assuming he ignores it."

I nodded, glad he'd mentioned John Wallace, Dahlia's husband. He was a good man, and though he didn't practice law for his day job, he still did pro bono and some specialty work alongside his brother and father's firm. Anything we could do to keep this creep from making further overtures toward her was good with me.

"How is she?" Bruce asked, and I heard the echo in his words. *How are you?*

"She's shaken up. Embarrassed she kept this a secret but also just scared. Upset. But I think she's hopeful we can get this shut down before it's anything more. I'm not talking to her about stuff we've seen…" I glanced at Wilder.

A little over a year ago, Wilder had found his now-wife and her good friend held at gunpoint thanks to a deranged stalker who'd come after Sarah's friend Madeline Reynolds while Saint Security had been tasked with protecting her. Sarah had worked at Saint. In the end, the leak in security had come from inside the client's house, so to speak, and the Saint team had learned a lot about handling stalker threats. That said, each case could be a superspecial little snowflake, and we needed to take this one as such.

"Hit Bloom in ten when it opens, and from there, we're with you. Say the word and you've got the Saint resources, no questions asked. If anyone gets nosy, send them to me."

Bruce was a handsome devil, but when he got that focused look, the one that said he wasn't going to let anyone harm someone, much less a woman who mattered to him and who I—well, who mattered to me a great deal, too—God help the person who stood in his way.

When I left Wilder's office, the hallway had cleared of the thick enmity between Jess and Beast, likely because their moderators had disappeared into a meeting with me. Kenny had left his post on the stairs, which freed me to speed walk toward Silver Street without interference.

The soft breeze and wildflowers blooming just past our building should've been beautiful. I should've been walking on clouds today after spending the night holding Jo, but there'd been very little romance about it. A sweet kiss to say goodnight with her under her comforter and me next to her on top of it and nothing else, because any physical pleasure between us wasn't going to come in a time of crisis. It wasn't right, and it certainly didn't adhere to the go-slowly plan.

Sharing a bed at all wasn't exactly slow, and yet leaving her hadn't been an option. She was scared and upset, and though it seemed unlikely she was actually in danger at the moment, I couldn't have walked out of there for all the money in the world.

The need to protect her rose up so strongly, my steps turned into a light jog. I wasn't panicking about this, but the impulse to torch the earth until I found this guy and put him in jail had never occurred to me until last night when I'd seen so much fear in her eyes, I could taste it.

I'd never experienced anything like this—this burning for her and for her protection and safety and happiness and ability to do what she wanted and share herself and her work with the world however she chose. This threat to so many of those things had me feeling practically feral.

When I walked past the bookstore, I saw her unloading a box of books, and thankfully, Darcy had also planned to be in the store. Was it too much to believe she needed me patrolling outside of her workplace right now?

Yes, yes it was. But I felt the pull toward her, even still.

Thankfully, Bloom was just a few doors down, and they opened early, bless them. I calmed my mind the way I'd learned to do years ago before a mission and focused on the outcomes I needed before entering the store.

"Hey—oh, hi," the woman behind the desk said. "How can I help you today?"

I didn't know her, but that didn't mean Dahlia wasn't in. "Is the owner here?"

She flushed and seemed to panic a little. "Uh, she is, but I'm wondering if there's something I could help you with? She's dealing with—"

"I'm sorry but I really need to speak with her. Can you get her, please?" I didn't want to push, but I needed these questions answered discreetly.

"Give me one minute," she said, a thin smile on her face.

She slipped into the back room, and I wandered the space. Dahlia had created a shop that felt at once homey and like something out of a fairy tale. Rich jewel tones on the walls and bright pops of green and color everywhere through arrangements and some strategically chosen home décor and garden décor items. It really was incredibly charming.

The timing was all wrong, but I wondered what kind of flowers Jo liked best. She wouldn't like anything fussy, but I didn't imagine her going for a simple rose or daisy either. I'd have to find out so that when all this settled down and the negative memories of having flowers delivered faded, maybe I could send her some of her favorites.

"Adam? Everything okay?" Dahlia Wallace smiled kindly at me, her dark hair pulled out of her face and an apron covering her clothes, with various tools of the florist trade stuck in the large front pocket.

"Actually, no. Mind if we speak privately?" I asked as quietly as I could.

"Maryanne is in the back, if this works." She stepped to the front door and flipped the sign hanging there to closed.

"I need information about a delivery Jo Malcom received yesterday." I showed her a photo I'd taken of the bouquet. "The arrangement was left at her building's door, not her apartment, though she was home all morning, so if someone rang up, she would've answered. There was no card."

She raised a brow. "Hard to believe anyone could compete with you."

I forced a smile but shook my head. "Not the concern. It's potentially a more dangerous situation than that. I need to know who ordered the flowers and what the delivery instructions were."

It'd occurred to me that maybe, *maybe*, Dahlia had delivered them as a courtesy rather than the stalker listing Jo's address. This would still be concerning but possibly a good sign.

Dahlia moved to the check-out counter and tapped on the iPad she had set up. "I wasn't the person who took the order. We're not actually even open to customers on Sunday, so I'm wondering if maybe they ordered them earlier in the week since we do deliveries that day."

She squinted at the screen, skimming through information. "The order for that bouquet was placed on Saturday morning, and the person picked them up that afternoon. Paid in cash. No delivery request."

The ambient noises of the shop—the whir of the refrigerated flower cases to the left and right of the register, the light music playing over the speaker, the sound of someone clipping the ends of flowers in the other room—they all blurred into a silence that hit me so suddenly it felt violent.

Paid in cash. Picked them up that afternoon.

"No name? No credit card?"

Dahlia's dark eyes were big. "No, sorry. We normally would take one, but they only have the description of the bouquet they wanted here, not the name of the person ordering…"

"Anything else you can tell me? Any requests the person made? Any description of the person?"

Dahlia's finger slid down the screen. "Not that I can see, but Mandy took the order. She's off today, but I can call her and ask if she remembers the person."

I was already moving toward the door after slapping my card onto the counter. "Please do. If she can come in or call me to tell me herself, it'd be a big help. Call me with anything you find, and I'll check back this afternoon if I haven't heard. If you can send us any security footage from your cameras, I'd appreciate it."

"Okay. Will do. Sorry!"

I didn't tell her she had nothing to apologize for—she didn't. I couldn't blame her or her employee for accepting cash or not insisting on the person's name—there was really no reason to be alarmed by that.

What she'd just told me had my heart thundering as I jogged next door to All Booked Up, firing off a text to Wilder and Bruce while at it. I stopped shy of flinging the door open and demanding Jo come with me right this instant. Instead, I took a moment, eyeing the people milling around the street and willing my pulse to slow so I wouldn't burst in there and terrify her.

My training was kicking in, but I still felt the tremor of genuine fear and something like rage creeping in.

He knew where she lived, and undoubtedly where she worked.

And it would only be a matter of time before he decided he wanted to see her face-to-face—if he hadn't already.

Because unless he'd paid someone to do the job for him, Jo's stalker was here in Silverton.

CHAPTER TWENTY-NINE

Jo

My heart flipped when Adam came in, right until it sank when I registered his demeanor. Not frazzled or concerned or even happy to see me. Just still. Calm.

But not calm in the serene way he made me feel when we sat on the couch and chatted, or the stillness that fell between us after a kiss.

This was different. The readiness in his posture spoke to the warrior side of him, and though he was a medic, he was absolutely a warrior, too. Sometimes, I forgot that. It was like forgetting Captain America wasn't just an altruistic sweetheart who looked great in his uniform and knew how to wield a vibranium shield. He was also a deadly fighter and a superhuman.

And okay, yes, I'd recently watched some Marvel movies, and yes, Adam reminded me more than a little bit of Chris Evans' bearded Cap.

Point being, *this* Adam Carter walked in with a subtext that read *you can take the man out of the Army but the operator never leaves the man.*

These thoughts flew by in a matter of seconds as he approached me where I was reorganizing our local-author shelf.

"Hey, did you talk to Dahlia?" Nerves knotted in my stomach as I searched his face for a clue or some crack in his preternaturally calm demeanor.

"Just stopped in. She called the girl who was working when the order was taken, so we'll know more soon."

His gaze felt heavy and purposeful as he surveyed me like he was checking for injuries, almost, and then he wrapped me in a hug. I slipped the book I'd been holding on to the nearest shelf behind him and hugged him back, resting my head against his shoulder.

He was so solid and built in a way that called to me. He was thoughtful and safe, and he smelled so good I had to stop myself from inhaling the scent of his skin.

We pulled back and he pressed a quick kiss to my cheek. "I'm going to bring you lunch later. Until then, I want you to stay in the store, hang with your dad, and I'll be back in a few hours."

"Is something wrong? You seem... something. I don't know what, but you're different." There was no point in pretending this was normal—his solemn vibe or the way he'd just lightly ordered me to stay put.

His gaze softened and one side of his mouth slid up into a smile that made me want to kiss him. Though to be fair, most things kind of made me want to kiss him. Now that we'd broken the seal, there was no going back.

"Just focused on figuring things out. I don't know for

sure what's going on, but I'm going to know a lot more in a few hours, and I just want you safe."

The slow uptick in my pulse skyrocketed. "You think I won't be safe leaving the store?"

He dipped his head and leveled our eyes. "You'll be safe in the store because I have someone from Saint outside at all times now. Your dad's here with you. And I'll be back soon."

I swallowed hard. If he felt like the store needed a guard, a *professional* bodyguard, this was worse than I'd feared.

"Okay. So... go, and then come back," I said, my voice a little wobbly with adrenaline.

His eyes tracked between mine for a split second, and then he hauled me in for a hot, quick kiss before releasing me. "I'll be back."

In seconds, he was out the door, and I followed, glancing out the glass there to see Beast settling against the wall to the right of the doors. He dipped his chin when he noticed me, and I returned the gesture.

"That man is intense with you." My dad came to stand next to me and gave Beast a friendly wave.

I chuckled. "*That* man is intense with everyone."

"Well, true. I meant Adam."

He waited for a moment, and I sifted through what he might mean. "Is that a bad thing in your mind?"

I couldn't exactly tell him Adam was legitimately concerned for my safety.

Or maybe I could.

Maybe it was time to be honest.

Dad's brows knitted together, and he scraped a hand over his graying beard. "I'm not sure. You've got so much life and vitality, and I can't help feeling like he's just so focused on you—like *you're* his purpose. It's not unlike

Wilder is with Sarah at times, but they've got such history. I just wonder if he's able to enjoy all of you, and the same goes for you with him."

I glanced at the door to make sure no customers were about to step in, then drew him farther away so no one would overhear if they happened to pop in.

"I need to tell you something."

Worry painted his face with lines. "Are you okay? Is he hurting you?"

"No! Gosh, no. Not at all. He's wonderful. But the intensity you've noticed is for a reason." A wave of nausea rolled over me as I began to explain. "I have a stalker."

His eyes bulged. "What? How did this happen? Are you in danger?"

I set a hand on his arm. "That's what Adam and the guys at Saint are trying to figure out. He asked Beast to hang out to deter anyone who might be up to no good, which I'm thinking means he has reason to believe the guy might be in town."

A different kind of sick feeling invaded now—not one born of nerves and a small thrill at telling my dad, but one directly rooted in actual fear.

A crush of both kinds of anxiety flooded me as I finally said it out loud. "I've been publishing books as Josie Wade."

He blinked, then looked to his right, toward the romance section. "Josie Wade."

I nodded. He knew the name because we kept my books stocked thanks to my book club's love and their proselytizing other readers to give them a chance.

The serious expression melted into one of wonder. "Josephine, that's wonderful. That's simply amazing! You're so well loved by your readers. You're—" He held my shoulders, then hauled me in for a hug. "You've been doing this for years now."

Throat tight, I managed, "I have."

"Why wouldn't you tell me? And all your friends? They'll be thrilled to know it. We'll do signings and launches and—"

"Dad, there are a few reasons I've kept this close, and they're mostly still in play. One that's developed over the last year or so is that Josie Wade started getting letters from a fan that turned into something more."

He sobered and his voice emerged just above a whisper. "And now, this person is stalking you?"

My bottom lip trembled like an unruly child completely ignoring the reality that if I started crying over this, I likely wouldn't stop. "Seems like it. I got flowers yesterday afternoon, and I told Adam thank you for them when he got to your house last night. We started putting pieces together, and that's why he was so serious." Weirdly, I felt the need for him to understand Adam could be intense, yes, but mostly, he was thoughtful and kind and forthright. "He can be really fun and he makes me laugh. He seems to like when I laugh. And he's the only other person in the world who knows about Josie."

"You trusted him to tell him..." His throat bobbed.

"He found out accidentally. I wouldn't have told him, but I have to admit I'm so glad it happened. And I'm so glad I didn't keep it to myself until something bad happened." I was choosing to believe that now that Saint Security had gotten involved, this would end without anything other than me stressing out. There had to be a way to resolve this.

"I'm glad he's involved, and Wilder. They'll figure this out. They do amazing things and they're highly trained. I know they'll figure it out." He glanced toward the door again. "And in the meantime, we'll stay here in our little bookish world, and you can tell me all about what it's been like to publish books."

I grinned at his determination to distract me from the problem and turn toward something good. If only I thought Elizabeth would be able to celebrate with me instead of feeling disappointed.

But Dad was one person who mattered, and maybe this was a small step toward being more open with my family and friends and everyone.... Right after we figured out how not to make it even more dangerous.

CHAPTER THIRTY

Adam

Dread and rage swirled in my gut as I opened the last of six letters from the stalker.

There hadn't been any letters from this guy when I'd gotten her mail after she'd hurt her ankle... had there? We'd talked about it that night, and I'd stupidly failed to sift through the pile with any real focus. I'd changed the subject when she'd gotten upset, not wanting to push her after she'd admitted what'd been going on... clearly, I should've.

"This guy needs serious help," Bruce said under his breath as he skimmed one of them we'd already opened.

"Indeed," Wilder said darkly.

Each letter had been written on college-ruled notebook paper. The handwriting was orderly and clear. The language was unfortunately mature—both in terms of vocabulary and sentence structure, which meant this was almost without a doubt an adult male and not a misguided teen.

And there was the content. The early letters I'd seen were mostly unhinged praise, until the last one where he'd veered into more personal territory about his feelings for *her*. But these last few were graphic in a way that made me ill and escalated the concern here to massive.

Things he wanted for her, and far worse, from her, and then what he'd do when he found her.

Yes. He'd been making clear for a long while that he was working to find her in real life and hoped to meet her—hoped to "unite" them.

I tossed the letter and must've made a sound like a wild dog, because Bruce and Wilder both paused and eyed me right as my phone rang. Bruce patted my shoulder, attempting to reassure me without words as I answered.

"Hi, Adam, it's Dahlia. Mandy came in and can tell you about the customer."

I put it on speaker and she continued.

"I also sent the CCTV recordings to your email on the card and copied Bruce since I have his, too. Let me know if there's anything else we can help with."

"Thanks, Dahlia."

"Here's Mandy."

A few minutes later, we had a description of a man who'd come in early Saturday wanting a bouquet that matched what Jo had received. He'd returned later and paid cash. He had light blond hair pulled into a ponytail she only noticed when he turned to leave since he wore a hat low on his head, slight build, and was about five-foot-seven, pale white skin, no facial hair. She guessed he was in his thirties or forties but wasn't sure. He'd been wearing nondescript clothes she couldn't recall, but we'd see those on the video soon enough.

It was better than nothing. We could take the description along with the letters to the police, and while there was likely not much they could do yet, Chief Whitacker wouldn't disregard it.

"Doc, I'm going back after lunch. Cookie's there now." Beast ducked his head in for the update. Bruce had set up a rotating schedule so there would be someone at the bookstore all day in two-hour shifts. After we learned more, we'd figure out the way forward. Handy to be a security company who specialized in personal security, so we knew exactly how to do this.

At least, we did in theory. I didn't know how to handle this when it was someone who mattered to me.

"What's going on? How can I help?" Jess peeked in, body as far from Beast's giant presence as possible. In the doorway of my office, that wasn't much, but she still managed it.

I looked to Wilder, not sure what to say. I'd made clear we couldn't let this out because of the personal information about Jo that no one knew. Beast hadn't needed the full explanation, but Jess would. She'd know this was about her friend with even the smallest bit of information, and she'd demand to understand the full story because not only was she excellent at anything we assigned her to, she was also a good friend. She'd be worried and want to understand what this meant for Jo, and I didn't know how Jo wanted that to come out.

I couldn't make that call without Jo's okay, and Wilder read it loud and clear.

"Still getting intel for now, but we'll let you know if we need you. Thanks, Pop."

Jess paused, absorbing the brush-off with a small drop of her chin, and she left. At some point, I'd circle back with her and let her know, or Wilder would. When it was okay with Jo and we could clarify it wasn't a problem with *Jess*, this was the situation. No doubt Jess felt the slight, and I couldn't ignore the fact that Beast, her rival whether we liked it or not, clearly had some amount of information she didn't.

Beast looked after her, all squinty eyes and hard mouth, then patted the doorframe. "See you this afternoon."

After thanking Wilder as quietly as possible, I gathered my things. I had no plan to come back to the office today. Anything I was working on before this could wait.

When I took Jo lunch and explained it was time to go the police, she seemed calmer. I didn't detail what we'd found in the letters in her PO Box, but I did clarify that the person was here in town.

"I figured it was something like that since you put the guys out there." Her gaze flicked to the front door, where we could see Cookie's tanned arm and profile.

"I didn't want to scare you before I knew more, but Mandy from Bloom confirmed it. That's an escalation and we need to let the Chief know, for sure."

"Thanks for your help with this," Darcy said, his hand outstretched to me.

I had nothing but good things to say about the man, but we hadn't had many conversations aside from book-related ones when I'd stopped in and missed Jo. He was a good man, and from what I could tell, a loving father.

Even through the haze of worry and fear shrouding Jo, I could see a glint of excitement. His statement revealed he knew—at least about the stalking and probably about Josie Wade, too.

"Hope we can get it wrapped up quickly."

He released my hand and gave me a kind, fatherly look. "Me, too, son."

And then he left us to settle into the reading room in the back for our lunch.

That *son* shouldn't have left an impression in my mind, but it did—one I didn't have time to take out and trace over right now.

Jo picked at her turkey sandwich, only managing a few bites, and soon enough, we'd reported everything to the police. She'd been strong and clear about everything she had explained, especially the number of letters she'd tossed. As much as she'd claimed to have put it all out of her mind, her subconscious had known something wasn't right and had been keeping track.

As expected, they couldn't do much, especially since we had no proof the flowers were from the stalker. We'd connected those dots, but in terms of proof and not just some nice person coincidentally giving the pretty bookstore girl flowers, we couldn't link them.

That said, the Chief and the people in the know at Saint all seemed to agree it was too coincidental, especially since no one recognized the guy, and in a town this small, it was unlikely a total stranger had bought Jo flowers. Not that she wasn't deserving, but it simply didn't add up.

After they took her statement, Jo's energy circled the drain. I walked her all the way inside her place and she slumped onto the couch.

"Let's get you a bag packed." I took a seat in the chair next to her.

She rubbed at her eyes, then blinked over at me. "A bag?"

I took her hand in mine and held her gaze. "Yeah. Until we find this guy, you're coming to stay with me."

She instantly shook her head. "No, Adam. I can't do that to you. This is—the police know now and it's going to be fine." Her eyes filled with tears. "Right? It is."

I moved to sit beside her and pulled her into a hug. "We're going to get it figured out. We will. But for now, will you humor me? Let me take you to my house. You'll have your own room, your own space, and there's no pressure on this. I just want you to stay somewhere this guy doesn't have on his radar, and while I'm hoping he hasn't found addresses for your family, he certainly doesn't know mine."

She pulled back. "This is too much."

Too much to handle? Too much for any one person to have to deal with?

Or was this woman worried it was too much for our fledgling relationship? Was she worried I wouldn't want her there but was doing it for her safety?

She couldn't know that half of this was for my own peace of mind. Granted, Bruce and Wilder had signed off fully on the plan to have her out of the place where this creep knew she lived, but still. I couldn't handle knowing she was staying where this guy could find her, even if we did have someone outside her door at all times. And how long would that go on?

Jo could stay with me for as long as she needed to—as long as she wanted.

And if that rolled into indefinitely, well... I shook away the thought, banishing it from my mind because I knew better than to go there. This was not the time to start thinking of anything I wanted, let alone something so far past what I knew I could do.

"It's not too much—don't worry about that. Unless

you're not comfortable, and in that case, no judgment or worry, we'll figure something else out. You can stay with—"

Her hand slid from my shoulder to my jaw. "No. That's not it."

Even red rimmed and full of worry, her eyes were so beautiful it made me ache.

"Alright, then. Let's get a bag packed and go get you settled."

She took a slow, deep breath. "At your house."

She said it like she was absorbing the information in a new way.

"Yes, honey. At my house."

CHAPTER THIRTY-ONE

Jo

Adam's forearms strained a bit and his biceps practically bulged.

"Grab the headboard for me."

I turned from the scene for a heartbeat to give myself a moment because *really, sir, are you actually trying to kill me?* I shouldn't have been thinking of the romance novel innuendos, but so far, we'd hit "Think it'll fit?" and now this, and I just couldn't keep the blush from my cheeks or the dangerous flutter in my belly.

Honestly, those words from his mouth, even fully out of context, were kind of a problem.

"Jo? I'm sorry about this. I honestly forgot I never finished setting this up."

He gave me a regretful look when I turned, but I couldn't keep from laughing at myself, or him, or maybe the whole situation.

"You're laughing at me now? I see how it is. I invite you to stay in my humble abode and you're—"

Rushing to him, I wrapped my arms around him. Yes, I'd been a little needy for his touch in the last twenty-four hours, but knowing someone was stalking me made me want to cling to this person who made me feel safe.

"I don't blame you at all. It's just, you keep saying these things that have... other meanings."

He tilted his head, completely confused. "Like..."

My cheeks downright burned. "Um, like, well, like, 'Grab the headboard for me.'"

He waited for more, but when there wasn't, he huffed a laugh. "Okay, you got me. I have no idea why that's funny."

I covered my face for a minute, then dropped my hands and laughed. "Um, yeah, so you know some romance novels are on the steamier side of things?"

He nodded, eyes keen.

"And one of the things that sometimes happens in some, um, steamy scenes is the hero will say that... but not while he and the heroine are moving furniture."

Twin flames lit his eyes, and then he threw his head back and laughed loudly enough I felt it in my chest. My blush deepened yet again, and he hauled me into a bear hug.

"Oh my, my, my, Josephine Malcom. You have a scandalous little mind, don't you?"

He ducked his head and his expression was so... well, honestly, it was so delighted and *loving*, it stole my breath.

"It's not *scandalous*. It's just aware of the wonderful world of romance and the many double entendres that apparently do happen in real life." His sparkly blue eyes were making my stomach all swoopy.

His grin widened and his fingers sifted into the hair on

either side of my head. "What am I going to do with you?" His voice was gruff and low now.

"You could kiss me, I guess."

His smile flashed one more time before he took my mouth with the softest, fastest kiss, it was more tease than actual kiss.

I kept my eyes closed, waiting for more, but none came. When I finally opened them, he gazed back at me, so much heat and longing there I could hardly get out the words. "Is that all you'll give me?"

He laughed softly. "Oh, Jo, that's so far from all I want to give you."

The kiss that followed was one that lit every nerve ending on fire and made me hunger to the point I ached. His hands in my hair, my hands in his short strands, he molded us together with such skill and confidence and command, I never wanted it to end.

Until actual hunger made itself known via a horrifying sound courtesy of my stomach. He pulled back and looked almost as delighted as he'd been before the kiss.

"You need food."

I wanted to wipe the amused little tug of his lips right off his face, but he was too handsome, and it was clearly true. "Why do you look so pleased by that?"

He shook his head, his expression sobering a touch. "I like everything about you."

That hit an unknown mark in me, a bullseye I'd never realized I had. "Oh" was all I could muster, because what else could I say?

He linked our fingers and tugged me along behind him to the kitchen, leaving the bedframe and mattress askew and his guest room a few steps shy of ready for me.

Adam in the kitchen was an unfortunate revelation. He

assembled a meal for the two of us in a matter of about fifteen minutes—penne pasta with chicken and summer vegetables in a lemony caper sauce complete with slinging the kitchen towel over a shoulder at one point. It was both simple and fancy, and when he produced a crusty baguette and slathered a piece with butter before handing it to me, I fell a little harder.

Had I only ever dated boys? Was that the difference here? Or was there something about these Saint men, or maybe men who'd served in the military, who were consummately capable in these earthy, obvious ways I couldn't resist?

I didn't subscribe to the idea that in order to be *manly* and appealing to a woman, a prospective partner for me needed to be a member of the warrior archetype. I had a fairly sensitive father—I mean my sweet dad had been a workaholic, but he'd been an accountant, and then he'd followed his dreams to a little mountain town and opened a bookstore. I hadn't exactly been raised with a paragon of what much of society would tell me was attractive.

I'd never wanted a man who was all muscular and couldn't cry because he was just too manly. Gross. And that was no doubt why meeting Bruce Camden and learning he was a faithful book club attender, guardian to his little sister, and a little bit of a romantic at heart had reached out and grabbed me.

Bruce was precious and just right for Nikki. The more I got to know Adam, the more I wondered... the more it felt like he might just be right for me.

He was this triple threat of sexy muscles, endless capabilities, and softness. Yes—he had his tender side for his friends he would never convince me was a failing. And all of it on display here in his clean, orderly home with sensible furnishings and a gloriously stocked fridge was nearly too much.

"Taste okay?" he asked after we'd been eating for a few minutes.

"Yes. It's delicious. I was just thinking I'm not sure I've had anyone cook for me—certainly not something they hadn't planned out."

One boyfriend way back when before grad school had tried to impress me. He'd made us rare strip steaks and an undercooked baked potato. I'd choked it down and then felt sick the rest of the evening—he'd been embarrassed and admitted he never cooked. Ah, well. It didn't end up working out, anyway.

"I'm decent at a few things. E's the real chef between us. He actually went to culinary school for a while after the Army."

"I don't think I knew that. He's a jack-of-all-trades, isn't he?" I smiled at the thought of my friend creating culinary masterpieces for his future partner.

Adam leveled me with his blue eyes. "He is that. And he's a deeply decent man. I'm really proud of him."

"Sometimes, you talk about him like he's... I don't know. I can't figure out what it is other than maybe self-deprecation or condemnation paired with your love for him?" It wasn't a particularly cogent question, but he nodded in understanding.

"I think I feel the difference between us so much more now than I did when we were younger. I'm not sure why other than that I see his hope for the future—the way he wants a family so much and the way I've avoided that for years. I've realized a lot of it comes from choices I made, yes, but also at having seen my mom miserable and single for most of my formative years, whereas she found our stepdad when Ethan was in junior high, right after I enlisted. And that really changed how he grew. I envy him sometimes, but I'm also grateful he had that experience."

A bittersweet smile flitted across his face before he continued. "He saw what a loving relationship looks like—how a man can make a woman happy in a healthy way. How it can work."

My throat cinched tight against a swallow. I heard the unspoken words there—*he saw it, and I didn't*. He'd argued he didn't know how to make a relationship work and this had to be part of it—not just his past failure with marriage but also his lack of a model he could emulate or even understand, maybe. But here he was, with me.

Right as I found my words, he spoke again. "Enough of that, though. I gather you told your dad about your writing. How did that go?"

I saw it for what it was—a need to change the subject. I'd give it to him this time, but we'd circle back to the matter soon because we'd have to. If this relationship kept going the way we were headed, and I certainly hoped it would, then we'd need to come back and face all of those fears down.

Lucky for him, I'd never been a coward.

CHAPTER THIRTY-TWO

Adam

Jo lit up as she recounted the moment she'd told her dad about Josie Wade. Her energy perked and she started gesturing with her hands—she was luminous with joy.

"He didn't cry outright, probably because of the whole stalker thing, but Adam... he was so genuinely happy for me. *Excited.* I don't know why I doubted he'd react that way, but it was amazing." Her eyes glittered back at me from her seat at the table.

Her seat. That felt right.

Not the time.

"I bet it's a dream come true for him."

Impossibly, her grin widened. "You think? Maybe I've gotten too wrapped up in my worries about people finding out to make a best guess on how they'll respond to the truth..." She shook her head. "I can't seem to shake the fear it's a fluke. Or maybe he's the only one who'll be like that."

"Happy for you? Excited? Is it just Elizabeth who wouldn't be?" I asked.

She ate another bite and took her time chewing before she spoke again. "It's definitely Elizabeth, but I think my mom, too. She was always so serious, and while I don't think she hates my dad, I think she resents that he moved here and opened a bookstore, and this will feel like a betrayal of her in some way."

I exhaled slowly. "That's a lot to take on."

"What is?"

"Your sister's expectations. Your mother's feelings about her first marriage, and in turn, her feelings about your father..."

Her lips flattened and she sighed. "Point taken."

I couldn't stop myself from tucking some hair behind her ear. Maybe this was the way I was appeasing the ever-present desire to run my fingers through it—so be it. "I don't mean to sound harsh or like I'm judging you for feeling the way you do. You know your family dynamics and your feelings are legitimate. But I'm glad you're willing to hear me out there, because you're putting so much pressure on yourself and I hate for you to miss sharing this part of yourself with the people you love *if* you want to."

She picked at her pasta and took another bite, evidently mulling over my words. After sipping her water, she set down her fork and squared her shoulders.

"You're right, though. I'm assuming my work has anything to do with... anything. My work is just that—*my* work. If Elizabeth doesn't agree with the choice, that's okay. That's *her* choice. And if my mom is mad at me for a while because she gets her feelings about my dad and our life here confused with my chosen profession, then that's kind of her and her therapist's deal to comb through."

Good grief, she was adorable when she was determined like this. "Very wise."

She tucked her lips between her teeth and squinted at me. "Yeah. I am."

I chuckled. "You are. Truly."

She dipped her head as though to say *yeah, I know*. "Which is why I also know it's one thing to say all of that, and it's another thing to believe it and actually function in a way that reflects it."

Well, damn. There she goes again.

I threaded our fingers together and brought her hand to my mouth for a kiss. "*That* is very wise. Can I make a suggestion?"

"Of course."

I took in the shadows under her eyes and the way the light above the table made her irises look like amber sunbursts in a richer brown now. "Go easy. Give yourself some grace with this change because, like you said, saying it and actually changing the way you think as a default is a process."

A soft smile curled at the corner of her beautiful mouth. "Fair enough."

"And while we're on the subject, how do you feel about us telling Jess sooner than later?" I didn't want to tell her about the moment earlier today when her friend had clearly felt shut out because Jo didn't need that kind of pressure on her decision-making.

She rubbed at one eye, exhaustion more and more visible on her face and in her body. "I need to tell her. I'm sure it's weird at work now. And I... I guess we don't know how long this is going to go on for? How long until we can... find him or whatever the goal is?"

My goal would naturally be to eliminate the threat, but

that couldn't be the end here. Ideally, he'd do something stupid enough to get him on the police's radar and scare him away from doing anything more serious, but who knew if we'd get so lucky.

"I don't know. Hopefully, we'll get a better picture of things in the next few days."

Our team was combing through every angle of every video we'd found in town. They were tracing the license plate on the car he'd presumably driven, and I hoped it'd be a matter of time before we had more information and could help her life return to normal.

"I need to send an e-mail tonight before I tell Jess, but I'll plan to talk to her tomorrow." She set her fork and knife onto the plate and folded her paper napkin neatly. "I don't really want everyone else to find out yet, though. Okay? I think I want to surprise them."

"Devious of you," I said, eyes glued to the little smirk on her lips.

"Not devious, but I feel like, at this point, it makes sense to wait until we get this situation more under control. I know I can trust Jess, though. And honestly, putting it off a little while gives me a chance to figure out how to tell Elizabeth and my mom. They won't hear it from anyone accidentally, so I should have plenty of time, but I'll feel better if we keep it close for now."

"Done. Everyone at Saint knows how to keep their mouths shut." We signed NDAs regularly and all of us had been used to keeping literal top-secret information compartmentalized and away from prying eyes and ears. No one would learn of her pseudonym from one of us.

We finished dinner and she insisted on helping with dishes. Fortunately, there weren't many, so we loaded the dishwasher, and soon, she was stifling a yawn, and I was steering her to the guest room.

"You take a shower and I'll get the bed fixed up so it's ready when you're done." I eyed the mattress and bedframe.

"Okay. We could also..." She swallowed and tucked her hair behind her ears. "We could just not worry about the guest bed."

Scientifically, the idea that my heart slowly thud-thud-thudded to a stop in that moment was entirely inaccurate. If anything, it took off at a sprint. Medically, if your heart stops, you have died. And I didn't die. I kept on living in a moment where Jo Malcom, a woman who was endlessly beautiful and thoughtful and tender, had just suggested we share a bed.

We'd done it last night, so this shouldn't have felt so earth-stilling as it did now. *Alas.* Last night had felt like an acute situation, and even though we were only standing here in my guest bedroom because this situation was exactly that—another highly unexpected scenario brought on by actual danger to her—it was also different.

"Or, no, I just mean, I don't want you to stress about this. I can help you. I—"

I stalked to her, and her words cut off as I cupped her face. "Don't backtrack. Don't try to take away those words when they are suggesting something good."

She blinked rapidly a few times, a thousand thoughts hiding in her eyes. "But?"

Her perception was excellent—she would've been a great operator in that regard. "But I don't think that's wise tonight."

She nodded slowly, mulling over my words. "Can I ask why?"

"Of course you can." I waited.

She rolled her eyes and shoved at my chest with a laugh. "Why?"

I let my hands slip down from her face to the slope of her neck where it curved into her shoulders. A devil on my shoulder pushed at me to tell her exactly why not, but the angel said to emphasize the situation.

"This is a stressful time full of unknowns. I don't think it's fair to make any decisions that would impact our relationship in that context."

The angel's answer had her lips spreading into a thin facsimile of a smile. "Right. Yeah." She turned toward her bag where it sat on the dresser and unzipped it, head ducked.

Seeing her curl into herself and knowing in my gut she'd taken it as a rejection, the devil won out. I crowded her from behind and slipped a hand around her waist to rest at her navel while the other smoothed her hair from her neck. Her head snapped up and caught my eyes in the mirror in front of us.

I dipped my head. My lips coasted along the line of her neck and up to her ear, where I spoke softly, breath brushing against it. "I should also make clear, Josephine, that I very much want to share a bed with you. I want to share everything with you. And because I know how much I want that, it's better for us to be smart or we'll ruin this whole taking-it-slow thing."

She swallowed hard and leaned into me, eyes never leaving mine. "Okay, then. We'll go slow."

I pressed a kiss to the shadow behind her ear, then her temple. "Thank you."

Reluctantly, I left her, savoring the knowledge she wanted closeness with me and knowing in a way I never had before that I wanted to give it to her. And believing more and more that perhaps, I really could. When I said I wanted to share everything with her, I meant it all, and for the first time, instead of instantly sensing doom, there was a pull toward believing maybe it was possible.

CHAPTER THIRTY-THREE

Jo

I spent a not-small portion of the night reliving several points in my day, first in line being the most recent incidence of Adam trying to cause me to spontaneously combust.

The way he'd touched me and held my gaze in the mirror, and then after I'd agreed... *I died.*

Fine. I didn't die, but I felt a little like I did, because the man could be rather unexpected. I had never imagined he'd say those things, his hands on me in a deliciously possessive way despite effectively rejecting me, and then he'd kissed right behind my ear before nipping at my earlobe.

Not a huge thing. A small, insignificant act.

Except for the reality that the heat coming from his body and touch and eyes spoke of so much hunger for me, his little bite had signaled a break in his self-control.

Afterward, he'd stepped away, focusing on the bed.

When I'd emerged from the bathroom, it'd been made with fresh sheets and a soft gray comforter with a pile of pillows and a note. *Whatever you need, I'm here.*

So it was the ear thing and the words and the admission of how much he wanted me and the moment earlier with the whole "I like everything about you" and his secret kitchen skills and his medical smarts and his general hotness because, though I wasn't a particularly superficial person, the man was gorgeous and I wasn't going to pretend he didn't absolutely do it for me in the looks department.

He was right that sleeping together wasn't a good call, especially in the context of knowing he felt strongly that his first marriage had been rushed and that had been part of the failure. But also because having a stalker wasn't romantic. Being with Adam was, and having him so focused on keeping me safe was apparently my kind of catnip, but when I wasn't just dreaming of being wrapped up in him, I could admit that part of me loved the idea of the distraction and not the escalation between us.

Well, maybe. I wanted more between us for sure, but I could feel him holding himself back. I'd known it from the beginning—though he'd agreed to date me, he wasn't saying he wanted forever. It was probably premature for me to want this, and yet I couldn't deny how every minute I spent with him moved me closer to envisioning it between us.

Even his refusal to share a bed—whether it meant sleep, or more—felt like the right choice and endeared me to him more. It felt like he was prioritizing something real between us, not just the satisfaction of desire, and this was one more way he was caring for me and our relationship.

Pump the brakes, woman! You're halfway down the aisle and he hasn't even agreed to be your boyfriend! One date does not a boyfriend make.

Ah, reality. There ye be.

But he doesn't want to date anyone else, and neither do you, and...

A knock on the door jolted me from my unhinged musings, and I swung it open to find a gorgeous bed-heady Adam. His slow smile did unnamable things to my insides, and then he reached up and gripped the doorframe on his side of it. His T-shirt sleeves hugged his biceps and slipped up with the movement, as did the torso of the material, so the taut skin at his waist and the cuts near his hips disappeared into his low-slung gray sweatpants.

Of course they do. Of course he is.

"G-good morning." Yes, I stuttered. How could I not when my tongue had tied itself in a knot right along with the majority of my vocabulary?

He grinned. "Hi. You get any sleep?"

"Not much."

Maybe I should've been worrying about the stalker, but instead, I was mostly worrying about how much I liked Adam and how close these feelings felt to some much larger L word I had no business feeling.

His brows dipped and he crossed the threshold into my room, sliding his hands around my back and tucking me into the place where I fit so perfectly, it made me ache.

"I'm sorry, honey. I hate that this is keeping you up, but hopefully, we'll make some progress today." He pulled back. "You hungry?"

Twenty minutes later, Adam served me scrambled eggs and toast with coffee at his now sunny table, and I wasn't sure my heart could take much more of this. Seeing him barefoot in his kitchen cooking for me... it did nothing to quell the future-gazing setting my brain had switched to in the last twenty-four hours.

After we ate, we parted to get changed, and a bit later, he was opening my car door and making sure I'd packed a snack.

That's right. He didn't want my blood sugar dipping while I was under so much stress. He'd sliced me apples and put them in a little baggy with a string cheese, and it threatened to turn me into a puddle of mush. *Note to self—have future book hero pack heroine a snack.*

Adam was a caretaker and I'd known this, but he'd hammered it home these last few days.

When he pulled up to Saint Security, I gave him a look.

"On the off chance anyone's watching the store, I thought we'd park here and I can walk you in. Beast's already set up, and when you're ready, text Jess and I'm sure she'll come right away."

We walked hand in hand from his work to All Booked Up, and every step we took, my pulse inched higher. By the time we turned onto Silver Street, I was shaking and clutching his fingers with a death grip. He slung an arm around me and pressed his lips to my head.

"You're okay, Jo. I'm not going to let anything happen to you."

He kissed my head again, and Beast nodded at us as we approached the door, then opened it for us.

"Your dad's going to be here again today. Said he had some inventory work to do."

I exhaled, relieved to know I wouldn't be alone in the store all day and desperately checking the windows and back rooms from paranoia. But as time ticked on, I fell into the usual pattern I so often did at the shop.

My dad checked in, Adam texted every few hours, and though I didn't get a response from her via text, Jess e-mailed my Josie Wade account a little before Adam came for lunch. She'd responded to the last e-mail I'd sent in, which had accepted the invitation to the book release party.

Her words were cheery and she used more exclamations than I ever would've imagined for a woman so steady and often serious, but it made me even more excited to tell her the truth.

I didn't anticipate a call from Elizabeth, and I briefly considered not answering, but she'd see that as a signal of something amiss more than me being a little cagey on the phone. Granted, she had a knack for ferreting out when things were off with me, so I was probably doomed to an inquisition either way. Best bet was to keep it as short and sweet as possible.

Since my dad was happily chatting with Dr. Corrigan, and Jamie Morris and his wife and two of their kids were milling in the children's section and always took their time, I slipped into the reading room and answered.

"Hey, Lizzy. How are you?"

"I talked to Dad last night and he sounded weird. What's going on?"

Ah. So that was why I was hearing from her again so soon. We'd talked last week, and usually, we didn't speak quite so often.

But also… "How was he weird? What did he say?"

"He didn't want to talk about you."

I blinked at the empty fireplace, bereft of its usual wood during the summer, waiting for more.

"He normally can't stop talking about everything with you, and all I could get out of him is that you're seeing a guy and you really like him."

She sounded so deeply annoyed by this, I had to laugh.

"And you assume that means something's wrong?"

Normal people gave cues in a conversation—a huff of

breath against the speaker or restless tapping in the background or *something* to indicate the person's mindset. Not so with Elizabeth Malcom.

"We both know something's going on, so why don't you just tell me?"

My heart shot out of the starting gates, galloping so hard, I sank into a chair to keep from getting dizzy. "It's nothing."

If I told her about the stalker, I'd have to tell her about Josie Wade. I could do that. I could. It would be okay, and even if she thought it was silly or frivolous or not living up to my potential, it was my life, wasn't it?

"Jojo, tell me."

Oof. For the jugular with that one, but it did the job. It reminded me of how she'd cheered me on, urged me to find something I loved and that made the world a better place— something that *mattered*. Would writing satisfy that charge in her mind?

And was it foolish for me to still be so worried about this?

But mentioning things being dangerous here wasn't the right choice anyway. She had an important job and needed her full focus there. I didn't know where *there* was exactly, but I knew she shouldn't be wandering around worried about me. She hadn't admitted anything was wrong, but this frequency of calling lately, and how she'd not only avoided talking about work but about anything in her life lately, clinched it for me.

So instead of anything emergent, I admitted something else. "It's Adam. I—I'm falling for him."

She hummed. "Well, is he a good man?"

I huffed a small laugh because of course she wouldn't be startled by my statement. "He's the best."

"Then what's the problem?"

This would be a better conversation for a time when I didn't have a potential audience for it, but after sneaking over to peer out into the main store, everyone was still happily browsing or checking out with Dad. He was occupied, so no chance of his overhearing either.

I paced around the small, cozy room. If I wasn't going to tell her the truth about the stalker, I could at least be honest about this—fully honest. And maybe for the first time, truthful with myself about why I'd started to feel both elated and scared in the quiet moments between me and Adam.

"Two things. First, when we met last summer, he stated very clearly that he had no plans to marry again. He's divorced and it was messy, he blames himself, and... well, I think that may be changing, but I know how stupid it is to believe he'd change for me."

A silent beat, then, "And second?"

I slumped onto the couch. "I'm scared. I mean, let's assume he miraculously does want a future with me. How do I know..." My throat locked up.

"How do you know it won't turn out like Mom and Dad?" she supplied.

"Right," I said, only a whisper. As if one of the roots of my romance writing hadn't been in righting the wrong I'd witnessed between them—writing stories that led to happily ever afters together and not apart. Granted, they'd both found new HEAs, and I truly delighted in that for them, but it ached thinking about the desolation of losing Adam in such a way.

She sighed then, long and loud into the receiver. "I know it'll shock you to learn this, but I'm not an expert when it comes to love."

This response made me smile. "No? I'm shocked."

"But Jojo, I think you are. You're naturally so loving, I think you've got a great shot at it. And I think..." She sighed again—*what is happening here?* "I think Mom and Dad broke up for a lot of reasons, but what I used to think would make it avoidable... I don't know."

This lack of certainty in her voice was the final knock against my thick skull to alert me. "Hey. You seem... something. Are you okay?"

Quiet on her side again, then, "I'm just tired. I'll be okay."

"Maybe you should come visit. See Silverton for yourself."

"Yeah, maybe."

I perked up at this idea. We had a lot of differences between us, but part of the reason I felt so far from her was because I was. We hadn't lived near each other in sixteen years. She'd visited me a lot more often when she'd first gotten started, even though I knew it had stressed her out to do so. Nowadays, I was lucky if I saw her once a year, and it'd been longer than that for both me and Dad. She'd never seen the shop or what our lives were like here.

"It'd be amazing to have you here. And you could meet Adam." The thought sent a thrill through me.

"Maybe I will." A sound in the background broke through, and she did the thing that always made me cringe. "I'll let you go. Hang in there."

"You, too, Lizzy. Love you."

"Yep. You, too." And she was gone.

She wasn't okay. Elizabeth wasn't the kind of person to say she was tired unless something was really wrong. This had justified part of my reasoning for not telling her about Josie Wade, and I felt that even more.

And her response about Adam... she hadn't given me empty reassurances that I'd never face the end of a marriage like our parents had. I appreciated this about her—she wasn't going to give me platitudes, that was for sure.

When all this stalker nonsense was over, I'd be brave with Adam. I'd ask him straight on if he thought we had a future together, and we'd go from there.

CHAPTER THIRTY-FOUR

Adam

Friday marked day five of sharing my house with Jo.

I was handling it just fine. It hadn't made me want things I'd long ago decided I'd never have. It hadn't made me question every promise I'd made to myself concerning her. It hadn't made me want to lock her inside and spend days satisfying her every desire as a way to distract us both.

What it had done? Made me a flaming liar.

The stalker was still on the loose, and this fact made clear he wasn't an average John Doe. He'd used a stolen plate on the car he'd driven through town the day he'd ordered and placed flowers at Jo's door. We'd canvassed the area asking people if they'd seen the guy after obtaining an artist's rendering, but no dice.

So days later, Jo was living at my house in my guest room, our team rotated between Beast and Cookie and me guarding her, and we waited.

No new letters and no overtures in person, either.

By Friday night, all of us were ready for some down time. Jo was thrilled to get together with her girlfriends, and since the Saint Security routine coincided with her girls' night, she had protection in place without drawing her friends' attention to it.

Weirdly, I'd found it increasingly difficult to be away from her. Actually, no. It wasn't weird. That reality was rooted in the worry I had for her, and getting used to having her close by at night and first thing in the morning. Sue me if having a beautiful woman occupy my usually rather empty house made my life a little better.

But tonight, the frustration from a week full of chasing rabbit trails paired with worry over how hard Ethan was working and how much Dorian was struggling and even the fact that Jess had taken off on a quickie remote assignment this week, so Jo still hadn't told her about Josie Wade... all of it had added up.

When Beast sat a highball of whiskey down in front of me, I toasted his and we drank. Bruce eyed our glasses as he poured a round of beer for everyone else—Kenny, Tristan, and Cookie.

"Rough week there, Doc?" Cookie asked, his dark hair flopping over his forehead in a ridiculously charming way.

"You could say that," I grumbled, then glanced to my right to catch sight of Jo.

My heart tripped, then did its best impression of splattering on the bottom of my rib cage. Graphic, and utterly nonsense physiologically. For the best, she was the author and I was the... what? No longer actually a medic. No longer a soldier. *Personal security guy.* Neat.

"You look like you're spiraling a little," Bruce said

quietly as Kenny launched into a story about who knew what.

"Frustrated. And..." I glanced around again. It wasn't the feeling of being watched. I knew that feeling and this wasn't quite it. More so, it seemed like we were on display tonight. Going through the emotions when we should be at home. When Jo and I should be wrapped in each other and I wouldn't have to share her with anyone.

But that's not how this works—not now, not ever.

I grumbled at my own thought.

"Sounding like me," Beast muttered under his breath as he nudged my glass toward me.

I took another drink.

"As soon as you're ready, let's schedule the first survival class. We'll get you something to focus on." Bruce patted my back like this news would cheer me.

It did on some level. "Sounds good." Bruce's statement was more reminder than news, but I appreciated the effort.

Tristan's presence next to me was steady and calm, as usual. Oak had been aptly named years ago during his selection and assessment, just like we all had. But was Doc really much of a nickname? It said nothing about my character or who I was at my heart—nothing of who I am outside of the military.

"Calendar's filling up for fall," Kenny said, leaning on the table and drawing my eye. *Barbie.* He did have a Ken-doll smile.

"Business is booming. I'll admit that when Julian Grenier told us he'd back us, I thought he was a fool. I never realized how many celebrities and high-profile clients would end up here." Bruce raised his pint glass to the center of the table, and we all touched our glasses together.

Mine was empty. *Odd.* Had I guzzled it down while I drowned in my own sorry thoughts?

"Grenier's a good man, for a billionaire," Cookie said, his mistrust of wealth not a surprise. His most recent overseas assignment with a celebrity had drilled that home, from what he'd said.

"We couldn't have gotten started without him, that's for sure. And we wouldn't be able to expand as quickly as we have either," Bruce acknowledged.

"Yeah, but you and Wilder are still the Saint Daddies." Kenny grinned, eyes sparkling, and he looked like he might start posing for photoshoots, he was so proud of his comment.

Bruce gave him his infamous Jaws look. "Call me Saint Daddy again, Barbie, and see what happens."

Kenny fluttered his lashes, but Beast, shockingly enough, broke in. "Pretty sure that specific title belongs to Wilder—according to Pop."

Everyone chuckled and Bruce patted his shoulder. "Thank you. Exactly. Wilder is the official Saint Daddy forever."

For his part, Beast looked pleased with the response as he emptied his glass. *Interesting.* Saving Kenny *and* dropping a reference to his enemy number one. Hard to believe a few sips of whiskey in that giant body could shake his rigidity loose, but he'd been under a fair amount of stress lately, so maybe he was trying.

Done with the attention, Beast disappeared for a few minutes while everyone else chatted—about the fall and how busy it would be rolling into the high season of celebrity appearances during the ski season, about travel assignments and leave plans people had, and all the while I stayed quiet, nursing my drink.

Beast had evidently slid a fresh one in front of me and I'd been brooding. I wasn't a brooder, nor was I particularly a lover of whiskey, but by the time Jo and Winnie came to the table and Winnie led Tristan away, I was feeling it.

"You ready?" Jo asked, a soft smile and tired eyes greeting me.

Beautiful. Damn but she was so completely beautiful.

"If you are. But I shouldn't drive." I knew that much.

"I'll drop you both. Nik and Kiley are doing a movie night since Kiley's sick." Bruce waved his keys and Jo accepted, looping her arm through mine.

"I'm sorry. I should've eaten, or slowed down, or both." I never did this—never got to where I couldn't drive and certainly not when I was supposed to be responsible for someone else. When I was tasked with keeping her safe.

She waved me off and Bruce got us home a few minutes later. We'd work out cars tomorrow. For now, I focused on not running my hand over Jo's bare knee next to me in Bruce's back seat. I begged my mind to clear enough so I didn't do or say any of the things that felt so close to the surface in the dark, as we watched Bruce reverse out of the driveway while we walked inside together.

What if this was it—just us, like this, indefinitely? What if you had her for good?

I locked the dead bolt and double-checked it, then turned and ran into Jo, whose hands came to my shoulders.

"What's going on in that head?"

Her voice was soft and a little rough like it sometimes got after a night out. I'd noticed it once months ago as we all left Craic after hours of laughing and talking together with the Saint staff and her friends.

"I'm sorry."

She ran a hand up my neck and scratched at the hair at

my nape. "Stop that. You're allowed to blow off some steam. No one is hurt. Nothing is wrong here. I'm not upset, and you don't owe me an apology."

I shook my head, marveling at her. So many things flooded to the forefront of my mind—how often my ex had been angry at me and how often I'd acted like I didn't care. How infrequently I'd apologized and how rarely she'd accepted if I did, much less told me there was no need.

It'd been years, but there they were, those memories, a direct counter to this moment.

"What is it?" she asked, pleading in the huskiness of her tone.

I took her in.

I want you so much I can't find words for it.

My pulse hammered in my neck just inches from where her fingers toyed with the too-long hair at the back of my head.

I think I might love you and the fact that I'm not sure shows just how broken I am.

I swallowed hard, drinking in the concern in her eyes, the intention with which she watched me.

All I know is I belong with you and I wish you belonged with me. I don't know how I'll handle this when it's over.

She jolted. "When it's over?"

On a sharp exhale, I dropped my forehead to hers and just breathed, waiting for my thundering heart to find a way to explain—to make up for what I'd said *aloud* apparently. For everything I'd messed up between us already and the fact that I had no intention of ending it here and now even though I should. I'd just admitted I expected an ending, hadn't I? But here I was, clinging to her instead of letting her go.

"Adam, I need you to use words now," she said, her

voice edged with an unbending will I'd rarely heard directed toward me.

I pulled back and steadied myself. "I don't know how to go forward, but I don't think I can stop with you. I don't want this to stop."

She gripped my forearms firmly, as though grounding us together in the moment. "Then let's keep going forward. See what happens. Be brave."

She sounded so clear and certain that was an option. She had so much faith in us, I felt it seep into me through her fingers and her palms against my skin.

"Okay."

And for the first time, I could feel in myself a genuine desire to be open—to let things between us unfold in a way that could actually mean forever, where one day becomes two, then three, then it merges and blends into an endless streak of days... That's how forever happened, didn't it?

I'd never imagined being in a place to want a future with someone again, but this miraculous woman had shown me how wonderful being with someone could be.

Jo made me not only want to try, but made me believe I could.

And so together, we'd be brave.

CHAPTER THIRTY-FIVE

Jo

I'd never seen broody Adam before, nor had I seen a tipsy one. But the way he looked at me now, with so much focus and the wrinkle in his brow spelling out his determination, it made the hope that'd been building and building in me explode into something unwieldy, too giant for me to hold alone.

So maybe here, what we were saying, meant we'd hold hope for each other together. Maybe it meant we could see the days merging into something without end down the line. It might not mean marriage and kids and happily ever after, but did anyone really ever see the horizon when they looked at their relationship? I'd had a vision of one version of life, and I hadn't given up on wanting those things, but just because they weren't instantly in my grasp didn't mean what I had, this precious fledgling thing in my hands, wasn't beautiful and worth having.

"Okay," I whispered, inching closer as my hands slid to the bend in his arms, then up the curves of his biceps.

His blue eyes followed the movement of my hands, flickering to meet my gaze, then dropping back as I drew closer.

When we pressed as close as we could get with my dress and his jeans and T-shirt in the way, I kissed his neck slowly, exploring in a way I'd never indulged in. Once I reached the line of his beard at his jaw, his hands sank into my hair and guided my mouth to his in one sure movement that made me tingly and aware from my scalp to my toes.

His kiss tasted like whiskey and Adam, and as much as I wanted a whole night with him, tonight wouldn't be it. But for now, I let myself sink into his kiss. After a few minutes of this in the entryway, we stumbled into the living room and he pulled me down right as I sank to straddle his thighs on the couch.

His warm, rough palms on the soft skin of my thighs, the demand of his lips, the feel of the punishing brush of his beard against my chin and cheeks... it made me drowsy with desire—drunk on it.

And that thought brought me back as I reluctantly pulled away. "Let's slow down," I said, out of breath.

He nodded, gaze glued to where his large hands rested on my bare legs, my dress rucked up scandalously high. I watched as his jaw flexed and his hand rose higher, sending my stomach into a flurry of flips, and then he gently pinched the edge of the silky material and slid it back down to more typical leg-covering territory.

"Good call," he said, his voice rough and rich and frankly, delicious.

"I'm going to head to bed, I think," I said, because there was no small part of me still considering we'd both said we were going to hope. Hoping was good. Hoping should be celebrated. Hoping was cause for big grown-up-man-and-woman-style celebrations.

No. Simmer down! He's not himself and this situation is messed up and you need to wait until your creepy stalker has been caught and you're not living at his place by default to keep you safe.

Okay, self. Fair points, if a little rude.

"Good idea," he said, eyes boring into me even as his hands found my waist and he guided me up and off him.

He stood once I stepped back, but he linked our fingers and raised my hand to press a soft kiss to the inside of my wrist.

"Thank you."

That low, gruff version of his voice was enough to turn me to mush.

"For?" I asked, not sure whether he meant the kissing or the stopping kissing or the conversation before, or even simply not being mad he hadn't thought driving home was right.

"For all of it," he said, as though he'd heard my thoughts.

With a lingering clutch of our fingers, we parted more than a little reluctantly. I worried I wouldn't sleep thanks to the rather intense last half-hour and the week over all, but the time with my friends had been wonderful, and my book would release in a few days. Jess would be back and I'd tell her everything so she'd be in the loop, and hopefully, every-thing would be fine.

When I woke later on Saturday morning than I had in quite a while thanks to not working a shift at the shop, I wandered out into the living room to find it empty. No bed-head Adam reading news on his phone or sipping coffee on his deck. There was a note on the counter that simply said

"Be back soon —A," so I poured myself some cereal and took my time eating while scrolling Instagram and organizing a few posts I had planned for the coming week. I'd spend most of my non-bookstore time working on social media and early reader campaigns, which meant these last few days before release were all just fun... and nerves.

I never knew what readers would think—would they love this book? And, would Adam read it? He might recognize a reflection of himself in the hero, and he'd absolutely recognize a few moments we'd shared during our book "practice."

The back door swung open and I jumped, then absolutely melted.

Butter in a hot pan.

Wax against a flame.

Other meltable things next to heat sources, because *goodness.*

"Morning. Sorry I wasn't here when you woke up," he said with a touch more of his accent than I usually heard, all smiles as though nothing was amiss. As though this magma-hot man hadn't waltzed into his living room shirtless and in a smallish pair of running shorts which showcased his strong legs and very well-honed muscles.

It wasn't like I didn't know he was fit. I did. He ran every morning, and when he didn't meet me for lunch, he lifted at work or at Grit, the gym right next door owned by my beloved stepbrother Warrick. He came from a job where his physical fitness and capability had been paramount, and I knew from having working eyeballs that everyone at Saint Security adhered to that standard in one way or another.

But this? This whole situation right now with the sun streaming in behind him and his breaths still heavy from exertion and how he'd dragged his hot fingers across my shoulders as he walked behind the couch where I sat and into the kitchen to get water? This was shoving my face in it a bit much, wasn't it?

"Good run?" I managed, because I was not about to sit here and let myself actually burn to a crisp in his presence, though I should probably make sure I hadn't fused to the couch.

"Not great after the whiskey, but cleansing. Got my head straight." He glanced at me, blue eyes having stolen some of the sky's natural coloring this morning and showing off with it.

"Good. That's good."

He rounded the couch and sat on the edge of the coffee table next to where my feet were propped up. "You good?"

I tucked my lips together and nodded. "Mm-hmm. Yup."

One side of his mouth quirked up, and he ducked his head a little. "You look a little flushed, honey. Are you feverish?"

My gaze had dropped to his chest and the flat arc of his pec, where a tattoo slashed into the space between muscles at his sternum. The lines were mesmerizing, and it felt shocking I hadn't seen this before. I hadn't even known he had a tattoo. *Does he have more? Where? Can I see?*

"Jo, honey, you okay?"

My gaze snapped up to meet his as heat rushed to my cheeks—no, my entire face. I was a blazing little tomato of guilt. "Totally fine."

"Just fine? Should I flex for you?" He raised an arm and flexed his bicep, and it was just rude because how dare he.

I shot out of my seat on the couch. "Ew! Don't!"

He laughed. "I'm just making sure you got your fill.

Forgive me for disturbing your view." He stood and set his hands low on his hips, because of course he did.

And yes, my eyes dropped to the tightly woven muscles of his abdomen. I'd felt his chest and stomach. I knew he had a solid body. But being confronted with it at first light of day after a fairly intimate week spent together, and especially after last night's admission and plan and kissing...

I waved a hand at myself, willing my face to cool. "It's a decent view, especially for your age."

His eyes narrowed and he was bounding over the couch and coming for me before I had a chance to scream.

"For my age, huh?" he asked as he quite literally slung me over his shoulder and jogged me around his living room.

"I take it back—everything I've ever said about you being a good man, a kind person, a helper. You're a menace." I swatted his—*yes, delectably firm*—butt. "Release me! This is—gross! You're sweaty!"

"I just ran six miles, so yes, I am," he said, still trotting until he finally made it to my room and flipped me onto my bed, then leaned over me, arms braced on either side of my head.

He stared at me, all stern and serious, as though waiting for another comment.

I refused, but staring at him like this, so close range, I couldn't stop the smile that crept over my lips. Soon enough, he was smiling back at me.

"No more objectifying me, Josephine."

I chuckled under my breath. "I'm sorry."

"And you won't do it again?"

"Do I have to promise that? You're so pretty."

His scowl returned, but then he pressed a searing kiss to my lips and pulled back. I grinned, and then he dropped his head and nuzzled into my neck—with his sweaty hair.

"Ew! Ewwww!" I practically screamed it and shoved him away.

"Payback," he said and sauntered out of my room.

I shuddered at the sweat but chuckled, too, and went right for a shower.

I liked him so much. He could be fun and lighthearted. He let me be silly and weird. He was just so...

Hope. We'll hope together.

CHAPTER THIRTY-SIX

Adam

We spent the weekend busy together—visiting with her step-nephews and nieces on Saturday for a birthday party up at the Saint Family Ranch a ways up the canyon, and Sunday, we had a quiet start reading on the back porch in the cool of the morning and sipping coffee before we visited Dorian.

Jo stayed in the car since I knew Dorian wouldn't be ready for new people even though he'd met her before, but I was nervous to see the state of things and didn't want to upset Jo or Stone.

Turned out, he was baking. Blueberry-lemon muffins. In an apron. And I couldn't have been happier or more surprised, though he'd looked at me like his baking habit wasn't news and I let him be. He even had plans with Kenny later, so how could I complain? His time with Dr. Corrigan had certainly been paying off.

It was Tuesday afternoon, a day before the release party, when Jess popped into my office with Ethan close behind.

"Wilder said you wanted to talk to me?" she asked, not fully entering the office.

"Actually, Jo did."

She seemed perplexed. "I'll see her tomorrow for setup before the release party." Her face lit with a giant smile. "Oh my gosh, we're all going to die with glee when Josie Wade walks in. Ah!"

I'd never heard the woman screech. She really wasn't like that around us, though it made some sense knowing she'd come out of a deeply male-dominated profession.

I grinned, something niggling at me. Probably the general concern over the event and wondering if it'd draw the stalker out. We would be securing All Booked Up better than any star-studded billionaire-attended event in town, that was for sure.

"Maybe drop by and see her tonight. She's closing this afternoon and getting the print copies organized after she locks up." Her dad would be there, and I'd go pick her up and take her to dinner before we got a good sleep to prepare for the big event.

Separately. We'd get a good sleep in separate beds. No matter how much I would like to share one with her. Yes, in every way, but just to hold her again—I hadn't savored it the way I should've that one and only time over a week ago.

Curse me for having a guest bedroom.

"I'll do it. I just have to finish up the AAR I didn't wrap on the plane, and then I'll head over."

"Sounds good."

She bid Ethan goodbye, and he sauntered in after her looking like roadkill.

"Whoa, buddy. You need a week-long nap."

He slumped into the chair across from me. "You're telling me. I cannot sleep. I'm not even working that hard—I just can't sleep. You're looking at a bona fide insomniac." He dipped his head in a faint bow.

"Worrying? Are you more stressed than usual?" Maybe that was a stupid question knowing he was a new business owner only slightly past the one-year mark.

He scrubbed at his eyes. "Maybe? I don't know. I just can't stop my mind running at night. But it doesn't seem to matter when I go to bed. And I own a coffee shop, but I've cut out caffeine just in case."

My brother loved coffee like some people love chocolate, so this was huge. "That's probably wise. What about exercise? Hydration?"

We ran through the list of things that might be stressing him, but I suspected it was mental more than physical. Most times I'd seen insomnia, it'd come from mental stress or anxiety far more so than physical causes. When we'd exhausted all the avenues, we came back to stress.

"I just don't feel that stressed. I don't get why that would keep me up at night. Joe's been in the black for ages. It's not like my partners are pressuring me for more results— they're both happy with the way things are going. And the community seems to like it. I feel settled here and I'm glad you've found someone you care about." His throat bobbed.

I heard it. The hint. "But you want that. You've wanted that as long as you've known it was a thing."

His gaze fell to his hands. "I have. I do. But that's not keeping me up."

I wanted to push him on it because he'd always been a little anxious, and it made sense he might've adopted more worries now than when he was in the full throes of setting things up last year. But I also knew he'd shut down if I did much more now. So I offered him the one tool I could think of for now.

"Take this. Just in case. I know a lot of people who've found her to be very kind and helpful."

Ethan took the business card for Dr. Corrigan and eyed it. "Therapy?"

I shrugged. "It's rare to be an adult in this world and not need it at some point. I haven't talked to her, but I did a lot of work with one as I transitioned out last year. I have friends here who've worked with her and would vouch for her—I can ask my friend about talking with you if you want." I couldn't exactly lay out her client list, but I suspected Wilder would vouch for her, as would Kenny or Dorian.

He nodded and stood. "Thanks. I'll think about it."

I pulled him into a hug, and he shoved me away eventually once it became unbearably tight—our stupid childhood tradition hadn't died off completely.

"You're an idiot," he said, shaking his head but smiling lightly now.

"Yeah? You, too." I winked as obnoxiously as I could, and he rolled his eyes. "You up for a hike this weekend?"

His brows raised. "Yeah. Of course."

"Why do you look so shocked I asked?"

"You usually go alone or with your work people. But yeah, I'm there. Let me know when and where."

With one more little wave, he left and I sat with his statement for a minute. Had I really not asked him? He often took weekend shifts at Joe when his employees had to call out or during shoulder seasons when their staff was running on a skeleton crew. I hadn't ever meant to stop asking, but I had. And these last few weeks, I'd been so absorbed with Jo, I hadn't made much time for anyone else.

Basically the opposite of every other relationship I've ever had. What a thought.

Historically, my problem was not prioritizing the person I was with, but lately, I'd been so focused on Jo, I'd hardly bothered with anyone but occasional checkups on Dorian. Well, and the occasional check-in with Kenny. But overall, I'd been consumed with Jo.

Easy enough to see why. The stalker had created a pressurized version of our relationship, where not only was my protective instinct activated but my professional training was, too, and all of it was directed at her.

In normal circumstances, she wouldn't be living with me and we wouldn't be so close. We wouldn't be having meals together and waking up to stare out at the sunrise or read next to each other.

I would be able to think about anything other than her. Right? I would. And chances were good that when all of this wrapped up, when normal life returned, my usual pattern of putting work and friends first would, too.

Wouldn't it?

"Excuse me." Jess's voice cut through, a slice of frustration issued from the hallway.

A grunt followed—classic Beast response, especially to her.

I rubbed my temples, wishing I could solve that problem but knowing it wasn't up to me. Or really anyone. Some differences between people just couldn't be *solved*.

Seconds later, Jess appeared in my office door again. "Heading over to see your woman. Any messages for her?"

Your woman. It was probably wrong how much I liked the sound of it.

"You can say hey for me, of course. Get over there and talk to your friend."

I didn't think Jess would be mad at Jo for not telling her about Josie Wade, but I knew for a fact Jo would be relieved when all of her friends knew. The lingering concern over Elizabeth and her mother wouldn't disappear instantly or anything, but I hoped letting more people in her life celebrate her success and even enjoy it with her would encourage her.

"Roger. See you, Doc."

When Jess left, the revolving door of visitors stopped, and I focused on a few tasks in my queue. When Jess wandered by my door twenty minutes later, I grinned, expecting to find her floating on the high of finding out her dear friend was also her favorite author.

Instead, she had no excitement to speak of. She seemed startled to find my office empty of anyone but me.

"Pop, did you find Jo?"

"I thought maybe she'd come here while I went there. She wasn't there."

Jess's response took a minute to register in my mind, but once it did, I sat up straight, fully alert. "She should've been. I dropped her off. She was having lunch with her dad and Jane, and now that the store's closed, she was going to work on organizing the books so you guys had less to do tomorrow..."

"I didn't see her," she said, the gravity of her words hooking into both of us.

My stomach dropped. "Could she have been in the back? What about Cookie—he didn't see her?"

"Cookie was at the door, but I thought maybe she'd gone out the back, though now that I say it, it makes no sense. I called her cell but no answer."

The moment snapped and we were both running, both of our phones already to our ears.

CHAPTER THIRTY-SEVEN

Jo

L uc, aka Cookie, slipped inside after the last customer left. "You doing okay here? Need anything?"

He was the nicest guy. I didn't know him as well as I did Bruce and Tristan because he hadn't joined the local Saint Security staff until much later, but he fit right in with the crew—gorgeous, kind, and apparently quite capable. He seemed like he probably fell between Kenny and Adam age-wise.

"I'm good, thanks. Why don't you take a break? I'll lock up after you, and I think Jess is going to be here soon to talk." I widened my eyes.

He nodded knowingly. He'd been briefed on the situation—my secret identity, the stalker, and also that Jess didn't know, but I didn't want her finding out from anyone but me.

"When's she coming? I'll just wait until she gets here," he said, checking his watch.

"Oh, any minute."

He gave me another polite nod and slipped out. Since he'd decided not to go until Jess came, I didn't lock the door behind me. I hoisted up a box of books to carry into the reading room, and nerves fluttered in my belly. I'd never done a signing before, and of course having my friends know I was Josie Wade—finally!—made it all the more intense and exciting.

A soft metallic *click* drew my attention, and I looked up to see a person with a hat standing just inside the back room's doorway, a hatch from the ceiling gaping open just behind him. *What?* There used to be an attic that connected into the closet of my apartment before it was renovated, but as far as I knew, it'd been sealed up for years.

"Josie Wade."

The man breathed out the name and everything in me reacted at once. Instinct or reflex or whatever it was had me throwing a book in his direction and bolting for the shop, but he beat me there, handgun pointed right at me.

"I don't want to hurt you, but if you run out there or if you start screaming, I will."

Fear scampered throughout my veins, chasing after the adrenaline already rushing, and I threw my hands up. "Please, don't shoot."

Should I scream? Should I run? I could probably bowl him over, but would he end up actually shooting me?

"We're going out back. Move."

Everything I'd ever learned about hostages and kidnapping said you don't leave the first location. You never leave. *I can't leave.*

"Why don't we stay here? I can sign some books for you and—"

"We're going now or we're dying here together. You choose."

In all my mental wanderings about this man, I'd never imagined him to be murderous. Creepy and overstepping and violating, yes, but I hadn't imagined him wanting me dead. What arrogance and foolishness had convinced me that somehow he actually *cared* about me and therefore wouldn't want to truly hurt me?

Idiocy. And maybe a heroic helping of delusion for good measure and my temporary sanity's sake.

"Okay. Sure. We'll go." I dropped a hand to my back pocket and, if possible, my heart sank further. No phone. I'd left it on the counter in the other room. I'd grown so hellaciously complacent, and I would never forgive myself for this.

"Move. Now."

I walked, and when the muzzle of his gun pressed into my back, I gasped and jerked forward. In a movie version of this moment, maybe I would've busted out some sweet self-defense moves. I had taken the beginner's class with Saint Security. But the fear and shock of reality blurred everything out, as did the feel of metal pressed against my spine. No amateurish move would keep me from dying if he decided to pull the trigger.

"Stop there!"

His voice rose, and for the first time, I heard nerves or maybe hysteria. Something unhinged, which made my mind scramble around for purchase.

A sticky shred of a sound came, and he grabbed my hands, then duct-taped my wrists together behind me. I was frozen with inaction, almost inert with the terror that this person had found me and he'd come prepared.

When he slapped a strip of duct tape over my mouth, I started crying.

"Shut up," he said, grabbing my arm and steering me toward the back door. Outside this building was only a little courtyard, but there were walkways in several directions. If he'd parked out front, someone would see. *Someone* would see this guy marching me out to his car.

But he went to the left and down the alley the opposite way I hoped, not to Silver Street. There was still good reason to hope someone would—

He shuffled forward and opened a car door. He'd parked right next to the alley's opening, and it was a slow Tuesday early evening. I stumbled as I entered the small sedan and cried out when he shoved my head hard enough and ordered, "Get down," then gently shut the door behind me.

The clock on the dash of the car said six minutes after five. I'd try to keep track, and maybe that would help me know where we were going. He got in and didn't speak a word to me, only began driving. I ran through every possible horrifying scenario my mind could think of before I willed myself to focus.

Someone would know I was missing very soon. They couldn't track me with my cell phone, but seeing it there at the store meant they'd know for sure something was wrong. And they were the best in the world at this, so in theory it wouldn't take them long.

Except this guy had come prepared and he'd planned this. This timing was too perfect—right when I was alone in the store—my dad had left to get dinner and Jess hadn't arrived. Before the busyness of dinner and—when did he get into my apartment? He couldn't have been there when I

was—the space was too small. I would've known…
wouldn't I?

A thrill of horror at the idea that he'd been there when I
was home watering my little house plant earlier sent a
shiver through me.

My thoughts scattered as he slowed and eased into a
garage, then parked. The rumble of the garage door shutting
came before he ever opened the door, though thankfully he
did turn off the car.

Once the door closed fully, he exited the car and got me
out, then forced me up a few stairs and into a home.
Curtains were drawn and my eyes struggled to adjust to the
low light after being in the brightness of the summer early
evening.

"Let's get you settled on the couch." He said this as
though we were having a nice conversation and he wasn't
gripping my arm a little too hard and shoving me forward.
"Have a seat."

I sat and my stomach lurched at the feel of the plastic
cover on the cushions. That was due to his desire to
preserve the precious materials of his couch and not for any
other reasons, right?

Maybe he lived here with someone—a grandparent?

Looking around, it seemed empty save a few pieces of
furniture. There was no way he actually lived here.

"I know what you're thinking, and I'll just tell you now,
there's no one here to bother us. This place hasn't sold, but
the old lady who used to live here is at the retirement home.
No one even knows we're here. It's just us."

He moved around with his back to me and my ears
strained to make sense of the sounds—maybe his keys
resting on the counter? He took his hat off and brushed back
some of the hair that'd escaped from his ponytail, then

flipped on a light overhead and sat across from me on the coffee table.

"I'm going to take this off now." His fingers brushed over my cheek before he peeled back the edge of the tape and then slowly removed it. His eyes got a dazed quality as he focused on my mouth. "You're so beautiful. I wanna do all the things you write about in your books."

"Like... rescue people from kidnapping?" I asked, because at this point, anger was starting to outpace fear.

"No. I'm gonna give you time to fall for me like Holden and Shailey in book two. And since I haven't gotten to read the newest book yet, maybe something from that one." He reached behind me and I ducked out of the way, but he grabbed my ponytail and ran his hands through my hair. "Then maybe you can write us an open-door scene and we'll act that out, huh?"

Tears hit my eyes. "Where is this coming from? Why would you think this is okay?"

"We're in love, Josie. I've seen your messages to me since the very first book." His expression was so full of assurance and love it was honestly stunning.

"What?"

"Your author's note. You always have something in there for me. I always find it." He grinned.

"I don't know you. I've never met you. How could I possibly be leaving you a message?" Not that I was completely surprised, but he really was unhinged. He'd fabricated a relationship where there was none. He didn't look familiar to me at all, and since I'd never done book signings or even sent out signed copies, there was no way we'd met and I'd forgotten.

He stood and walked away, but kept talking. "Oh, but you do. It's always something for L. 'I miss you so much, L, and I'm so proud of you,' or, 'To L, you mean so much to me and inspire me every day."

I nearly screamed. I very nearly lost my mind with frustration. Because those had been notes to my sister, to Lizzy, who would never read the books but I'd still wanted to acknowledge her. But did I really want to give this sicko any more information about my life, or upset him?

My best bet was to play along as long as I could stomach it—maybe not agree we were destined to be together or whatever nonsense he'd spun for himself, but keep him talking and happy until Adam could find me.

Adam would find me. Or Jess would. Or Wilder. They'd come for me like they'd found Winnie, because they weren't fictional.

They wouldn't stop until they found me, so it was just a matter of time.

CHAPTER THIRTY-EIGHT

Adam

We'd swept the place, pulled all security footage, and it was him. The creep had broken into Jo's apartment and entered the store through the old attic entrance. He must've found old building plans in order to even know it was there, which meant we might be able to find out who this guy was if he'd left any traces at City Hall when requesting the plans.

The store's back entrance was always locked, so we hadn't stationed security there, and he'd taken her out that way—since we'd never known he was inside the store, we hadn't been worried about him exiting that way. Cookie had been on duty in front, but he'd never been so far as the floor of the bookstore, so Cook had had no chance at seeing him.

At some point in the future, we'd use this as a training model—as a reminder that people will go to any length to get what they want. We'd always considered those kinds of factors on active duty and we had to do better now. That this had happened with Jo made fire burn through me.

Jess hadn't seen any sign of struggle, and since she'd reasonably thought maybe Jo had come to see her plus she hadn't been briefed on the danger surrounding Jo at the time, she hadn't second-guessed that Cookie hadn't seen Jo exit.

We were working with the local police on getting a way to track his plates through town and see if we could tell which direction he'd gone.

"I can't believe this. I can't believe this." Jess was muttering the words under her breath as she frantically clicked through images on her computer while the rest of us —literally every other person on staff at Saint who'd been available—worked the problem.

Bruce was on the phone with Chief Whitacker while Wilder was sending out an alert to local businesses. Cookie, Kenny, and Tristan were combing the streets of downtown looking for hints, though we'd hit a dead end outside the bookstore.

Darcy was at the store and I'd just left there. I'd be back there as soon as I could... as soon as I had a lead.

"Chief's sending footage in just a few. Heads up," Bruce said.

"On it," Beast said, head buried in his computer. He was one of the best with tech, and we needed him to work his magic.

For once, Jess didn't gripe. She continued searching online for hints about this guy. We had an irrelevant license plate from his last foray into town, but I wondered... would he have a different car?

"Search every silver Honda Civic in town. Let's see who's registered here and cross them with our guy." The plate would be different since we knew he'd had a false one, but what if he was still using the same car?

Jess's typing escalated, her fingers practically smashing the keys as she searched. My heart pounded as I saw the links come in for the roadway footage.

"Same car," Beast confirmed, and Jess said less than a minute later, "Pulling the list of registrations now. I'll cull it."

We went on like that with quick verbal updates as we worked the problem. Thankfully, red light camera video from just north of town showed the car we believed to be his turning into a local neighborhood rather than taking the canyon road out.

"Can he really be this close?" My heart sprinted and I grabbed my keys.

"Hold it. We need a plan. Beast, give me the layout of the most likely destinations in that neighborhood. Pop, find out who we've got living in that neighborhood and if any of them happen to be a single white guy in his thirties. Wilder, call your mom. That's not too far from her place—does she know anyone who lives there? Any local gossip we can use?" Bruce directed and gave him a nod of appreciation.

Taking point on this wasn't an option for me. Ever since Jess's visit, I'd been in a low-level panic. She'd said Jo was gone, and my only thought had been that I'd failed her. I'd failed her. I hadn't kept her safe.

Quickly replacing that self-pity was the determination to find her, to get this guy as cleanly as possible so he could be arrested and put away for a nice long time so Jo didn't ever have to worry about this again.

"Doc, let's get you kitted up, and then I want you to go update Darcy. I know he's out of his mind. We'll come get you on the way."

Good. I would do whatever needed to be done to get Jo to safety. And then, if I had the chance, I'd make sure she knew how amazing and loved she was. All those petty hesitations and fears about not being capable evaporated in the face of this nightmare.

I'd let my early failures and the statements from a wounded woman dictate the way I'd thought about relationships for far too long. Yes, I'd played my part, but as E and Jo and Bruce had begged me to see, that didn't mean I couldn't change.

The truth of who I was—Doc to my fellow soldiers and friends, Adam to my family and Jo... that man was caring. Innately. And though I might not've had that nailed down at twenty or twenty-five, I'd learned how to care about people since then. I'd learned just how much being able to take care of others mattered to me—in my work, yes, but in my day-to-day, too. It was how I loved. It was as natural as breathing.

I'd been doing it with my chosen family in the military, I'd done it with E, and I'd been doing it with Jo practically since we'd met and certainly since I'd discovered her secret.

As a man, I'd learned to commit to people. I hadn't demonstrated that romantically, but I'd learned it in other places. And then Jo... Jo came along and taught me so much. She reminded me how much I had to give—endless wells that somewhere along the way, I'd lost sight of. I'd missed how the devotion and love I had for my friends and family were signals of the growth and maturity in me—were proof that I wasn't the same man I'd been all those years ago when I'd failed my ex and myself.

That marriage hadn't ended out of nowhere. We'd ended because Marlee and I had both made choices. And this meant that going forward, there were more choices to make. Time, experience, maturity... these things *could* inform my future—they could mean different choices.

I wouldn't take away from what I'd felt for Marlee. I'd been infatuated, yes, but I had loved her in the way I'd known how. The way a boy could love someone he wanted to keep but wasn't sure how to cherish. What I felt for Jo was so much larger, with roots running deep underground and branches arching into the sky. I could hardly contain the feeling now that I saw it for what it was.

Jo had held up a mirror and demanded I look and see— not just that I could have a future with her, but that I didn't need to bury myself in the sins of my past. She made the difference here—she'd urged me and taught me to hope, and now I couldn't imagine doing anything else but running toward her and grabbing on with everything in me, breath- less and wild and full of determination to see what we could be.

The door to our command center room burst open, and a woman with dark hair and dark eyes searched the room until she set them on me. "Adam Carter?"

"Yes."

Her nostrils flared and she ground her teeth as though making an effort to calm herself. "Where. Is. My. Sister?"

I rushed to her. "Elizabeth?"

She gave me a dead-eyed glare that likely terrified an average man. Lucky for me, I wasn't average, and I was in love with her sister, who I was bound and damn determined to recover as soon as possible, so I had no time for cowering.

"We've got her location narrowed to a small neighbor- hood north of town. We're working on the house exactly, but we're moving soon."

She took my measure, then her gaze sifted around the

room, all kinds of thoughts racing past, but not one of them on display on her severe face. Then she held out her hand.

"Elizabeth Malcom. I'll need a weapon."

And that was how I met my girlfriend's sister.

After Eddie James vouched for Elizabeth Malcom with stars in her eyes—apparently Elizabeth was a very big deal in the Kappa Sector where Eddie had worked until the last year or so—we'd quickly vetted her and read her on to the situation.

She ended up riding shotgun in my vehicle as we rolled up to the street we'd identified as the location, and soon enough, Elizabeth Malcom, Jo's mysterious and intimidating sister, rolled out of the vehicle with me and followed Bruce's direction as we closed in on the house where her sister's stalker held her hostage.

CHAPTER THIRTY-NINE

Jo

My stalker and kidnapper—Lester, as fate would have him named—became increasingly erratic as the minutes ticked on.

He'd been pacing back and forth across the living room and had, much to my very freaked out dismay, picked up the gun again.

"I don't see why anyone's expecting you. Why would they know? They should know you're safe with me." He rapped the side of the gun against his forehead. "Don't they know that? We're meant to be together. I've been telling you this. Why didn't you tell them?"

The plan to placate him had gone out the window when he'd asked me if I loved him. I couldn't do it. I couldn't. I told him I was in love with someone else, and that had been the wrong choice.

He'd screamed at me like I'd betrayed him, then started

this pacing when I'd said the person I loved would know I was missing. That my dad and my friends would be looking for me.

And here we were.

"I can't tell them that. It's not true. I don't know you."

He ran up to me and grabbed my arm. "You do know me. I've been writing to you for over a year. And you wrote back—at the beginning, you wrote back. Why did you stop writing back?"

He was talking faster now, and he was dragging me with him to the front room, but he stopped when headlights flashed through a slit in the drapes.

It'd been less than an hour of sitting here, and I felt like I might crawl out of my skin. I'd made a plan, though—he hadn't bound my feet. If he tried to touch me in any way other than moving me place to place, I'd kick him, even if he did have the gun. I wasn't sure where I was, but we couldn't be far from Silverton. I could walk or even reliably run for a mile or two if I had to. Those headlights gave me hope, though.

He yanked me to the side of the window and moved the curtain with the gun, holding it back to look out the door right as the doorbell rang and he jolted. I started to yell, but he clasped a hand over my mouth.

"Shut up. You just *shut up.*"

His hand pressed against me so hard it hurt my teeth, but then he shoved me back into the kitchen and slapped more duct tape over my mouth before moving me into a bedroom and then into a closet.

I tried to speak. Tried to say, "No, no, don't do this," but he must've known that whoever was at his door was looking for me.

"Get down. Get down on the floor." He pushed me

until I was face down on the floor of the small empty closet. "I will shoot you and then myself if you move or scream. I'll shoot your boyfriend and your dad and anyone else you care about if they're here and you start making noise." He shut the door as the bell rang again.

Hope raced through me. This was it. They'd know something was up, maybe come in and be able to tell something was off. Or maybe they'd see his gun and wonder why someone was carrying a gun around their house on a Tuesday afternoon.

Find me, find me, find me. Adam! I'm here! Please come get me!

I screamed it in my head but could hardly move, much less make a sound. Having my arms behind my back made moving at all a challenge, but I eventually curled on my side into the fetal position, then sat up. Thanking goodness for free feet, I leaned against the wall and inched myself into standing, then nudged at the door until it creaked open.

"Thanks so much for stopping by—very welcoming of you. Yep, you, too, have a good one." Lester's voice came before the sound of his door clicking shut, and I froze, paralyzed by what to do now. I'd hoped to get into the front room and rush out to see whoever had rung the bell. Even if they were just neighbors, they wouldn't ignore someone bound and gagged like this.

Now what?

"No!" Lester shouted, and I jumped, plastering myself against the hallway wall as he ran toward me. "No, no, no!"

Before he reached me, a body burst through the garage door and covered me.

Lester screamed. "Not you! She's mine! Leave now! You can't be here! She doesn't want you."

"Put the gun down, man," Adam said, his voice steady and calm.

Adam! Desperate for him, I leaned my head against his back. He had his hands raised, gun in one of them and disappointingly not pointed at my kidnapper.

"I will shoot you both. Both of you! Leave! You have to leave!" Lester was raving now, just totally nonsensical.

"Easy. Everything's fine."

Adam's voice was so spectacularly calm, I wouldn't have believed he was being threatened by someone waving a gun around while yelling at the top of his lungs. But that's when I saw it—my eyes flicked to the movement over Lester's shoulder, and I jolted as my sister stepped into the kitchen, weapon raised.

Everything happened at once.

Elizabeth yelled, "Drop your weapon, now!"

Adam shoved me behind him down the hallway and rushed Lester, knocking the weapon from his hand before he got a shot off as Elizabeth collected the gun and kept hers trained on Lester while Adam zip-tied his hands. At this point, Bruce, Wilder, and Jess were all inside, and I heard sirens wailing outside.

Then Adam was with me, slicing through the duct tape at my wrists and easing the strip away from my face. I gingerly moved my arms, my shoulders screaming after being constrained for so long.

"You're okay. I'm so sorry. You're okay," he said, clutching me to him, one hand at the back of my head and one wrapped around my shoulders.

"Thank you. Thank you," I said, the flood of fear and anxiety cresting and dropping out into an emotional release that left me ineloquent and relieved.

"I'm so sorry he got by us," he said, his voice fierce.

"I'm glad you found me." I'd never doubted—honestly, I'd never for a second believed they wouldn't find me—*he* wouldn't find me.

"Let's get you checked out with the paramedics, okay? Are you hurt? I mean... more than this?" His thumb arced over my cheek where my skin was raw.

My hands were shaking—my whole body quaked, a total overload of adrenaline. "I think I'm okay. It's mostly the tape. Maybe a bruise. But I'm okay." And then I was crying in earnest, so relieved to be able to say it and mean it.

I was okay. He'd come for me and—wait. "How is Elizabeth here?"

He chuckled softly, holding me close. "I'm pretty sure she's a Valkyrie. She got to town right after I left the store, I guess. You two will talk soon."

Just then, my sister stepped up and gave me a wry smile. "Hey, Jojo."

I laughed and then it switched to an absurd sob as Adam stepped back and she wrapped me up. I sobbed harder than I could remember, the relief and happiness and ridiculousness of the situation jumbling together into a tangled, cathartic mess. After a few minutes, I tapered off and pulled back.

"Better?" she asked, her face so familiar to me even after so long.

"Yeah." I sniffled, working for composure. "Think so. I'd like to leave this creepy house, though."

She grinned. "Fair enough. Why don't you have Doc take you out to the EMS and we'll wrap up here. I think I need to chat with the Chief."

Behind her, someone was leading Lester away. Hands cuffed in front of him, he trundled slowly, then looked up and lunged toward me.

"Josie, I'll always love you. I'll never stop loving you. We'll still be together. I'll figure it out. I'll—" The officer escorting him picked up the pace and shuffled him out of the room with the help of someone else.

Elizabeth's eyes went wide. "Yeah, let's get you out of here. We have some things to talk about, I think."

I laughed sheepishly. "Yeah. We do."

Clearly, the Josie Wade cat was out of the secret-pen-name bag, and I could only feel grateful.

Funny how being kidnapped by a stalker had granted some perspective on things.

Across the room, Jess caught my eye. She widened her eyes and shook her head, a multitude of thoughts passing between us. They must've briefed her on who I was, and I hated that she'd learned the truth this way. I mouthed, "I'm sorry," and she just huffed and shook her head, whispering, "Later."

Yes, I owed her a more thorough explanation, which I'd intended to give her earlier. But for now, this would suffice.

"Ready?" Adam asked, holding out a hand.

Clasping our hands together, I felt the words down to my soul. "Ready."

CHAPTER FORTY

Adam

Long after the police had dragged Lester Deets to jail and every one of us had given our statements and Elizabeth and Jess had both confirmed Jo really was okay even after the paramedics gave her the all clear, we lay side by side in Jo's bed at her apartment.

The police had searched her home and ascertained he'd gotten in through the front door, so we'd already had the locks changed and we'd resecured the old attic door he'd used to get into the store. I'd offered to take her to my house, but she'd been determined to reclaim her space, and I couldn't fault her for wanting to face this head-on.

Damn, she was a marvel.

Lester had been convicted of stalking once before, and scarily enough, he'd gotten better at it. He'd left so few traces prior to taking Jo, we couldn't find him before he acted. He'd been sloppy enough for us to see his license plate, and thanks to Jane Saint, who'd noticed an unfamiliar car parked in front of a house in her neighborhood on and off the last few days and tipped off Wilder, we'd narrowed down where exactly he'd been blessedly fast.

Fortunately, Deets hadn't hurt Jo too badly, and he'd be tucked away for a long, long time since he'd actually kidnapped her.

"Thanks for staying with me," she said, her eyes shut and face slack enough that I'd thought she'd fallen asleep.

I pressed a kiss to her forehead. "Thanks for letting me."

Her mouth stretched into a smile and she opened her eyes. "Maybe we should thank my dad and Jane for insisting Elizabeth come home with them."

I chuckled. "I've never been more grateful that Jane's a little pushy."

She grinned full-out. My heart thudded and the words I needed to say were *right there*. But I didn't want to overwhelm her, and after hours of wrapping up with the police and then my team, and finally, her family, I'd just wanted her to myself.

What a selfish jerk, right? I couldn't blame myself. I couldn't pretend it wasn't true, either.

"I love Jane Saint and all the more so now. Though seriously, my head is exploding that Lizzy's here and she's meeting Jane finally and my dad can show her the shop and she knows about Josie." She huffed and sat up, scooting back so she leaned against the headboard.

"Lots to talk about still," I said, settling into the space next to her.

"Yeah. But"—she took a deep breath—"it feels small now. Not like what I want to do is small, but like, I don't need to clear it with anyone else. Like I should choose to do something with this one life that I love. And I love writing. I love telling stories. And I kind of think that after today, I'm going to love meeting fans who are just kind of normal reader fans and not planning to duct-tape me and lecture me on their plastic couch."

I hauled her to me, my pulse quickening at the reminder of what she'd been through. Not that I would ever forget, of course, but the fact that she was joking about it was good, even if it made me a little ill.

"I don't know if I can take you joking about it yet, but I'm sure it's probably a good sign." I pressed a kiss to her temple.

She tipped her head up, and I took the offering with a soft kiss. She leaned up, opening her mouth, and I deepened the kiss at her command but pulled away.

As much as I wanted the physical connection with her right now, we had things to discuss. Her brow furrowed slightly, and I touched a finger at the small vee.

"I wanted to say I've had some clarity in the last few weeks. Today clinched it."

Her brows arched high, and then she snatched my finger and dragged it down from her head. The soft touch of her lips to the pad of my finger made something in me shudder with wanting.

"I've had this identity for so long—Doc. And I've seen it as something tied to medical training—being an operator medic, and then even taking on most of the first aid training and such here. I deal with any kind of medical situation, I accompany any personal security work where there's a higher risk of injury or illness, that kind of thing. But I think I want more. And I know I already mentioned the survival training, so we're starting that soon. I haven't mentioned that the team approved it, but they did."

She flung her arms around me and squeezed me. "That's amazing."

"Thanks. And thanks for encouraging me to push for that. I don't know why I didn't. I think I thought I'd step into the security thing and it'd be a fit, but it's different. I knew that would be the case, that it wouldn't feel like active duty, but I'm glad I have a way forward."

She ran a hand through my hair and seemed so genuinely happy for me. "I love it. And I have to say, I think Doc nods to more than just your medical training. You're a caretaker. You've admitted how much you worry about others, and I know you don't like to own that as a good thing, but I think it means you're a nurturer. You care about people, and you want to do what you can to help them. That's how we ended up here, after all."

"Is it?" I asked, marveling at her assessment of me. As much as I'd pushed against the idea before, it rang true. And why had I resisted the idea of seeing myself that way?

"I'm afraid so. We're all your fault."

Her eyes flickered around my face, and her soft smile made me want to thank God for my own existence and the privilege of sharing this moment with her.

"All my fault, huh?" I asked, though my words were a bit breathless.

She shrugged. "Yep. I was just minding my own business and there you came, offering to help me figure out how a guy would pin a woman to a wall and kiss her." She fluttered her lashes and we both burst out laughing.

I took her face in my hands and just... marveled at her.

"What?" she asked, voice quiet in the stillness of the moment.

"I'm just so in love with you."

She swallowed hard and her smile melted away. "What?"

I nodded. "I am. I've spent the last year talking myself out of this and telling myself how bad I would be for you or how you deserved better. And there's probably always going to be a part of me that worries those things are true, but—"

"They're not! They're not true, they're not," she said, smile blazing as she laughed and kissed me.

"I think I get that a little more every day. And I'm trusting myself more. I know that's thanks to you—that you trusted me first, and it gave me a reason to try it out—to see if we could do this."

"I think we can. I know it's only been a little while, but we've been through some craziness and I think it's still going pretty well," she said, a little shrug like she was casual about it.

A chuckle skipped out. "Yeah. I think so, too. So, if you're interested, I'd like to keep this going. Keep trying. See where it goes without a plan to deal with it when it ends... just a plan to hope together, like we said."

She kissed me again, then pulled back. "Hope together. Work together. Practice kissing scenes together."

She laughed against my lips when I tackled her and toppled us back onto the bed, legs threaded together and bodies close. She hadn't said it back, and as much as I didn't want to beg for it, I would if I had to. I'd tossed my pride out the door a while ago, but I held on for another moment, just waiting.

"Aw, you've been so patient. What a good boy."

I dropped my head to her shoulder and laughed, shaking my head at her. Her hand on my jaw urged me up to look at her.

"I love you, Adam 'Doc' Carter. And I'm in love with

you. And I'm so happy you're not going to quit on me." She kissed me then, a claiming kiss I'd remember for the rest of my life.

"Never," I said, and I knew it in my bones. I would never quit on her or myself. I'd never quit on us. And I couldn't wait for what lay ahead.

CHAPTER FORTY-ONE

Jo

The crowd outside All Booked Up was shockingly large.

More than one person had suggested we delay the party, but this felt right to me. I didn't want to focus on the bad that'd come from this—I wanted to move forward with hope and focusing on the good. Based on the people hovering outside, the support would undoubtedly overwhelm me in the best way.

"I can't believe this," I said, voice shaking enough that Adam rubbed my back.

"Nerves are normal, but I *can* believe it. You're amazing and people want to support you." He dropped a kiss to my cheek.

"Thank you. I just hope everyone's happy..." I always had doubts about whether readers would enjoy my books, but because I only interacted with them online, I never worried about looking someone in the eye and seeing disappointment. *Yikes.*

"Ready? They're here..." Jess peeked in through the doorway from the main store into the reading room, then scuttled to me and hugged me. "I'm so freaking proud of you. This is going to be amazing."

My sweet friend hadn't been able to wait until too much later to find me after the craziness last night. She'd just said, "You're really her?" and I'd laughed, tears in my eyes and said, "Yeah. Surprise!"

She'd launched at me, hugging me tightly before giggling in a way I could only describe as maniacally, and then she did a thing I wasn't sure I ever imagined my badass friend Jess doing—she had jumped around and clapped like a child. "This is so cool! This is so, *so* cool!" And all those worries that she'd hate me or feel betrayed? She had put those thoroughly to rest.

Since she was in the know, she got to be the guide for the rest of our friends.

"I sure hope so." Nerves knotted in my stomach, and I was sweating, which I really didn't want to do. I'd worn a cute navy dress that coordinated with the back cover of my book and strappy sandals to match. My hair was down and wavy, and overall, I felt put together and comfortable in a "Hey, I made an effort!" kind of way.

But this was it. In seconds, my friends would be the first inside for a special few minutes so they could learn the truth before the party officially began.

"That's my cue," Adam said, then cupped my face. "It'll be great. I'll see you in a few."

And then, he abandoned me to my fate after a soft kiss to my lips.

"Oh, hey, Adam."

I could hear Catherine's voice right outside the door. Of course my friends would greet him because they knew him, and they were friendly and they probably hadn't expected to see him. Because they weren't expecting to see me.

"Ready, ladies?" Jess asked, a smile audible in her voice.

One of them screeched—Dove, if I had to guess. I exhaled out my nerves and rolled my shoulders back, finally facing a moment I'd been dreaming about more and more lately.

Dove, Elise, Catherine, Nikki, and Winnie all shuffled through the door followed by Jess, who said, "Ladies of the Silver Ridge Romance Readers Club, I give you, Josie Wade."

"Wait," Elise said, her eyes flicking around the room.

Nikki and Winnie shared a look while Catherine eyed me.

"What? What?!!" Dove's exclamation rose.

And then they all broke—Winnie and Catherine were laughing, Nikki beaming, Elise cackling with a full, throaty sound that was pure joy, and sweet Dove was shrieking, "Oh my gosh! Oh my gosh! It's you! You're her! She's you!"

I'd never known a moment so full of elation and love and excitement and relief as this one. They all ran to hug me, their words coming from all angles.

"I can't believe it!"

"I can toootally believe it!"

"This is amazing."

"This is the best day ever!"

I swiped at my eyes and Dove dabbed at hers, too. Winnie sniffled a little, but everyone else seemed to have held it together. We found our usual Romance Reader Club seats and Dove burst out first.

"Okay, tell us everything. I need to know how it started

and how it's going and what Adam thinks." She wiggled her brows like this was salacious.

I chuckled, but Jess cut in. "Of course we want all the details, but the signing starts in five minutes."

Dove clapped but Elise grumped. "Ugh. Fine. But we will expect a comprehensive report on all things Josie Wade, *and* you will buy us guacamole as your formal but entirely unnecessary apology for keeping this from us."

My heart swooped low. "I really am sorry I didn't tell you. You have no idea how much I wanted to. But between the letters I was getting and some other things, I just..."

"You don't need to apologize. You made the best decision based on what was right for you, and we can't fault you for that." Winnie understood a little something about hiding things since she'd kept the *convenience* part of her marriage to Tristan out of our discussions when we'd all met her. But it'd been right for her then, and we'd understood.

Of course they were forgiving, or even, absolving, of me now.

"It's true. I would love to have known all this time, but I'm so glad to know now. I'm sorry you had to keep it from us, and I'm so, so sorry for the problems you've had." Catherine reached for my hands and squeezed.

Jess had told them Josie Wade had a stalker and that was why she didn't tend to do signings, but they didn't really connect with the fact that it was me until right now.

Stricken, Dove's eyes widened. "Oh my gosh. Josie Wade has a stalker so *you* do... Are you okay? What can we do? Can Jess find him?"

Jess grinned and I stood and hugged her. "That is a story I will tell you after tonight, but for now, I promise he's not a concern."

"It's time," my dad said, leaning into the room. "Come get in line, girls."

We moved into the store, and my heart threatened to beat out of my chest with pride and joy and excitement, and yes, still nervous energy. The store looked fantastic and had been slightly rearranged so my signing table would be right in front of the romance archway. Two rolling shelves had been brought in and filled with my books—I'd told my dad it was likely overkill because so often people brought their own books, but he'd refused to listen and had rushed shipping.

Adam waited by the door, and I noticed at least six other Saint Security employees scattered out front, and Tristan was tucked back behind me. Though they had no concerns about Lester anymore, Adam had mentioned they were all coming to support me.

Evidently by support, he meant create an imposing security presence.

Although honestly, given that my books were about hot veterans defending their women, I couldn't be mad at the preponderance of capable, muscular men peppering the area.

My dad opened one door, and Adam pulled open the other. Dad stood in front of the store before anyone entered. "Thank you all for coming! Since the store is small, we'll ask you to stay in line and enjoy the summer evening until we invite you in. Thank you for coming to celebrate Josie Wade's book release!"

Cheers rose and I giggled, red in the face, until I'd signed each of my friends' books. The line kept moving, and Dad and two other store employees were running checkout and helping with the lines while Jess jumped in and took photos for people.

I hadn't seen Elizabeth yet since my dad and Jane had kept her busy meeting her stepsiblings, but I had called my mom this morning. She hadn't seemed upset, though she hadn't been ecstatic like my dad had been. That was okay. Even if she didn't like the path I'd chosen, I felt better being honest with her. Now there were no secrets.

Elizabeth knew the truth, but I wanted her buy-in. I wanted her on my team for this, and nothing had drilled that home more than the relief and amazement when I'd seen her last night.

The sheer number of familiar faces coming through the line floored me. There were the expected ones—Jane and Sarah Saint, Calla and Wyatt, Sadie and Warrick—but they had to come, didn't they? Jane would've strong-armed them into it, though I suspected, based on the way this family showed up for one another, she didn't need to.

The Morrisons all showed up, too, and though I didn't know all of them personally, I recognized them and so did nearly everyone else in town because they were Silverton Royalty. Liam and Wells Morrison, Danny and Mia Morrison, and Leo Morrison and Jonas Bauer, but then came Jamie and Bel Morris, whom I and everyone else in the world knew thanks to Jamie's rock-star status. Dahlia had brought a huge bouquet for me, and John squeezed me tight. Kieran, the Irish pirate as we'd come to know him thanks to Kenny, came by and gave me a quick peck on the cheek after getting his copy signed. *Adorable.*

Some people had come from Salt Lake and others from Brigham City. Someone had driven all the way from Las Vegas, which was amazing because we'd only advertised the signing since last night when Dad asked what I thought, and in a show of freedom I hadn't experienced since I'd first read the turn in Lester's letters, I'd said yes.

The line slowed eventually, and then each of the Saint staff came through. By now, my friends had all pulled up seats and were chatting happily around me, my own little entourage. Bruce came by and bought a copy even though Nikki clearly already had one. Kiley had already come through with a group of friends.

Ethan swung by and gave me a huge hug. "You're quite the entrepreneur, Jo. But I'll admit, coffee and books—perfect combo."

I beamed at him. "Absolutely. I'm so grateful to be your partner with Joe. You're doing an amazing job."

He swallowed hard, like he'd needed to hear that. The store was doing great, and he seemed to have a knack for it, but I hugged him again. "Thanks for coming."

Tristan brought his collection—yes, he had all of my books—and added the newest release to the top of the pile. "Proud of you, Jo," he said, and his quiet comment was one I'd treasure because he was both an actual reader, and an actual soldier, and my friend's husband.

Beast's arrival was a genuine surprise.

"Oh, wow. I didn't expect you to want a copy."

He blinked at me. "Why not?"

I laughed. "Uh, fair point. I don't know. And, thank you again for yesterday and these last few weeks." I couldn't imagine standing outside the bookstore was fun, but he'd done it faithfully, back and forth with Cookie.

"My honor," he said, then his gaze flicked to Jess's, then away.

Naturally, mine did, too, and her thunderous glare wasn't a shock, but it still surprised me. Beast held the book up in farewell, and I smiled at him.

"Oh, hi," Elise said, her voice having an odd, breathy quality that hardly sounded like her and drew my attention.

"Hey." Cookie's response came with a soft smile for her and *ohhh*. As though he had to pry them away from my friend, his eyes found me as he shifted down the table. "Mind if I get your autograph?"

I laughed and my friends snickered. "Of course not. And thank you for all your help."

"Anytime. Though I do hope there's no need from now on." His smile was so charming and friendly. I'd never really looked at the man but goodness, he was handsome.

"Slide along, soldier. I need to hug my sister." Elizabeth stepped in front of me at the table, and I bolted from my chair and around the table so I could hug her.

"Thank you for coming." My throat was tight around the words, but I refused to cry.

She pulled back and held my shoulders.

"I wouldn't miss this." Her smile was huge and genuine and hiding nothing from me. No mask for this moment—just her. Just *Lizzy*. "I'm so proud of you. I can't believe you kept this from me all this time, but I'm so happy you found something that makes you happy."

"Really?" I said, voice watery.

Her brow furrowed. "Of course. It's amazing. I wish I had something like this."

"Wait, *really?* I honestly thought you were going to be disappointed. I mean, what am I doing for the world? I'm not changing anything, I'm just..."

She shook me a little, her hands firm on my shoulders. "You're bringing joy. Distraction. Love. Light. Beauty. Hope... You're giving people a reprieve from the harsh realities of this world and giving them something to laugh or cry or think about that isn't something overwhelming in their real lives. That is a gift and it's wonderful, and I won't tolerate you disparaging it."

My mouth fell open, her words so deeply meaningful to me, I couldn't find my own to respond with.

"Hear, hear!" Jess said, and my friends and family nearby joined in to echo it.

I laughed, swiping at my eyes for what felt like the hundredth time in this dream of a night.

"I'm going to go and let you wrap up here, but we're going to lunch tomorrow, right?" Lizzy said after one more hug.

"Yes. Can't wait."

Kenny jogged up to the table right as my dad shut the doors to the store. He was fumbling with his phone and looking a little harried, and started talking before he'd even reached the signing table.

"Sorry I'm late, Jo. I needed to grab something at work and then—" Kenny's words cut off and he froze, still as death, when he glanced up to see my sister's face. The air gusted out of him and his lashes fluttered. "Liz."

Her hands had dropped away from me, but I could sense she'd stiffened at his voice. She turned her head ever so slightly and met his eyes for half a second, dropped her chin, and then left.

My sister, the conqueror of bad guys and badass woman I looked up to, had just practically run away from... Barbie?

"Do you know Elizabeth?" I asked, because what?

Kenny's gaze had followed her to the door, and he was still craning as though stretching his neck would help him see where she went.

"Kenny?" I prodded.

He shook himself and flashed a smile. "Right. Yeah. We've met. Anyway, will you sign? So proud of you, Jo. You're awesome. Seriously. So awesome. I assume at least one of your heroes is based on me?"

I chuckled. "Oh, definitely all of them, obviously."

He grinned. "Naturally." He held up a hand and I high-fived him, then he sauntered off like he had not a care in the world.

"Okay, we all saw that, right?" Dove asked, surveying the group.

"Yes, we did," I confirmed as my friends nodded.

An hour later, we'd cleaned up and closed the shop, parted ways with my family and friends, and Adam walked me to my door.

"Are you coming in?" I asked, eyeing the way he hadn't followed me inside.

His blue eyes pierced me and my stomach flipped.

"I want to, but the crisis is over and I think it's best if I go back to my place." He shifted forward like his body wanted to follow me even if his mouth had just drawn a line between us.

I wouldn't jump to conclusions here because we'd been through so much. Maybe he just needed time to himself. "Is everything okay?"

He reached out, his movement lightning fast, and gripped my waist.

"It's better than I've ever hoped for. And that is the reason I'm not going to come in and mess it up." He dropped his forehead to mine and exhaled slowly, eyes falling shut. "Even if I desperately want to."

A light laugh slipped out even as I clutched at him, not wanting him to go. "You can come and just sleep, just like last night."

He was already shaking his head. "I'm a strong man, Josie, but I know myself. I know how much I want you. And I know that we made a promise to take things slow." He released me. "So we're going to do that. And we're going to keep our promise to each other. And then, when we're ready, we're going to make more promises."

My mouth dropped open. "More promises?"

He nodded, all confidence. "Yeah. More. Some might even call them vows."

I laughed outright at that. "You have it all planned out, huh?"

I sounded flippant but oh, boy was my heart racing and hope winging around like a deranged butterfly in my chest.

He leaned on the doorframe and dropped his face so he was as close as he could be without touching me. "Planned, not so much. But I sure am hoping."

EPILOGUE

Adam

The time had come.

Jo was writing the epilogue to her current book, and she'd lightly hinted she wanted to practice some element. I'd been waiting for something like this—the right idea to click and run with it.

Everyone had joked with me that I had to do something huge to propose to Jo, but they didn't get it. It didn't have to be huge, it just had to be right for her and for us.

Yes, this was coming a little sooner than I might've imagined, but at this point, I couldn't think of anything I wanted more than to commit my life to hers. I already had, and I wanted the vows and the paperwork to go with it. *Wouldn't mind the sharing a house and bed and all that, too.*

"Hey, you're here."

Jo beamed at me as she came in through my front door. She had a key, and even though we didn't live together, we spent a great deal of time together and having access to each other's houses just made sense.

"I made lunch, but did you want to knock out that practice scene or whatever you needed first? I have to head out for the weekend after this." My last fall survival weekend trip. I'd miss them over the winter, but I wouldn't miss being away from Jo. Leaving her today, if all went to plan, was going to kill me.

She set down her laptop and unloaded a notebook and water bottle. "Yes. Let's do it. So he's going to do the traditional thing. Obviously, it's not hard to imagine, but I want to look at the details like your hands and biceps and all of that. So kneeling, pulling out a ring, holding it up and pretend spiel, all that."

Perfect. When she'd mentioned needing to stage a proposal weeks ago, the clock had started ticking. I always enjoyed hearing what she was writing but knowing this scene was coming, I'd been on tenterhooks.

I'd known Jo was my future for a long time now—much longer than I'd originally admitted to myself. It'd take time to accept that I didn't need to be a different person—I could be myself and embrace who I was, and that would allow me to embrace what we had between us.

When I'd seen the book I'd helped her with and read the dedication page, it had confirmed that the heroes Jo was writing were fictional, yes, but that wasn't what she needed, because she saw me as someone special and, dare I believe it, right for her.

To Doc, the inspiration for this story and so much beyond it.

She'd decided on that dedication long before the book had been published, likely when we were still skating around each other, while I was still in denial about who she was for me.

I'd never stop thanking myself or the people around me for surrendering the stubborn insistence that I couldn't love her well enough, and today was the next step in our story.

"Okay, so… maybe let's go outside. It's so nice out," I said, walking toward the deck.

"Oh, sure," she said, grabbing her notebook. She liked to either do a writing sprint or at least jot down notes when we did these kinds of things.

The leaves in my backyard had fallen and created an orange, yellow, and red carpet. The sun was still high and the air crisp but not too cold yet. Another week or two and there'd be snow higher up and we'd be getting hard freezes indefinitely.

She stopped at the top of the deck, pausing to enjoy the view. From where she stood, she could see Silver Ridge Peak and the sisters over the trees, especially as they thinned with leaves changing and falling.

Her hair blew around her, and she nudged her glasses up the bridge of her nose, then tucked her notebook close to her body like she'd caught a slight chill. She was so completely beautiful, and nothing in me doubted what came next. That was a gift she'd given me.

"Come here, Jo." I held out my hand.

She grinned, suspecting I was beginning the practice. *Little does she know.* She set her hand in mine and descended the stairs. I led her a few steps away from the bottom, then knelt.

"Jo, I—"

She laughed. "You don't actually have to say anything."

I squeezed her hand and held her gaze. "Josephine."

Her smile fell and her expression grew serious, like suddenly she saw through me.

"I never believed I could love someone well enough to ask them to share my life. You've not only taught me how misguided that belief was but you've taught me to see the way I've been learning to do that with my whole life, not just with you. And that speaks to how boldly and beautifully you live and love—you do it so well that just by being around you, people are better."

She sniffed and pressed her lips together, so I kept going.

"I love your persistence and determination to do what you love. I love the way you enjoy your friendships and care for your family and soak in your community. And I love *you*, the woman you are and the way you share yourself with me."

She sucked in an audible breath and chuckled a little, not quite crying or laughing but clearly full of the moment. My voice wavered with the same as I continued.

"You gave me the courage to try and helped me see what I couldn't on my own. You helped me hope for more, and honestly, the day I met you, I started wanting more than I'd ever planned."

She beamed and chuckled at this.

"I want to keep hoping together. I want to commit to a life together and work together, but I want to keep hoping and loving each other until our last breaths decades from now."

Her chin wobbled and her eyes filled with tears as she nodded. I released her hand for a second and pulled out a small velvet box, flicking the top open to reveal the ring, and held it up.

"Jo, Josie, Josephine…"

She laughed loudly at this, a little puff of air releasing from her like a pressure release valve

"I love you so much, it's mined new depths in my soul. I want to keep loving you. Will you do me the incredible honor and inconceivable joy of accepting this ring and becoming my wife and partner for the rest of our lives?"

She laughed and cried all at once, shoulders shaking and eyes leaking as she nodded. "Yes, yes, of course."

I slipped the ring on her finger and she pulled me up, then pounced, wrapping me in her arms as I did the same to her. Her kiss was frantic and punctuated by laughter. After a moment, we pulled back, and I smoothed the tears from under her eyes with my thumbs.

"That go okay?"

She just laughed and shook her head.

"Should we do it again?" I asked, beaming and a little teary-eyed myself.

"No. I think that's good. I don't think I'll forget any of it."

With a soft kiss I couldn't resist, I held her close. My friend, my love, and now my fiancée. "I love you so much."

She held on with as much determination as she did everything. "I love you, too."

Thank you for reading Jo and Adam's love story! Don't miss the bonus epilogue to get a sneak peek from dear Beast's perspective! And don't miss Beast and Jess in their book Fighting For You.

BONUS EPILOGUE

Beast

I've wanted Jessica Korbel from the very first minute I saw her. Yes. Instant attraction.

Interest.

Infatuation.

Did I love her then? No. Who can love someone based on one visual? That came later, though admittedly, not much later.

She'd walked into training, one of three women in a group of fifty people, and she'd had the attention of everyone there. Her counterparts had also been under inspection, but she'd had this fire I couldn't look away from.

Or, maybe it'd been those dark brown eyes and her dark hair twisted into a tight bun at the back of her head. Full lips and delicate-looking ears and a voice that sounded like she hadn't gotten a full night's sleep in a while—a little husky and rough.

And back then? She hadn't exactly smiled at me, but she'd extended a hand. "Jess Korbel."

My hand had swallowed hers, though that wasn't unusual for me, being larger than the average bear. "Jude Rawlins."

And then it'd happened.

"Jude," she'd said, like my name—*my name*—had charmed her.

So that was the moment. Call me a fool or whatever you want, but that was the moment I fell for her. After that, it was all downhill. No stopping, no turning back... even when she fell for my best friend.

I couldn't have guessed how it'd all turn out—how things with my best friend would blow up and how he'd ruin everything. How the choices we all made would get people hurt and how they'd steal the one thing I'd ever wanted.

How they'd turn Jess Korbel into my enemy.

I lived off glimpses of her, swallowing down even her ire when it came at me, since that was better than nothing. I'd given up hoping she'd change, that she'd see me as anything more than a villain. I wouldn't beg her to be my friend again.

So I gave her nothing—less than nothing—and felt my heart harden into granite against her.

She avoided me—literally traveled around the globe to escape me. But now, she'd returned.

And the circumstances had come together in a way that would mean she couldn't avoid me any longer.

Our team at Saint Security knew we didn't get along, even if they didn't understand exactly why we couldn't bury the hatchet. They'd done everything to keep us separate, likely as much for their own sakes as for ours.

But this weekend, Saint Security had signed on for an advanced team to scout a high-end resort for a celebrity client, which meant we'd go in undercover and report on their security. The assignment was for a husband-and-wife cover story.

Jess was slotted as our female agent, but I wasn't going to get anywhere near that, until Cookie got sick. Wilder was gone, Tristan couldn't do the job, Bruce had another tasking, and down the list it went.

So I said yes.

Because I needed a change.

And because something in me said it was time to push back.

There'd be nowhere for her to hide now.

And me?

I had nothing left to lose.

Don't miss Jude (Beast) and Jess's story, Fighting For You.

AUTHOR'S NOTE AND ACKNOWLEDGMENTS

Thank you for reading Inspired by You! I had so much fun writing this book and I hope you had a blast reading Jo and Adam's story. I'm going to have to figure out how to include some "let's act out this scene from my romance novel" in more books because weee! That was fun!

Thank you to my babe of a husband for being a persistent supporter of my publishing business. Thanks to my kids for letting me point out story structure in basically any movie we watch or book we read. Thank you to my neighbor and dear friend BR Goodwin for being a source of delight and encouragement and an excuse to walk to Starbucks and drink a shaken espresso. Huge thank you to Genny Carrick for letting me whine and sharing in so much life but in our "old-fashioned" e-mail correspondence way. Tentacles in the next one for sure ;)

Thank you to Zee Monodee for her excellence and willingness to stick with this until it was just right—your patience and persistence are a blessing! Thank you to Amanda Cuff helping me navigate my hatred of the past perfect, ha! Thank you to Jamie McGillen for friendship, brilliance, and final sweep for any errors.

Thank you to my amazing beta readers Amanda and Genny. Your thoughtful reads always help me find the places where I need to dig deeper or adjust to make the story the very best it can me. I appreciate you SO much.

Thank you to Suzan, who takes prime placement in

ARC thanks because she sees the book first and is such a staunch supporter! Thank you also to Elise, Joanna, Darla, Rebecca, Aubrey Ann, Jordan, Hannah, Kayleigh, Rosy, Abby, Tiff, Rachel, and so many other wonderful bookstagrammers who do so much to help share and spread the word about my books. I truly can't tell you how amazing you are and how grateful I am for your time, talent, and energy you give to the indie community and to sharing my books! I'm honored!

And finally, many thanks to you, reader. I thank you last only because it's hard to verbalize just how amazing it still feels that you've chosen to spend time in this world of mine. Thank you. Truly.

Now it's time to see if we can get those enemies in the same room for more than a few minutes...

ABOUT THE AUTHOR

Claire Cain lives to eat and drink her way around the globe with her traveling soldier and three kids, but is perhaps even happier hunkered down at home in a pair of sweatpants and slippers using any free moment she has to read and cook. Or talk—she really likes to talk. She has become an expert at packing too many dishes in too few cabinets and making houses into homes from Utah to Germany and many places in between. She's a proud Army wife and is frankly just really happy to be here.

You can also join Claire's facebook reader group for exclusive content and fun: https://www.facebook.com/groups/clairecain/

Website: http://www.clairecainwriter.com

E-mail: Claire@ClaireCainWriter.com

Newsletter sign-up for new releases, exclusives, and freebies, including a free book:

http://www.clairecainwriter.com/newsletter

amazon.com/author/clairecain

bookbub.com/authors/claire-cain

instagram.com/clairecainwriter

facebook.com/clairecainwriter

goodreads.com/clairecainwriter

pinterest.com/clairecainwriter

www.ingramcontent.com/pod-product-compliance
Lightning Source LLC
Chambersburg PA
CBHW061636190726
48289CB00006B/1625